DESTINY'S CALL

*Steve and Lesley –
Hope you enjoy this story as much as I do!
Scarlett Dean*

Praise For Destiny's Call

"Scarlett Dean has created an exciting, enthralling mix of romance, suspense, humor, and horror. *Destiny's Call* features the ultimate dysfunctional nuclear family; a trio of bloodsuckers. Dean's expert touch puts a fresh spin on the vampire legend. Fans of P. N. Elrod and Sherrilyn Kenyon will love this!"

—J. A. Konrath
Author of *Whiskey Sour*

"Move over Anne Rice and Poppy Z. Bright for Scarlett Dean, and all those Larel K. Hamilton fans will flock to Scarlett Dean's novels should word get out of Dean's layered and complex set of characters, who happen to be caught up in the fire of erotic vampirism…great read, un-put-down-able!"

—Robert W. Walker
Author of the *Instinct & Edge* series
and *Fire & Flesh,* as Evan Kingsbury

ALSO BY SCARLETT DEAN

Unfinished Business

DESTINY'S CALL

BY

SCARLETT DEAN

AMBER QUILL PRESS, LLC
http://www.amberquill.com

DESTINY'S CALL
AN AMBER QUILL PRESS BOOK

This book is a work of fiction. All names, characters,
locations, and incidents are products of the author's imagination,
or have been used fictitiously. Any resemblance to actual persons
living or dead, locales, or events is entirely coincidental.

Amber Quill Press, LLC
http://www.amberquill.com

All rights reserved.
No portion of this book may be transmitted or
reproduced in any form, or by any means, without permission in
writing from the publisher, with the exception of brief
excerpts used for the purposes of review.

Copyright © 2004 by Scarlett Dean
ISBN 1-59279-823-3
Cover Art © 2004 Trace Edward Zaber

Layout and Formatting provided by: ElementalAlchemy.com

PUBLISHED IN THE UNITED STATES OF AMERICA

*To my parents, who taught me
to stand strong in my beliefs and pursue my dreams.*

Thank you to Sue Heneghan of the CHPD for her police insights.

*Also, a special thanks to Darden Hood of
Beta Analytic Lab for lab specifics.*

PART I

Tainted Kiss

CHAPTER 1

Brasov, Romania, October 1973

Golden fireplace flames licked the frigid bedroom air and captured Emelia Von Tirgov's melancholy gaze. An ornate hearth of carved wooden cherubs gave the impression of heaven's doorway, wide open. A vaulted ceiling loomed above cream walls and thick peach carpet, complimenting Emelia's favorite room in the castle. She finished her diary entry, suddenly jerking back a bloody finger. The paper cut burned as she pressed it to her lips and reread the passage...

October 21, 1973

Vladimir will be leaving in the morning for Bucharest. I will miss him so. He loves his country and feels for its people, and so he goes to plead mercy from President Ceausescu. Although we have played host to many a diplomat under the President's rule, this trip could be dangerous—not so much for his life—but for our stability. It is our wealth and Vladimir's political ties that have saved us from losing our home or having to stand in line for food. One wrong word reaching President Ceausescu's ear could change that forever and put us at odds with the administration, leaving us targets for the police known as the Securitate. I pray for Vladimir's safety.

I try to remain positive, and the child I carry inside is already bringing me joy! Happiness is never far away, and I feel so alive. Perhaps Vladimir is right—it is a daughter. She will be beautiful with dark eyes like her father and a determined spirit to make her strong and safe. She will have the added security of her two-year-old brother, although little Michael does not quite understand when we speak of the new arrival. The birth is many months off, yet my arms already ache to hold this child! However, patience must come in the form of hope, and the promise that all is well. Our wonderful future lies ahead.

She basked in the fire's warm glow and reclined in her favorite nightgown. The sheerness aroused sensual feelings; sensations of being young, beautiful, and so complete as a woman. The recent weeks had been kind to her figure, which had become slightly fuller yet shapely. Her blonde tresses cascaded over creamy white breasts that amply filled her lace bodice. How she loved the life inside her—how she loved life itself!

But ashen waves of sadness washed over her as her own mother could not be here now to enjoy her grandchildren. Although she'd lost her mother at the vulnerable age of twelve, she carried the loss close to her heart...

Emelia clutched her mother's limp hand against her chest, and felt its coolness. "Mama?"

Her father's hand rested on her shoulder. "I'm sorry, Emelia, she's gone."

"No, she's just sleeping. You said she'd get well. She promised she'd never leave us!"

She grabbed her mother's shoulders and shook her. "Wake up, Mama! Wake up!"

She clung to the woman as her father tried to pull her away. She wanted to drag her mother from the dark abyss.

Finally, it was her older sister, Mira—always Mira—who'd come and comforted her. They sat on the bed beside their mother, talked and said their good-byes. Led gently away, Emelia glanced back once more making a promise to one day destroy the dark enigma called death—

Emelia jumped at a sudden crash against the balcony's French doors. Eyes wide, she slowly rose to investigate. All remained quiet except for the crackling fireplace and a low moaning wind outside.

She cautiously approached the doors and saw a thin fracture in one of the glass panes. Until now, she hadn't been aware of her hand resting protectively over the small swell of her abdomen. Her nerves sharp as talons, Emelia felt the blood pounding in her temples. Then she saw it—something on the balcony. Frozen in place, she squinted into the darkness through the glass.

A gray mound lay in a heap near one of the doors. It did not move. She bent for a closer look and gasped in horror as two wide, circular eyes peered back at her.

"My God, it's an owl." She opened the French doors wide.

The unnatural twist of its neck and the blood smeared on the windowpane caused her stomach to churn.

"It's just a baby," she cried.

The bird's transfixed, ebony eyes refused to release their stare. Suddenly Emelia's chest grew tight and waves of nausea gripped her stomach.

The wind caught the doors and blew them wide. Emelia grabbed both handles and slammed them closed. Shaken, she sank to her knees. She tried to convince herself her reaction was due to the pregnancy, but looking out into the blackness of the night, hot tears streamed down her face. In an instant, everything had changed; she could feel it, sense it. Their lives had been altered forever, for she knew her safe haven, Von Tirgov castle, stood in danger.

CHAPTER 2

Vladimir Von Tirgov peered out the window on his right to see Brasov's train station well lit against the night sky. The locomotive's high-pitched shriek announced the overdue arrival and the end of the long train ride home. Mechanical problems produced a late start and then halfway between Bucharest and Sinaia there'd been a further delay when a herd of sheep decided to cross the tracks.

The platform clock displayed the eight o'clock hour. He should have been home long ago and Emelia would be worried. He was glad his visit to Bucharest was at an end and that he'd had some success with President Ceausescu. There remained political milestones to overcome.

As the other passengers departed, he collected his belongings—a leather brief case, several magazines, and his coat. The extended trip hadn't been kind to his bones and he tried to stretch in the cramped seat before standing. He looked forward to kissing his beautiful wife and taking a long hot bath.

He made his way down the aisle and hoped all was well at home. Emelia had been frightened and deeply upset by the baby owl dead on her balcony, convinced it was a bad omen, and as a result, he shouldn't go to Bucharest. He smiled knowing within the hour he would hold her in his arms and gladly tell her how wrong her prophecy had been.

He smiled at the thought of her and realized their life together had been paradise. With a twenty-three year age difference between them, he'd never heard her complain once that she'd married an old man.

Now there was growing concern on his part over the truth of his past and the curse of the seventh generation. He'd told no one outside the family, except Emelia. He showed the signs early on, and some in the family thought his strange powers bordered on witchcraft. It actually proved more powerful than witchcraft, and it gave every seventh generation male his ability to communicate with the dead.

The train lights flickered inside, and he hurried to vacate the cab. On his way toward the lot, he squinted in the darkness to see his car. With only a few vehicles remaining, he easily spotted it in the far corner. He hurried as a bitter wind chilled the air and turned his breath into smoky dart-like wisps. Inside his pocket, he groped with frozen fingers for the keys. He turned when a rustling sound beside him caught his attention. At first, he saw only darkness. Then a flash of red.

A gypsy dressed in bright colors rushed him. Vladimir dropped his case to defend himself. He tore at the man's tattered shirt and clawed at his bare chest, but the man possessed incredible strength for his size. Vladimir's six-foot frame and impressive build was no match for the five-foot willowy assailant. A low growl and rancid breath wafted close to his face as the man effortlessly pinned him to the pavement.

Vladimir pleaded. "Take my wallet and leave me! I've done nothing to you."

Against the bright moonlight, Vladimir saw the gypsy smile under black gleaming eyes. His grip grew tighter against Vladimir's shoulders as a mournful wail rose deep in his throat. The man's eyes penetrated Vladimir's, and he opened his mouth to expose yellowed fangs.

"No!" Vladimir screamed. "Get away!" He fought as the man bent close. Knives of pain tore through his neck. He was paralyzed as the man began to feed. Vladimir felt his blood draining as the man drew hard, and a strange euphoria lifted above the pain and fear, and he calmly lost the desire to resist.

Warm blood—his blood—trickled down his neck as the gypsy suckled like a babe at breast. Vladimir closed his eyes and rode the pleasant floating wave. Weightless now, as if his physical body no longer existed.

Suddenly, his chest seemed to explode from within. His eyes widened in panic. He couldn't breathe. The attacker fled, leaving him to die. Vladimir clutched his throat, his hands sticky with blood.

"Help," he cried. "Help me." The empty parking lot surrounded him in the solemn darkness. Hot shards of pain shot through his chest and spread upward. At last he succumbed to the fire in his head, and sunk into a void blacker than night.

* * *

Vladimir startled at something nearby. Where was he? Had it all been a terrible nightmare? A dimmed lantern illuminated the room enough to see he lay in a small tent on a narrow cot. The clothes he wore reeking of smoke and mint, were not his own.

Muffled voices seeped through the canvas, but offered no clue whom they belonged to or where he might be. His stiff neck had been bandaged with strips of soft cloth, and he smelled the aroma of blood. He tried to sit up, but found he had no strength as every muscle screamed in agony. Before he could call out, the tent flap opened and an elderly gypsy woman came to his side. Her dark eyes sparkled against the lantern's light as she smiled tenderly above him. Long gray braids hung on either side of her chubby face and lay over a hefty bosom. Her bracelets jingled as she prepared to remove his bandages.

Vladimir caught her wrist as she reached for him, their gazes locked in silence. Finally, he asked, "Where am I?"

She pulled from his grasp and continued her work. "I must change your dressing."

Too weak to fight, he allowed her to remove it. "Who are you?" he whispered.

"I am Zarina, mother of Sirelle. *He* did this to you."

"What happened? Why do I feel so strange?"

She stopped cleansing his wounds briefly then continued. "You rest now. When I finish, you must sleep."

"Your son, Sirelle. Is he mad?"

Her leathered complexion appeared to soften as tears brimmed her eyes. "He is not the son I knew. May God show him mercy." With that, she set the remaining bandages aside and started to leave.

Vladimir grabbed her multicolored skirt, and pleaded, "Please tell me what has happened. I feel so numb, as if I don't really exist."

"Everything has changed," she said, dimming the lantern. "Sleep now." The tent opening swung closed behind her, leaving Vladimir alone in the dark.

Against the ebony darkness, somewhere nearby an owl hooted a familiar refrain. Vladimir fought the urge to sleep. He must get home. Every nerve tingled—every physical sensation magnified. He glanced over his surroundings and discovered he saw everything clearly through a pale gray veil. From the gypsy camp, although silent on the surface, there came the breathing of many sleeping souls. Vladimir, fully awake now, sat up without the slowness he usually possessed. His arthritic limbs did not creak with stiffness or ache from immobility. Not even the vigor of youth had ever fit his body so well. He'd never felt this strong and alive.

He tore the bandages from his neck and stroked the place where Sirelle had pierced him. The wounds and pain had ended—gone. He wondered if he'd ever really been injured. Perhaps he'd hit his head in the struggle with Sirelle and had dreamed the rest. Vladimir searched the cluttered dwelling for his own clothes, knowing the gypsy garb would only frighten Emelia when he returned home.

When he passed the wooden crucifix on a nearby stand, he was overcome by an odd tingling sensation. It felt alarming, like a warning. He quickly moved away, distracted by a desirable scent. He followed it to the darkest corner of the room where he found a pile of discarded clothing—his clothes. They smelled of blood. The aroma caused a stirring within so deep as to be primal. His throat tightened, his loins ached with desire. He brought the bloodied shirt to his nose to breathe in the sanguine scent of his own blood, his eyes closed in longing. The blood was sticky, and he could not quell the desire to taste it. He plunged his tongue into the wadded mass and began to suckle the area like a hungry child.

Repulsed by his own behavior, he tossed the clothing aside. What could possibly be happening to him? Was this the act of a loving husband and father? How could he face his family again? He behaved more animal than human.

Suddenly the room began spinning. He squeezed his eyes shut, but this did nothing to end the vertigo. His legs, weak and leaden, Vladimir stumbled toward the tent opening to find Zarina. He threw open the flap and saw a blazing campfire surrounded by several tents. Three gypsy men with rifles guarded the camp, one sleeping on the ground. The spinning sensation slowed, and he gripped the tent for support.

"Help me...please," his voice sounded distant.

Immediately, the men stood, with their guns pointed directly at him. One of them barked orders to a comrade without taking his eyes or his aim from Vladimir.

The sleeping soldier, now fully alert, ran to a nearby tent and disappeared. Vladimir fought to maintain his stance for fear any sudden movement might get him shot. The brightly dressed sentinel remained stock-still, his eyes wide in what appeared to be fear. Knowing that gypsies were naturally leery of strangers but seldom afraid, he wondered what might they possibly fear from an unarmed man?

A dark shadow moved against the largest tent and Zarina came into the camp light. Vladimir then lost his grip, and fell to his knees.

"Zarina...what's happening to me?"

The gypsy woman commanded, "Put down your weapons, they are useless! Help him to the wagon."

"What are you talking about?" he asked her.

The men half carried, half dragged him, afraid of getting too close, and Zarina climbed into the back of the wagon ahead of him.

He lay back against a soft padding of blankets and closed his eyes while a moon glared above, a solitary, mournful eye behind a black veiled face. His hearing became suddenly acute, and the surrounding forest seemed to come alive in the darkness. He heard twigs cracking, small ground animals scurrying out of breath. He clapped his hands to his ears. As the wagon started through the woods, barren tree limbs hung overhead, reaching for him with stark, brittle fingers. He trembled and in turn reached for Zarina.

"You must tell me the truth. What is happening to me?"

She lifted his head onto her lap and stroked his forehead. "It is not *happening*. It is already done. We are taking you home where you will be safe. But there is much to consider, as...as your life has been altered forever."

"What do you mean? Am I...dying?"

Her solemn expression grew darker with eyes reflecting the moon's eerie glow. Zarina's hoarse whisper penetrated the night. "You are not dying, for you are now as my son, Sirelle. You are the living dead, a vampire."

He felt the world spin out of control. Zarina's words echoed over the wagon wheel's rhythmic lull. *"Vampire...vampire...vampire!"*

His breath became shallow and his slowing heartbeat pounded in his ears as he struggled to remain awake. A heavy blanket of numbness enfolded him, and he felt himself pour like blood over the mountain edge of eternity.

CHAPTER 3

Tears brimmed as Emelia read her latest journal entry...

May 1, 1974

My absence from you has been justified. The past months have consisted of chaos and grief, when they should have been full of joy; our lives forever changed the night the gypsies brought Vladimir to me—for their kindness and hospitality I'm indebted. Now our lives are about to change once more with the birth of the child. How can all of this be? My husband exists in our home as vampire and yet he is about to become a father?

I feel the life inside and find no gladness, for what will the child be told of its father? He is cursed...he is dead...your Tata is but sleeping. The children and I will visit his grave as I have been doing out of duty and show, but he is not there. I'm sure the household staff wonders why I spend so much time in the cellars of the castle, locking myself behind bolted doors for hours each evening. Perhaps they justify it to themselves as the grieving widow gone temporarily out of her head.

Each evening, my husband awakens from his deep, troubled

slumber and I spend precious time with him, alone. We've shared many happy moments there, although it is damp and cold for me at times, it doesn't bother Vladimir. In this unusual, heartbreaking way, he has been able to watch his child grow inside me, weeping inconsolably upon feeling the baby's kick for the first time. While he is vampire, he is still a loving father.

He has never attempted to take my life or blood and seems to remain under control in my presence. I don't fear him, but miss our old life so much. It was the gypsy woman, Zarina, who counseled me that first night, explaining, "You must allow him to rise up and go in the night. It is now his way. Do not judge, for he must do this evil thing. You cannot change what has happened or stop what he does. May God have mercy on you."

That is why each evening after I visit him; I make an excuse to go before it is too late. I know he would never ask me to leave, but he must feed before the sun rises. At times, I despise what he has become, wishing to destroy him for my own peace as well as his. Yet, I'm still drawn to his tender nature. And so, this is how I see him, night after night, and he is still my Vladimir; the true love of my life.

He pleasures me greatly, for his body has become frozen in eternity, forever strong and virile. Even now with my misshapen figure, he offers unrelenting, tender passion no other earthly delight can provide. My cries of ecstasy mingle with tears as I revel in the splendor of his new life, one without aging or pain, yet I mourn the old life where we would have the opportunity to age together. We remain as man and wife with no bond broken between us.

I am grateful yet concerned over the impending visit of my older sister, Mira, from America. She has written that she will arrive next week to help with the baby. Again, I must play the grieving widow so she will not be suspicious. Mira is very perceptive and not easily fooled. I believe our nursemaid Olga has doubts of her own, but is too afraid to voice them. Great caution is called for during the next few weeks or all will be lost.

* * *

Green eyes gleamed at Vladimir through the thick brush of the forest, watching him take his kill. The scantily clad whore, oblivious to the danger, sputtered an inebriated giggle and unbuttoned her blouse.

"Come to mama," she ordered, and grabbed Vladimir by the hair to press him to her breasts.

Daegon watched in disgust, knowing novice vampires often made the mistake of taking too long to seize their victims, ultimately resulting in the kill's escape. His knowledge of such things had allowed him to take his place as master of the vampire community. After more than two hundred fifty years, he had much experience in all vampire matters with powers developed far beyond any of his flock. Daegon ruled with vengeance and strength. No one dared to question his authority or challenge his place as coven master.

This particular vampire, Vladimir Von Tirgov, was new to the dark side and not part of any coven, yet. Daegon had decided with lust in his heart that this one would become his own. He would instruct him in the ways of vampire and cultivate Vladimir's powers to rule beside him forever.

The harlot's raucous laughter distracted him and he saw her lay down, enthusiastically hoisting up her skirt. As Vladimir mounted, Daegon wore a wry smile as the woman's wanton expression turned to shocked horror. The painful pleasure she'd received had not come from between her legs, but from her throat. As Vladimir drained her life force, she continued to buck and push to gain her freedom. Gradually, her struggle ceased and her bare legs fell limp. Daegon found satisfaction at her vacant, wide eyes. Vladimir had done well, even without a master's tutelage. He would be great one day.

Vladimir pushed away from the whore and wiped her blood from his mouth. A sinister remorse filled him after each kill that made it impossible to view his victim afterwards. He turned away knowing the feeling would pass; it always did.

His nerves were electrified with fresh blood and he felt his strength return. How these acts repulsed him and forced him deeper into the abyss of self-loathing. Yet the need was more powerful than any human drive he'd ever experienced. It overpowered his sense of right, and his life-long quest for peace and fairness. He brushed the dirt from his clothes and stepped over the corpse. His desires were satisfied; his appetite was quelled. Until next time.

Vladimir stopped. Someone was near; he could smell their scent. The nearby brush shook briefly as a tall figure stepped into the small clearing. The man stood well over six feet and wore a black hooded cape that obscured his face. Long fingers clutched the cape at his chest as he moved closer. Although no words were spoken, Vladimir *heard* what the man was telling him.

I am Daegon Enescu, coven-master to our kind. You are not alone.

If these thoughts were meant to put him at ease, they'd failed. Vladimir's nerves were razor-sharp, ready for the challenge presented. He attempted an introduction. "I am—"

Vladimir Von Tirgov. I know who you are!

Vladimir was uncomfortable that their communication had been one-sided, but before he could offer a complaint, the man spoke in a deep, archaic voice. "My power of the mind disturbs you. Very well, I will speak as you do."

Taken off guard, Vladimir sputtered, "You read...you heard my thoughts?"

"Of course. It is but *one* of my gifts—gifts I generously offer to you as my student."

"Your student? What for? I've learned all I need to know to survive this curse."

Vladimir hadn't gone two feet before he fell to his knees. He clutched his head as Daegon's voice roared like fire in his brain.

"Ingrate! I would give you the world!" He spat his words as if they were bitter. "Would you prefer to simply *survive*? I can bring you to your full potential, to a level others in the coven only dream of." His tone softened. "You are weak. Sirelle is only a rabid vampire, not created in love. He is doomed to run wild for eternity seeking peace from his altered existence. But you—*you* are unique. I can make you truly great."

"Sirelle did not take me out of love I can assure you; therefore I too, am rabid."

Daegon lifted a bony hand to brush back his hood. Vladimir stared into the pasty face of death, yet the vampire's emerald eyes were hypnotic. He forced his gaze away from them.

"It is not too late for you, Vladimir, but time is essential. If you take one in love for your own, you will be spared a lifetime of torment. I must warn you, the longer you wait, the more desperate you will become. In the case of Sirelle and others like him, he waited too long and his soul is insane. He is unable to save himself. It is too late. Do not allow this to become your fate."

Vladimir's anger boiled at Daegon's words. "What you're suggesting is mad—*you're* mad! I could never lay this curse upon someone I love, and if you yourself could, then you're a sick, disgusting animal in need of destruction. Now leave me and take your false promises and deranged righteousness with you."

Daegon's leathered complexion tightened into a frown. "What is it you cling to in this life? I've offered you the world."

"Something you'll never have, even with all of the powers and principalities at your service. It's a foreign and unattainable concept for you—it's called love. And it's *my* great gift, Daegon, the one capable of overpowering and incinerating yours to mere ashes."

Vladimir turned then and vanished into the forest leaving Daegon with his thoughts.

Oh, foolish Vladimir, your so-called power has just become your destruction.

CHAPTER 4

Emelia turned sideways before the full-length mirror to scrutinize her figure. "There's only one word for it. Fat!" She plopped down on her bed rubbing her temples as she fought for self-control. Her condition wouldn't last forever; the baby was due any day. With all of the twists and turns her life had taken over the past few months, this one would end with beauty and good. It would bring forth life instead of death. Hope was not lost.

She rested a hand on her abdomen and spoke to the child within, "If only we can both hold out a while longer, little one. Unfortunately, the contractions I've had lately haven't been the real thing. Meantime, we need a distraction. It's been a while since I've visited the horse stables and my horse, Borak. Perhaps he'd like a short walk around the grounds today?" Emelia felt the baby's strong kick inside as if signaling agreement. "All right, a walk it is."

Before heading out to the stables, Emelia peeked in on her napping son, Michael. Surrounded by his favorite stuffed animals, several pair of glassy button-eyes kept watch as faint snoring drifted from the crib. Butter-colored ringlets covered the toddler's head against an orange satin pillowcase. Emelia beheld every inch of his small form and tenderly adjusted his blanket. She frowned and pulled the child's thumb from his mouth—a habit she'd been unable to break him of—then she smiled when his rosy lips stayed slightly parted. He was truly a wonder, their angel. She kissed him on the cheek, taking in his sweet smell. He squirmed a little, and returned his thumb to his mouth. Emelia tiptoed out and quietly closed the door behind her.

Outside, the late afternoon sun still warmed the spring air with a few dark clouds in the distance. A forceful neigh sounded from inside the stable as she approached. It seemed Borak was in full spring spirit today, as well. Emelia recalled the day she'd received the proud red stallion as a wedding gift from Vladimir. The horse had taken to her immediately and they'd formed a bond no one could have predicted.

He sputtered and stamped inside his stall and Emelia could see at once her four-legged *child* was ready to play. The stable smelled so good, even the less pleasant odors. She loved the way the sweet aromas of sun-baked straw and fresh oats mingled with the horse's natural scent. She missed these things most since Vladimir's accident. If only life could return to normal.

She nuzzled Borak's neck and rubbed his side. "Have you wondered about me?"

Borak neighed in response and allowed his cheek to be stroked. She led him outside past the inner yard toward the grounds where he could graze. An emerald grass carpet stretched into the distance where mature trees bordered the castle's property in a gradual slope that met a natural stream. Just past the trees on the west side was a small clearing where she and Michael had shared many picnics and had proven to be the perfect romantic hideaway for she and Vladimir.

Today the clearing provided a quiet place to contemplate the last few months and what they might mean for the future. Limbs heavy with buds fanned in the gentle May breeze over the gurgling stream below the short ridge. Borak caught the wind with a raise of his head and stomped at the ground. Emelia laughed at his impatience and pulled a large carrot from her pocket. "You know I wouldn't forget your treat."

The horse crunched noisily and offered no rebuttal to his master's sudden confession. "I'm afraid for my family now that Vladimir is cursed. Although he's immortal, he is more vulnerable than ever. I fear the staff will find out the truth, especially after the baby is born. What then? Do we leave our home and dwell in a cave somewhere? If they discover the secret, they'll kill us all. I can't share these things with Vladimir; it would hurt him. He has always been the strong one, but now *I'm* the one who must remain courageous and protect *him*."

She felt a sudden cool breeze and looked at the passing clouds overhead. A small funnel of dead leaves blew up in the clearing and the air smelled like rain. She thought she saw someone standing in the brush, but when she looked again there was nothing but a squirrel.

"We'd better head back, Borak. It's quite a walk and I can't race you like I used to."

She took hold of the reins to lead him, but he lifted his head and pulled away. Another gust of wind whipped a mass of hair across her face and she briefly let go of the reins.

"C'mon, baby," she coaxed. "The skies are getting dark. What's wrong? The weather has never bothered you before."

Borak stood close to the trees, his tail sharply twitching back and forth. Emelia clutched the straps tight, realizing she had to get him moving. She grabbed the reins. This time the horse reared back and raised his front legs into the air. Emelia kept a firm grip on him and refused to let go. Borak's high-pitched neigh heightened her own fears that an animal might be in the nearby brush. Then lightening cut a jagged streak through black clouds and sent Borak into a panic.

Emelia saw his muscular chest rise with his legs kicking. He landed inches before her and started to rear up again, forcing her backwards. Suddenly, her foot slid out behind her on the slick mud and she tumbled over the mossy ledge. She grabbed a nearby branch and felt a painful jerk up her arm. Carefully rolling to one side, she pushed with her feet to gain a stronger grip on the branch, but her shoes slipped against the wet soil.

Thunder shook the sky and Borak flew into another round of helpless thrashing above her. She watched his feet pound the ridge's edge, drawing closer with each landing. If he slipped off, he would trample down on top of her. Sharp slices of pain traveled up her arms as she clutched the branch and continued to struggle for a foothold. Suddenly, the branch gave way and she rolled downhill toward the stream.

She screamed as jagged rocks slashed her arms and she slammed repeatedly against the rugged hill. At last, she was hurled against a huge boulder at the stream's edge where she lay bleeding and disoriented. The first heavy raindrops splattered her muddied cheek as she attempted to rise up. She cried out, as knives seemed to cut through her arms. Her legs felt like lead posts and she was unable to move them. She squeezed her eyes tight to stop the spinning sensation.

As the rain soaked through her clothes, she shivered. "My baby...my baby," she cried softly. Tears mixed with rain down her cheeks as she fell silent and drifted away.

* * *

Vladimir's eyes bolted open into thick blackness; every sense told him it was far too early to rise, yet he could not deny a sudden overwhelming fear. An emotion he found alien, unusual. He feared so little. He listened carefully now in the darkened cellar for approaching footsteps or anything unusual. Nothing.

Suddenly, a flash of red went off in his mind. Vladimir's nerves tingled like the night in the gypsy camp, and he was sharply aware and on guard. He closed his eyes and focused on the flash of red. Then he saw Emelia's tortured expression, heard the sound of two slowing heartbeats and he knew. *Emelia and the baby are dying.*

Without regard for the light that might still be clinging to the evening, he unlocked the door, but found the cellar completely dark. He sped through the unlit winding passages of perspiring cement and mortar, eager to find Emelia. He could not smell her familiar scent. She was not in the castle.

Muffled voices behind the stairwell door told him he was near the first floor, close to the kitchen. He knew the staff mustn't see him, else he might lose Emelia forever. As he cloaked his body with invisibility, he decided his newly learned hunting skills would serve him well. It had been useful many times when stalking a kill. The ability to cloak himself from view, Vladimir had found, proved a simple trick played on even simpler minds.

Vladimir carefully pushed open the door to the kitchen and saw two staff members, speaking in hushed tones, their expression grim, preparing the evening meal.

"They've looked for Lady Emelia everywhere, but she's not here. She took out her horse, and never returned. Borak came back alone."

The other cook tossed a handful of chopped potatoes into a pot. "I always feared that cursed horse. Did you ever see his eyes? He's an evil one, I say." Her expression softened. "Oh, I hope Lady Emelia is all right."

Vladimir stepped into the kitchen and willed his presence to go unnoticed as he avoided eye contact. The two cooks continued in hushed conversation, as Vladimir hurried past them and to the front foyer where he left the castle undetected.

A defiant bulwark of gunmetal clouds crashed into an angry purple sky. Lightening exploded, setting the sky ablaze for one blinding moment, ozone hanging in the air like a poisonous gas.

Driving rain pelted Vladimir's face as he lifted his arms and rose into the air. He could smell Emelia now in the night, even through the heavy downpour. He soared like a great eagle to the forest clearing. Two heartbeats pounded in his ears, so close now—one dangerously slow, the other nearly gone all together. He heard Emelia's labored breathing becoming shallower. Finally, over the clearing ledge, he saw her broken body next to the stream.

Vladimir flew over the steep incline and landed solidly beside her. He stroked her muddy face and noticed a familiar smell hanging like a cloud overhead. The stench of death. He grabbed her up and jumped with great power back to the top of the ridge. They rose into the air and sped toward the castle like two spirits riding the night sky. They soon reached the huge double doors, and Vladimir kicked them open with one powerful thrust. He no longer cared who knew what he'd become. Just as he reached Emelia's bedroom door, Michael's nurse, Olga stepped out of the nursery and into the hallway.

"My God..." She crossed herself. "It's true, you are not dead!" Her eyes narrowed as she came forward. "Now you've cursed Lady Emelia as well."

Vladimir could smell no fear in the woman. He met her gaze and commanded, "Open the bedroom door. She's not dead, yet."

On the bed, Vladimir stripped Emelia of her wet clothes. "Hurry, Olga, get some blankets. She's dangerously cold."

As he held Emelia close, he saw her struggling to hold on to life. With her skin ashen, he saw that her respiration was almost nonexistent. He laid his hand over her swollen middle and felt a sudden rush of warmth. The child remained yet alive, but barely, its heart rate slowing fast. He cradled Emelia and tenderly kissed her, his tears mingling with the dirt on her face.

"I can't lose you, my love. I cannot lose you both." Her cheek was cold against his palm. "Please forgive me, darling. I beg your mercy and understanding. Don't hate me for what I must do."

He turned her head to one side and bent close to plunge his fangs deep into the icy blue flush of her neck. Her body stiffened briefly, then fell limp. Her blood tasted warm and sweet and filled him with strength as well as tremendous grief. When he'd nearly drained her life force, he raised her lips to his own and spilled the last of her blood into her mouth. As she swallowed, the color returned to her cheeks and Vladimir imparted the last few precious drops to her.

Emelia's eyes opened slowly, and she took in a sudden large breath, as if for the first time. Vladimir watched as her broken body healed within seconds, her color becoming that of a spring rose.

"Vladimir," she whispered and buried her head against his chest.

Olga returned to the room. "Great Jesus, our Lord! What've you done to her?" She rushed to Emelia and took her hand, dropping to her knees in prayer.

"Yes, pray for me, Olga, for the pains have begun." Emelia looked lovingly at Vladimir and said, "Our child will be born tonight."

Emelia sat up and pressed herself against the headboard, clutching her abdomen. "It's time!"

Olga used the blankets to prop her up, then lifted the foot of the sheet to examine her. "Oh, my Lady, the baby is almost here."

Vladimir held Emelia as another contraction took her, and Olga commanded, "Push! Push hard!"

He watched in awe as Emelia grew suddenly stronger and grabbed her bent knees, again pushing with great force. Her final scream bled into the cream colored walls and faded into silence as Vladimir heard the strong, sudden cry of his infant daughter, and he instantly knew her name: Arianne.

CHAPTER 5

Emelia stayed close to Vladimir, hidden in the shadows, while they waited for two members of the President's Securitate to pass. Moments before, she'd watched as the soldiers had beaten a peasant for stealing a loaf of bread and left him lying in the street bleeding. Emelia was drawn to the scent of his blood. It awakened a hunger inside she'd never known.

Vladimir seemed to sense her urgency and forced her to stay back. She heard his thoughts as if he were whispering to her.

Wait. It is too soon.

The men trudged on, with their boots heavy against the cobblestone walk as they moved down the street. Emelia's body ached as if her muscles were on fire. Her hunger had become intense and she knew it was time to feed.

Earlier, she'd pleaded with Vladimir to find some other way to survive. The thought of drinking human blood filled her with guilt and grief. She'd brought forth a life the night before and tonight she was expected to destroy another's. Vladimir reminded her their children needed her and she must do this in order to survive. There was no other way.

The poor peasant lay curled against the curb, crying. Emelia could see the man's bloodied face, and bone protruding from his upper arm. He'd been defenseless against their power. Angry at their vicious brand of justice, she realized she'd have no remorse in taking one of them.

Vladimir moved beside her and nodded that it was time.

The soldiers stood together on the street corner with their cigarettes glowing in the dark. Emelia felt disgust for them as they joked about the man they'd beaten, and her jaws began to move downward to accommodate her fangs. Her body had gone through so many changes in the past twenty-four hours that she found herself in awe. Her husband's instructions for a successful kill remained clear in her mind and she prepared to take the man closest to her. She prayed she would be quick enough.

In a flash, Vladimir grabbed the tallest soldier. The man screamed as Vladimir's fangs sunk deep. Emelia yanked her victim back by his hair and dropped him to his knees. Such strength she'd never known. His neck lay exposed as he struggled for release. She smelled his fear and saw the disbelief in his eyes.

His cries filled her ears as she bit deep into his neck. She felt his pulse pounding against her lips and eagerly drank the warm liquid. Gradually, the man stopped his struggle and lay limp in her arms. She knew she must stop or the man would die. Her throbbing muscles no longer burned and her strength was renewed.

Vladimir knelt beside her and laid the man aside. "It's time to go."

"What will become of them?" she asked.

"Eventually they'll go mad."

Emelia realized her power over death and smiled. She'd finally defeated death as her enemy. This was her new life.

* * *

Mira Brasov peered out the train window at familiar landmarks. The station wasn't much further. She saw subtle changes here and there, but everything looked the same. The past five years away from her homeland had passed quickly. It had broken her heart to leave family and friends when she went to America, but when the opportunity arose, Mira's adventurous spirit couldn't say no. She felt there was no future for her in Romania under Ceausescu's rule and sought out friends who'd left the country before her. When the letter came that housing had been set up with a Romanian family, she was ecstatic and hurried to make her plans. Only twenty-four at the time, she packed the very basics and sailed off to the United States, knowing only the names of the family she'd be staying with and that they'd come from Romania several years before. She was convinced she'd be all right, after all, if she'd survived tough times in Romania, surely the U.S. would be easy.

The first year had proven her theory wrong. Jobs were hard to come by and she struggled with the language even though she had been taught English in school. Finally, she landed a bakery job doing what she knew best—creating pastries and cakes. She vowed to one day own her own bakery and perhaps a catering business on the side. Right now, those dreams would have to wait, however. She toyed with the silver locket she wore around her neck as her mind replayed the telephone conversation with Olga, her sister's nanny, only days before. She knew something was wrong by the woman's tone.

"Is this Mira Brasov?" the hushed voice crackled over the line.

Mira recognized the familiar language. It sounded strange after hearing mostly English for so long. "Yes. Who's calling?" she answered in her mother tongue.

"I am Olga Covasna, your sister's nursemaid. You must come to Romania now."

Mira felt her blood turn to ice. "Olga, has something happened?"

"There isn't much time. I fear for the children. Please hurry."

"Olga, what happened?"

"There's danger. Emelia died during childbirth."

Olga's cryptic call did little to answer the question of what had actually happened. What danger could there possibly be if her sister was dead? It was hard to say if the woman was the superstitious type, or if it was simply a matter of concern for the orphaned children's welfare.

Mira winced as though she'd been slapped. Her sister was dead. Guilt coiled around her conscience like a boa constrictor—she should have gone to Emelia when Vladimir died. What kind of sister was she? Family should be there for one another, and she and Emelia were all that were left. Now it was too late. Instead of celebrating a birth, she would plan a funeral.

The lights inside the train flickered twice to indicate they were approaching their destination. Mira dug in her purse for a mirror. After a ten-hour flight and a long train ride, she probably looked like hell. She didn't want to frighten poor little Michael; it would be difficult enough to explain that he'd be coming to live with her.

She ran a comb through her auburn tresses and felt a grip of remorse when she saw her china-blue eyes so much like her sister's reflected back at her. They shared the same thin shaped nose and high cheekbones and could have passed for twins except for her two years seniority.

She caught a glimpse of her necklace with the Brasov family crest as it glinted against the window's light. She and Emelia both had been given one as a gift from their father on their twenty-first birthdays. It had kept her grounded during the rough times when she first arrived in America, and reminded her she was a Brasov—strong and sure. She was proud of her heritage and never took the necklace off. As far as she knew, Emelia didn't either. Inside the large silver lockets, they both kept a tiny pearl of their mother's. Someday, she would pass Emelia's locket down to Arianne.

The train's whistle shrieked as they slowed into the station. She hoped Olga's nephew, Peter, would be on time to meet her, because the thought of waiting alone at the station where Vladimir had been murdered frightened her. She stepped out into the warm sunlight and felt a wave of relief. Peter stood nearby, looking much the same as she remembered, with a pair of thin anemic lips pasted above a long chin. He greeted her with no more than a nod, took her suitcases and headed toward the parking lot. She shivered against the spring air with a feeling of dark foreboding.

Inside the small car, she began to unwind. The worst of the trip was behind her. She needed to collect her thoughts and decide the best way to tell little Michael he'd be leaving the people and life he'd always known. It would be no less of an adjustment on her part, she decided, as she went from single and carefree to raising two children. Just as she'd done five years ago when she'd set out for a new life in a new country, she held tight to the philosophy that all would be well. They would start a new life together.

Mira had dozed on and off for most of the ride after several failed attempts to engage Peter in conversation. As he pulled up the long stretch of road that led to Von Tirgov castle, Mira found she was fully awake, and leaned forward to take in the beauty of the castle's grounds with its mature trees and luscious landscape. Dusk crept over the evening sky in pale shades of purple and burgundy, and she rolled down the window to take in the view and breathe in the heavy scent of honeysuckle. Her hair whipped across her cheek and undid any hope of a neat appearance, but she no longer cared—she was home.

Her stomach grumbled and she realized the light meal she'd had on the trip was a faded memory. Suddenly, she gasped when she saw the castle up ahead—her appetite temporarily forgotten. It was just as she remembered, yet somehow grander, taller, all-consuming. Peter brought the car to a halt under the lofty archway near the front doors and cut the engine. Mira let her mind fill with memories, slowly getting out of the car. While Peter went to fetch her bags from the trunk, she stepped back in order to take in the full height of the residence.

Wooden double-doors with decorative metal bolts nestled under the archway between two wide steeple towers. Still as solid as the day it was built, the dark brick and mortar hugged tight after hundreds of years of foul weather and battles. She crossed the courtyard to the entrance and lifted the L-shaped handle to push open the heavy door. Peter came up behind her as she entered the spacious foyer. He dropped her suitcases onto the marble floor with a thud, and disappeared before she could thank him.

The vaulted ceiling made her nearly six-foot stature feel small. She continued into the parlor and called out, "Hello? Olga are you here?"

Her voice echoed in the large room as her eyes scanned the parlor and settled on the portrait above the wide fireplace. Emelia and Vladimir stared back at her with smiles that spoke of hidden secrets. They were a handsome couple. Her throat tightened as she remembered her sister, her best friend. She looked around and saw the home did not portray any signs of danger as Olga had led her to believe. Perhaps the nursemaid had over-reacted.

The mantle clock reminded her it was nearly seven o'clock. "Time to eat," she announced to herself. "Now, if I can remember where the kitchen is—" she turned and stopped. No words would come. Her clammy hands trembled as she raised them to her mouth. Emelia stood in the doorway.

Mira braced herself against the love seat. She couldn't take her eyes from her sister. Emelia was more beautiful than Mira ever remembered and looked far from dead. She wore a long ivory gown with a lace bodice that exposed opalescent skin against the light. Her lips were full red blossoms in a thin smile. Mira watched her carefully, for although she obviously wasn't dead, there was something terribly wrong with her little sister.

Emelia approached her with arms outstretched. "Mira," she said softly, "I've missed you. I'm so glad you're here." She pulled back and cupped Mira's chin with icy fingers. "You look wonderful. The American lifestyle makes you happy?"

Confused, but relieved to see her alive, Mira embraced her. She held Emelia close, but felt no warmth to her skin or softness of her body. It was as if she were made of stone.

Mira bit her lower lip hard and tried to contain her anger. She'd been led to believe her sister had died by some insane nanny and now

Emelia stood before her as though nothing had happened.

"Emelia, what the hell's going on here? Where's Olga?"

Emelia's blue eyes narrowed and her tone was cautious. "Olga is in the nursery. Why do you ask?"

"Your nanny called to inform me of your recent death only three days ago! But here you are, obviously alive. Now what's going on?"

Emelia's smile faded and twisted into a deep frown. "I'd hoped to have some time with you before having to explain. It seems Olga has caused a change in plans. Come with me, sister. I'll give you the answer you're looking for. But I warn you, in this house the truth will not set you free."

She led Mira out of the parlor and into the kitchen to the cellar door. Mira stopped feeling something was very wrong.

"Where are we going?"

"You'll see. Please trust me." Emelia opened the door.

They made their way inside where the air was cool and musty and the lighting was made poor by dusty wall sconces. The steep stairway wound down toward the first hall of cellars, and Mira followed her carefully, wondering where she was taking her.

Emelia glanced back to explain, "The staff has been ordered to stay in their quarters after dusk. Olga is the only one permitted to leave her room because she cares for the children. She knows the truth."

"*What* truth?" Mira hesitated.

Emelia moved ahead without an answer.

Mira held tight to the railing as they descended, her heart slowly breaking for her sister. She'd lost her husband and now she'd gone mad. "Emelia, you're ill, please come back upstairs. I'd like to see my new niece."

When they reached the bottom step, Emelia continued. "Arianne is beautiful. She looks so much like Vladimir, with her black hair and dark eyes. He is very proud."

Mira stopped briefly to decide whether to continue to go along with the sick charade or hurry and find Olga.

Emelia motioned for her to follow. "Not much further." Her gown dusted the musty cement floor as she walked.

Mira followed behind and kept an eye out for any unwelcome cellar creatures. The evening was growing into an impossible nightmare.

Emelia stopped before a wooden door at the end of the hall and pulled a long brass key from her gown pocket.

"I'm entrusting this secret to you, Mira. Remember, you asked for the truth. My life...my family, will never be the same and we need your help." She pushed open the door and stepped aside for her to enter.

Mira rubbed her arms to fight the frigid air and squinted to adjust her vision in the darkness. The room was the size of a small bedroom, furnished with a bed, and a long metal table against the far wall. Shadows climbed the painted panels by the light of two lanterns and offered little warmth or comfort to the cramped surroundings.

"What is all this, Emelia? Why did you bring me down here?" Mira asked.

"This is our home. Vladimir and I stay hidden here during the day and come out only at night."

"Vladimir? How could that be? He's dead." She regretted her harsh tone.

"Please try and understand. We are cursed, never to be clean again. We are vampires. There is nothing anyone can do."

Mira felt the sting of tears at her sister's sick display of insanity. Her grief for Vladimir had consumed her and stolen her mind. Filled with compassion, she pulled her sister close to embrace her like a child.

"My little sister, how I love you. I'm so sorry things had to be this way. But you must think of the children and be strong. Vladimir is gone and I don't understand the sick hoax Olga has played on me, but I'm so happy you're alive."

Emelia jerked back. "I am *not* alive! Not as you would believe. I will walk in darkness for eternity at my husband's side, for we have overcome the ultimate tragedy of mortality. Why can't you believe me?" Her eyes blazed against the lantern's fire and Mira tried to pull free of her vice-like grip. Emelia's lips formed into a sinister smile and then opened wide. Pearl-white fangs glistened sharply.

Mira turned her head. "No! Get away. Stop!"

Emelia drew closer, her breath hot on Mira's neck. She felt her sister's pressure against her skin grow more intense until she wanted to scream, then suddenly it stopped. Her arms ached where her sister had gripped her. She stumbled back from the abrupt release.

Emelia's voice was a coarse whisper. "You believe me now. Do you see what I've become—how your little sister has had to adapt in order to survive?"

Mira still trembled while she tried to make sense of it. She'd seen for herself the monster lurking inside Emelia. Olga was right. Emelia was dead, and in her place was a damned spirit, cursed to exist in eternal torment. She reached out to touch Emelia's arm. "Yes. I believe you, what choice do I have? But how can you live this way? Surely your staff will find out!"

"As far as they know, I died giving birth. Olga has asked them to stay until my funeral. It would be too risky to keep them."

"What about the children?" Mira's voice cracked. "What will happen to them?"

Emelia's expression softened. "We need you, Mira...the children need you. You can stay here, have free rein of the castle, come and go as you please. Olga will tend to their needs, but they need loving guidance from someone close to them. You're their family, please say you'll do it."

Mira's mind spider-webbed in several directions. How could this be? It was still surreal to her. Finally, she shook her head. "What you're asking is impossible, Emelia. I will gladly take them as my own, but we will leave Romania. I left here once for freedom and now it is for safety."

"Vladimir and I can't leave our motherland. It is too dangerous. There are those who seek to destroy us. Please say you'll think about it, Mira. Don't answer yet."

She grabbed Mira's hand before she could respond and led her back toward the stairs. "Now, let me take you to meet Arianne. I'm sure the choice will be easy once you hold her in your arms."

Mira followed her out of the cellar in silence. Emelia was right the decision *was* easy. She already knew what she must do. The only problem now was how to escape with the children.

* * *

Mira slept little that night, awakened from nightmares several times. Her mind was filled with images of giant black shadows that clawed for her with long bloody fingers. Finally, she arose to escape their terror and form her plan. She'd seen with her own eyes the truth of Emelia's claim; she was indeed a vampire. Although she had yet to see proof of Vladimir, there would be no reason for Emelia to lie. The fierceness with which her sister had attacked frightened her. Was she in real danger? As long as they needed her help to care for the children she felt safe.

Her blood ran cold when she thought about Arianne and Michael. Could they be in danger as well? If Emelia thought they would be taken from her, would she become desperate enough to kill her own sister? Her sister's words remained clear in her mind, *"My beautiful daughter is so like her father. She is already half vampire. In time we shall rule the night together."*

Tears slid down her cheeks as she recalled seeing little Michael asleep in his crib as she cradled the infant Arianne in her arms. She'd slept soundly with black silken lashes nearly touching her fair skin, unaware of the darkness and potential danger around her. It had been while she rocked the child she realized a tremendous void in her life had been filled. Her well of emptiness now overflowed with love and peace as she bonded with her niece and nephew. These precious, unblemished lives were entrusted to her by fate, through the most horrific circumstances ever known. The children would be raised as her own.

For now, she would go along with Emelia's plan until she could secure Olga's help. After the funeral, she would have full custody of both children, as she was the only living relative. Only then could she set her plan into motion to save their lives, and possibly her own.

CHAPTER 6

Emelia stretched in her bed, refreshed but already fighting the familiar gnaw of hunger. She sensed the late hour from deep in the cellar. It was time to hunt. She cherished her nighttime rides with Borak as they raced the wind through the damp air rising from the marshes. How strange it was that she had come to love the night, and no longer missed the sun's light or the explosive multicolor hues of an evening sunset. She knew she had changed, and held no regrets.

Vladimir stirred in the bed beside her and watched her dress for the hunt. "Are you sure the sun is down?"

"Yes, I can feel it. It's going to be a beautiful night." She slipped into her dress and pleaded, "Come with me, we can feed together."

He rose slowly. "You seem to find a pleasure in killing that I don't share. When I feed it is a very intimate, private thing. I see no thrill. It's only survival."

The flames from the wall sconces flickered and cast a dim yellow light over the damp cellar room. Shadows danced on the walls. Vladimir's eyes reflected the light as she moved beside him.

"See this gift for what it is," she said, touching his cheek. "I embrace it as my final accomplishment of a vow made when my mother died. You have given me everything I could want, this home, two beautiful children and now the greatest gift of all—immortality. We have defeated death don't you see? Never again will I weep over death's power in my life. My children will never suffer the loss of their parents as I have. If only the world could see there is a way out from under mortality."

"It's a curse."

"Many of our kind feel differently." Emelia nuzzled his cheek.

"They share your view?"

She shrugged. "I'm sure everyone learns to accept it in their own way. Some despise the fact they're forced to kill and drink blood to survive; others embrace it—and realize it is the only way."

"No. I don't accept it. And just as you vowed so many years ago to abolish death's power, given a chance, I would choose to release myself from the shackles of this immortality."

Emelia offered no reply. There was nothing to say. Vladimir had made his choice. She leaned close and kissed him softly before she turned to go. The night awaited her.

* * *

Later, deep in the cellar shadows, Mira waited. It was nearly dawn now and she knew Emelia must return soon. Her mind still fought to dispute the truth she'd come to know. She wanted more proof of the evil monster her sister claimed to be.

Her eyes widened when she saw what her heart had told her was impossible. Emelia passed through the wall itself. Her pallor was gone and she wore a pink flush, her lips still soiled with the telltale splatter of blood. Her ethereal motion reminded Mira of a gentle spirit gliding in the wind, but she knew no human could move like that. The truth hit her hard and she choked back a sob. Emelia was truly a vampire and the children were in danger. The sooner they were out of their parent's grasp, the safer they'd be.

* * *

Several days later, Mira struggled with shaking hands to button her blouse. The mirror reflected a pale woman with wide blue eyes and a nervous smile; a reflection she barely recognized. The past week had drained her of physical and emotional energy she couldn't afford to lose. Acceptance of Emelia and Vladimir's fate had not come easy, but that night in the cellar had given her no choice. With Olga's help she'd formed what she prayed was a solid plan. Today those plans would be set into motion with Emelia's funeral.

She checked her watch and noted it was time to leave. The car would be waiting to take her and the children to the church ahead of the guests. She couldn't be late.

At the nursery door, Mira paused and watched Olga cooing softly at little Arianne as she swaddled her snugly. Her throat tightened as tears bit the corners of her eyes. Now is not the time, she chided herself.

Mira forced a smile as she bent to straighten Michael's bowtie. "There now, don't you make a handsome young man? What a big boy you are."

Olga gently placed the baby into Mira's arms, then turned to Michael. "Now you be good for Aunt Mira. Listen to her and help her with your sister..." Her expression shattered like crystal in a tempest as she turned back to Mira. "May God...be with you."

"Olga, please leave as soon as possible. It's not safe for you to stay."

The nursemaid gave no immediate reply and escorted them out of the nursery. "It's time. You mustn't miss your flight."

* * *

In the church, incense floated over the pews as the large group of mourners gathered like black shadows. Bright sunlight pierced the stained-glass saints of the windows and created colorful prisms on the pale tile floor. Before the altar where the priest prepared to offer solace, strength, and hope eternal, a linen-draped mahogany casket basked in the prayers and grief of the parishioners. The organ began to rumble a low funeral hymn and the last of the mourners rifled sideways into their seats.

* * *

In the car, Mira bowed her head and whispered a prayer over Arianne as they sped toward their destination. She watched Michael stare out the window as the fields and livestock rushed by in a blur. Not too much further, she thought with a sigh. The finality settled in her mind like a closing door. Soon it would be over.

She met Peter's glance in the rearview mirror, and his expression betrayed unspoken anxiety. She cradled her niece tighter and took in the sweet aroma of baby powder as she wedged herself firmly in the confidence of her actions.

* * *

At the cemetery, the open grave gaped in a hungry expression as the coffin rested on supports. The priest's touching eulogy and prayer evoked more tears, and with a final blessing, he dismissed the mourners to their pain.

* * *

Jets blasted overhead at the airport as Mira covered Arianne's face lightly with a hanky against the heavy fuel stench. She took Michael by his sweaty little hand and glanced once behind to see about Peter. He moved at an annoying pace and she stopped herself from barking orders to *step it up*. She couldn't walk fast enough with the terminal now in view.

* * *

After the last of the mourners departed, the first shovel full of warm soil splayed over the casket below. Several cemetery workers pitched heartily, each toss bringing them closer to a hot meal and their fill of plum wine. The work continued in a steady rhythm to bring the day— and Emelia Von Tirgov's life to a close.

* * *

Mira felt claustrophobic as the fasten seat-belt signs lit up overhead. The jet's engines whined louder and the plane began to move. Michael had fallen asleep beside her and Arianne cooed softly in her arms. They were on their way. She forced herself to breathe deep as her heart hammered inside her chest. She knew she should be relieved that everything had gone as planned. Still, an uneasy feeling gnawed at her soul. Mira jumped as Michael suddenly cried out in his sleep, "Mama!"

* * *

As the daylight faded over Von Tirgov castle, deep in the cellar below, Emelia abruptly awoke from her cryptic sleep. She'd heard Michael's cry. Her senses told her that her children weren't in the house. They were far away from her now. She knew it was still daylight and realized she was a prisoner in her tomb, unable to reach them. Her guttural scream echoed the damp walls against the silence of an empty house and heart. Her children were gone.

CHAPTER 7

Emelia breathed in the night's musty scent. She would take no pleasure in the hunt tonight. Several weeks had passed since her children's' abduction. No trace had been found, but she knew where Mira had taken them. Olga had nearly paid the ultimate price for her betrayal, but Vladimir had stopped her. He'd reminded Emelia they needed Olga to care for their home and guard their secret. It was understood she could not leave, or Vladimir would be forced to silence her. Olga's nephew, Peter, had stayed on as well to care for the grounds and tend the horses. The Von Tirgov castle remained alive in appearance only.

Emelia's black skirt draped over Borak's back in graceful folds as she rode. They'd traveled for hours during the night, over hills and through forests to finally reach the caverns near the Alps. Her acute sense of smell told her there were no humans near, only a faint metallic scent. It had been a full day since she'd fed and the tight opalescent skin across her bony hands alarmed her. The craving inside for the taste of human blood would soon drive her mad.

Suddenly alert, Emelia dismounted and tied Borak to a nearby tree. The damp leaves padded the sound of her approach through the thicket. An owl's hoot questioned her intrusion from a thick branch above. She raised her head to take in the air and hurried past the watchful bird. Beyond the trees ahead, she detected the smell she'd sought—a human scent.

She peered through the heavy brush and saw a figure in the

darkness. Emelia's throat tightened in anticipation of her feast. A young woman stood alone in a small clearing and Emelia wondered why.

The woman turned as Emelia approached; there was no scent of fear around her, it seemed she expected to meet someone. Emelia kept her eyes fixed on the victim without a word. As she reached for her, the woman was jerked away.

A tall, hooded figure wrapped an arm around the woman's waist. At once she surrendered, exposing a creamy white neck. Emelia raced forward and severed the hold with a knife-like sweep of her arm. This was *her* meal. The woman fell to the ground, but before she could crawl away, Emelia grabbed her by the hair.

Emelia's chest felt as though it might explode from hunger. Her jaws gave a powerful thrust as her fangs emerged. She bent to take her kill.

Suddenly, the figure drew back the hood and exposed a man with long white hair and blazing green eyes. His twisted sneer revealed razor fangs of his own. Emelia heard his throaty laugh as he swiftly thrust-kicked her in the chest. She flew backwards and landed hard against a tree.

With one fluid movement, the vampire picked up the woman like a rag doll and plunged his fangs into her neck. Emelia watched with frustration and desire as blood trickled toward the woman's breasts.

Emelia lunged. "I'll kill you for that!"

She scrambled to her feet, hissing, and slammed the man hard. The woman's limp body dropped to the ground and he briefly stumbled back. His eyes fixed on Emelia as he wiped blood from his chin.

His expression never wavered and he clutched Emelia by the throat with one hand, lifting her. "I would welcome it," he said, and suddenly released her. She dropped to the ground beside the victim, face to face with eyes frozen wide in a stare of surprise. Emelia looked longingly at the blood, now drying on the woman's skin and felt the ache return.

A heavy hand rested on her shoulder, its large ruby ring inches from her cheek, as the vampire's voice filled her head. *I am Daegon Enescu, coven-master. Come with me, Emelia, and you will never hunger again.*

She knocked his hand away and got up. "You're Daegon the thief! And how do you know me?"

He smiled at her discomfort. "You are Vladimir's wife."

"How do you know Vladimir? Did you steal from him, too?"

"I know many things. For example, you haven't fed for over a day, your horse is tied just beyond those trees and you would do anything to retrieve your children." His final words were acid on her bleeding heart. Her desperation rose.

"What do you know about them? Tell me."

"I'll do better than that. I will show them to you." Before she could react, he reached out and cupped her chin. Immediately a vision formed in her head...

Beyond a white fence, Michael ran through a small yard of thick green grass and chased a flock of black birds. As he reached for them, they rose up in flight and scattered into the bright blue sky. He clapped his little hands and called out, "Wee! Birdie!"

Mira chase after him and scooped him up in her arms. Michael giggled as she tickled him and they entered a petite, white bungalow. Inside, Emelia followed the vision past a tidy kitchen and down a narrow hallway, where pictures hung in neat rows. Gilded frames housed faded black and white photos of their parents and homeland, telling the Brasov family history.

She watched Mira head into the first doorway on the right. Emelia's heart pounded hard as she saw Arianne kicking and wriggling in her crib. She'd grown so much already and her wide, dark eyes were alert to Mira's voice. "Where's my girl? Are you ready to play?"

Emelia's arms reached to hold her child close and smell her sweet baby aroma. She closed her eyes tight as the vision faded into the darkened forest around her. She grabbed Daegon's arm and fixed her gaze on his emerald eyes. "Show me how you do this," she commanded. "Teach me to be like you!"

Daegon's long chin lifted slightly as he looked down at her. "Ah, it seems you are a great deal wiser than your husband."

Emelia was cautious. "What do you mean?"

"He declined my offer to bring him to his full potential as vampire. Together, we could have ruled the night. But he prefers to wallow in guilt and self-pity."

"Vladimir never mentioned you. He's very strong and doesn't need your help."

Daegon smiled. "You're quite right. Now that he's taken you as his victim, he is no longer rabid and his powers will grow much stronger. Believe what I tell you, for my two centuries as vampire have been quite the learning experience—experience I'm willing to share."

Intrigued, Emelia refused to let him know it. "I'm only interested in getting back my children. What good is eternal life if your will to live has been taken?"

"Vampires have no use for a will. You are immortal." He seemed to read her thoughts and finally said, "But I can help you. Your powers are crude, but not beyond polish. What I have shown you today is but a taste of the potential you hold. You can have what I have."

"At what cost?"

Daegon arched a long gray eyebrow. "You would put a price on your children?"

Emelia's cheeks burned. "I asked you what cost. I didn't say I wouldn't pay it."

He pulled his hood back over his head and stepped over the dead woman as he disappeared into the woods. "All I ask is your allegiance."

* * *

"Here we are." The clean-shaven attorney slid the paperwork across the cherry wood desk. "Arianne's last name is now Brasov."

Mira scanned the documents and struggled to comprehend legalese. "It went smoother than I'd anticipated. I hope the orphanage will work out as well."

The man's expression spoke volumes, when his eyes wouldn't quite meet hers. He shuffled a stack of papers. "I'm sure it won't be a problem, Ms. Brasov. Adoption is big these days, especially children from other countries." He set the stack aside. "If you'll excuse me, I still don't understand why you aren't keeping both children."

Mira squirmed in the cushioned high-back chair and felt her cheeks grow warm. He seemed to be cross-examining her over the decision to put Michael in an orphanage. Wasn't he supposed to be on *her* side? She couldn't share the real reason—that both children were in danger as long as they were together. She knew Emelia and Vladimir would stop at nothing to get their children back. Her escape to the United States had only bought time, not safety.

She forced a reassuring smile. "It was not an easy decision, Mr. Peck. But I am unable to care for more than one child," she lied. "I feel little Michael will be better off at St. Paul's Orphanage. There, he will get the proper education and have a chance at adoption. Believe me, it is the hardest choice I've ever had to make, but it is necessary."

* * *

Vladimir reached the castle just before dawn to find Emelia absent. She'd grown more brazen against the day light, often returning as the first rays penetrated the morning haze. He feared she no longer cared for her life and welcomed the searing death the sun had to offer. She'd become desperate in her search for Michael and Arianne, although they both knew where their children were. She had become adept at seeing their daughter through her mind's eye, a trick the coven-master, Daegon, had taught her. Vladimir knew he could not be trusted and feared for Emelia, yet she would not give up on the hope he would help her.

They knew Arianne was well and living with Mira, but their link with Michael had been broken. He realized they had to make contact with her before they lost both of them, but they could not leave their homeland and risk destruction. Every day he could see Emelia dying a slow, agonizing death at her loss, and he knew of only one way to obtain the power he needed to save her. However, he'd vowed never to return to the curse he'd denied so long ago, although there was no other way.

Vladimir allowed his mind to enter the depths of a trance, drawing into the world of the dead. He had neglected his gift for so long, yet it came easily as he focused his mind. The familiar weightless sensation filled him as he drifted among the gray fog of the spirit world. He needed to find a desperate soul willing to do his bidding at any cost. Tortured spirits cried out for rescue and peace as he passed through the void. Their sunken eyes cried tears of blood as they clawed at his presence. He pushed through them toward an intense feeling of pain that seemed to call to him, and reached out for a nearby shadow.

Vladimir winced and drew back from the raw agony before him. He saw a man in eighteenth century attire come into focus and bow before him. "Master. Save me from this torment!"

Vladimir knew he'd found his servant at last; the one who would become Arianne's dark conscience and eventually force her to return home.

CHAPTER 8

St. John, Indiana 1995

Mira ran the open scissors along the ribbon and watched it curl into a springy peach tendril. She secured it atop the tiny white gift box and smiled at her decorating attempt. Arianne would be very surprised by the contents. It had never been a question of *what* she would give her niece for her twenty-first birthday, but rather what style. Mira wanted to give her a locket similar to the one that had been given to her on *her* twenty-first birthday. But fashion had changed and she knew the locket would have to match Arianne's taste or it would end up in the dresser drawer under a pile of dilapidated pantyhose.

Her own locket was identical to Emelia's—a two-inch diameter mother-of-pearl oval, with an embossed silver cursive *B* for Brasov. When times were tough in their lives, she and Emelia both stood firm on the foundation of their heritage and let it build them up to meet any challenge. Mira smiled. There had been many moments over the past twenty-one years raising Arianne, that she had found herself clutching her locket. Through temper-tantrums, chicken-pox, cheerleading, and puberty, she'd held firm to her locket *and* to her belief that she'd done the right thing so many years before.

On her way to Arianne's room, she spied the parade of hallway pictures that had grown considerably since she'd moved in. The walls read like a pictorial time line of her life with her niece. From kindergarten through high school, the photos reflected a bud of a child with wide dark eyes and blue-black hair to a glowing beauty with full, pouty lips and creamy olive skin. Arianne was Mira's pride and heart, yet so much like her father in looks.

Mira propped the gift on Arianne's dresser jewelry box and glanced at the snapshots framing her niece's mirror. The little girl room had slowly changed over the years into a young woman's, as she traded Barbies for a bra and teddy bears for a telephone. On her nightstand were several college books in place of glamour magazines. Arianne knew what she wanted out of life and already referred to herself—in Mira's company only—as Dr. Brasov.

A knot formed in Mira's stomach when she considered that one day soon she would have to reveal the truth to Arianne about her parents and the past. Although she'd never heard from Emelia since she'd taken the children, Arianne could be in danger now that she was grown and soon to be on her own. She needed to know the truth. Dread filled her like a dark shadow seeping into her simple, content life. The painful secret must be revealed in order to protect her.

Mira jumped at the sound of the kitchen screen door and hurried out of the bedroom.

"Aunt Mira?" Arianne called. "Where are you?"

"In here." Mira settled into the living room recliner with a book.

Arianne's cheeks were flushed with excitement. She quickly scanned the bookshelves and tabletops as she chattered. "I aced that biology exam and found every book I need for my research paper in the library. What luck, huh?" She planted a kiss on Mira's forehead and plopped onto the couch, briefly checking behind the pillows.

Mira grinned. "Lose something?"

Arianne shrugged. "Maybe."

Mira casually turned another book page. "Can I help you find it?"

"I think you can." Arianne moved to the floor beside Mira's chair. "It's a huge box with a large red bow," she fully extended her arms, "and it has something special inside."

Unable to stand the game another moment, Mira reached over and hugged her niece, whispering in her ear, "I think you'll find it on your dresser."

"Really?" Arianne was already on her feet.

"Happy birthday, baby."

Arianne grabbed Mira's hand and pulled her from the recliner. "I can't believe you fit a Porsche in my room!"

Mira rolled her eyes and smiled. *Not on a baker's salary.* It had taken months to save for the locket. Although she'd been able to use the sizeable inheritance from Emelia and Vladimir for raising Arianne, Mira had chosen to keep it separate, putting it in trust until she turned twenty-one.

She and Arianne had lived comfortably off of her salary, using only some of the inheritance for big ticket items like her high school class trip, a prom dress and, of course, college tuition.

She watched Arianne's reaction as she tore off the wrapping paper and opened the box. "Oh, Aunt Mira, it's beautiful. It's like yours!"

"Well, not quite. I chose something a little more modern. It opens like mine, though. Here, let me show you."

The gold-faced, oval locket displayed a bold B font in emerald birthstone accents. The tiny side latch opened the piece with places inside for miniature photos.

The young girl wrapped her arms around Mira's neck. "I love you Aunt Mira, and I'll never take it off."

Mira stepped behind her and draped the necklace around her neck. "Now, let me give you the speech my father gave me when I received my locket." She secured the clasp and turned Arianne back around to look at it. "Grandpa Andrei said, 'Never forget your roots—where you come from. You will always be Brasov!'" She smiled and added, "And you'll always be my girl."

A faraway look settled over Arianne's bright expression.

"What is it? What's wrong?" Mira asked.

Arianne clutched the locket gently. "I'm not being ungrateful, Aunt Mira, but when you said I should never forget where I came from, I draw a blank. I know I came from Romania after my parents died, but that's all I know. What *are* my roots?"

Mira barely heard her question. Her palms were suddenly wet with perspiration and her heart galloped hard in her chest.

"Aunt Mira? Are you all right?" Arianne asked as she followed her aunt's gaze across the room.

There on the pillow of the bed lay a long-stemmed, red rose.

Arianne picked it up and took in a full breath of its scent. "I didn't even notice it till now. It's beautiful. Thank you." She put the flower to her nose once more.

Mira's limbs felt like ice and she sat on the edge of the bed. "Arianne, today you are a grown woman and you're right—you should know your background. But now it's for your safety as well as heritage."

Arianne put the flower aside. "I don't understand."

Mira wet her lips. "I didn't give you the rose. It's a message from your parents."

* * *

Black eyes watched from the shadowed corner of Arianne's bedroom as Mira explained the sad truth about her parents. Shylock shifted silently as the story continued.

"So you see, Arianne, it's very important that you understand, and that you watch yourself. I hate to bring this to you on your birthday, but they've made contact and your life can never be the same."

Arianne crossed her arms over her chest. "Ha. Ha. Now what's with the Halloween talk, Aunt Mira? Is there another surprise for me?"

"I'm afraid not. It's the truth. Your parents are vampires."

"But they don't exist."

"Yes, they do. I saw your mother...what she does to survive. She isn't human, and that makes you half mortal and half vampire."

"That's impossible." Arianne felt her chest tighten.

"I understand this sounds unreal to you, but you must believe me for your own safety. I can't protect you anymore. You must be strong and alert, because I don't know what they'll do. The only thing I'm sure of is that they want you back with them, in Romania."

Arianne sat beside her. "I can't believe this. It can't be true. How insane! But I know you wouldn't lie to me. The hurt in your eyes is so real. Are you sure there isn't some other explanation?"

"None that I know of. I saw the proof myself."

"So my parents are alive?" Arianne looked hopeful.

"Not really, Arianne. They're just...shells of what they used to be. But I'm afraid they want you back."

"No way. It's finished as far as I'm concerned."

Mira frowned. "What do you mean? It can never be finished."

"I intend to finish it. I promise you, I'll never let my parents have their way—I'll never return to Romania."

"But aren't you the least bit curious about them?"

"How can I wonder about people I've never met? *You're* the only parent I need. We have no one else—we're family."

Shylock watched the two women hold each other as tears were spent. How touching, he thought bitterly. He moved from his isolated space and stood close enough to touch them as he fanned his hand over Mira's head.

Dear Mira. You've forgotten a very important part to the story. Wouldn't Emelia be disappointed with you if...

He leaned close to her ear and whispered, "...she knew you'd left out little Michael?" He chuckled to himself as she abruptly drew up stick straight.

Mira gasped. "Did you hear something?"

Arianne shook her head. "What was it?"

Mira trembled inside. "I'm not sure, but I heard...no, felt something."

"Let's go have some tea. I think we both need a break from the subject."

As the two women left, Shylock departed, deep in thought. Vladimir was wrong. His daughter was not going to return so easily. He must find a way or lose hope for his freedom forever. Things were not like they once were, long ago, when he had made the rules, and then broken them, a time when he had no master. If he wanted to taste freedom again, Arianne's cooperation was not negotiable.

CHAPTER 9

Arianne returned to her bedroom still trying to digest her Aunt's news. Vampires? It couldn't be. She was a modern woman, in a modern world, ready to go after her dream of becoming a doctor. None of it made sense. She didn't believe in ghosts, and she certainly didn't believe in vampires. It broke her heart when she considered seeking professional help for Mira.

She jumped when icy fingertips grazed her cheek. Her reflection in the mirror showed nothing there. All this talk of the walking dead was making her skittish.

When she turned, she gasped to see a man in black.

"Good evening," he said.

Arianne squeezed her eyes tight. Her mind told her this couldn't be happening. Victorian gentlemen didn't just appear. When she opened them, he was still there.

"Who the hell are you?" She stepped back.

He bowed curtly. "I am Shylock Duval, your dark conscience."

"Get out."

"Not until I get what I came for." He adjusted his cape.

Her eyes narrowed. "And that would be?"

"You."

"My parents sent you, didn't they?"

"I am here at your father's command."

Arianne threw the rose at him. "What are you? Some sort of ghost?"

"I've already told you. I am your dark conscience. I'm here to remind you that your place is in Romania with your parents."

"What's in it for you? What did my father promise?"

Shylock looked away.

"Well?"

"My freedom. Eternal rest."

"Ah, then you *are* a ghost. Well, let me save you the trouble. You're wasting your eternal time."

He began to fade, but his parting words were clear.

"You can never be clean, Arianne. The curse is upon you."

* * *

Months had passed since Arianne's twenty-first birthday and her visit from Shylock. When she'd told Aunt Mira, she'd broken down, asking Arianne's forgiveness for not telling her the truth sooner. She'd worried that his presence in Arianne's life could have somehow been prevented if she had. But Arianne had assured her that wasn't the case and she would deal with the annoying apparition in her own way.

"I'm stronger than you think. And I'm not afraid of some specter with an attitude."

Since then there'd been only a few signs of his presence with an occasional long stem red rose appearing in odd places, and the eerie feeling she was being watched. He stalked her to a park bench one afternoon where she'd tried to ignore him. Finally, she'd suggested her parents come and get her themselves. His answer had been vague and he'd quickly disappeared afterward. If that was the most he was capable of, she decided she could live with it.

The school year was set to begin. Gratefully, she'd found her growing excitement and busy schedule had occupied her mind. She set aside the college paperwork and reached for her journal. There was so much to tell, yet too much to consider.

August 12, 1995
Dear Journal,

Another school year will be beginning in two weeks. I'm anxious to continue my studies. It is sure to be a long road, but one with a foreseeable end, a happy ending. My life situation, however, does not seem to have that luxury, considering Aunt Mira's confession regarding our past together.

Through it all, my dear Aunt Mira risked her life to bring me out of my parents' evil world and raise me as her own. She has given me the sense and courage to continue. Yet, somehow, I get the feeling she's not telling all. Could there possibly be more to this somber tale? I won't let her down and insult her years of sacrifice by returning to Romania. When I reach the end of my path, I will be Dr. Arianne Brasov, holding firm to the roots of the woman who means everything to me.

My quest now, is to find the way to make me whole again, to cleanse my darkened soul. Can this ever be?

A knock at the door interrupted her writing. "Come in," Arianne answered.

Mira peeked inside before she entered carrying a can of soda. "I thought you might like a drink. You've been in here quite a while."

Arianne closed her journal and shoved it aside. "Thank you, Aunt Mira. I've just been collecting my papers and thoughts for school. I can't believe it's only two weeks away."

Mira sat on the edge of the bed. "Me, too. This summer flew by. But you're on your way to becoming the first doctor in the family. I couldn't be more proud."

"I'll miss you, you know. Dorm life can be fun, but it's not the same as home."

"Well, I'm here for you anytime. Call me when you get lonely, and I might just do the same."

Arianne traced an imaginary line across her desk with her finger. "This will be my first year away with Shylock haunting me. Most students bring their clothes, books, and favorite stuffed animals—not their dark conscience. But then, I'm not like most student's, am I?"

Mira's expression turned serious. "I was frightened when you first told me about him, but from what you've said, I believe you can handle Shylock. Remember, he has no real power over you. He's only here by your father's command to entice you. Nothing more." She smiled and added, "He might even prove entertaining when you're trying to stay awake, burning the midnight oil."

"I could do without him. And one day I will. There has to be a way."

"I'm afraid he won't rest until you do as he asks. Your parents want you back at any cost, so watch yourself."

"Yes, Shylock explained their desire for my return to the homeland, so I asked him why they simply don't come and get me? He said it isn't safe for them here."

Mira rose to leave. "Well, I have confidence in you, Arianne. Stick to your convictions and he won't sway you."

After Mira left, Arianne undressed for bed. She hadn't told her aunt about her recent feelings of doubt and curiosity. Could she hold off forever in the fight to ignore her parents' wishes? Would she eventually give in and find herself in Romania? Her troubled dreams were filled with visions of places so familiar to her, yet she'd never actually been there. In her heart, she knew they were of her native home. At times, her soul ached to stop the fight, embrace the truth, and accept her fate. Yet, in the morning after the night's shadows burned away in the dawn, reality always confronted her at the breakfast table in the form of Mira's loving eyes.

She clutched her locket with new determination. This torment could not last forever. She must know who she is!

Through her clouded senses, she became aware of the scent of roses. She turned to find Shylock.

"What do you want?" she asked bitterly.

He stepped from the shadows. "Why must you fight so? Surely, you understand your peace of mind is very simple to obtain." He continued past her, his cape fanning the pages on the desk as he strode. His expression remained thoughtful as he stroked his long chin and made his way to the window. She watched him warily. With his palms pressed against the sill, his ribbon-tethered ponytail lingered over his collar like a snake wearing a bowtie.

Arianne sneered at his proper *gentleman* ways, able to see beyond the white gloves, and suave demeanor. She knew he was nothing but a puppet trying desperately to regain his own soul.

"What's your story, anyway? How did you get into this mess?" she asked.

"It's a long, boring story, dear."

"I've got all the time in the world. You're from what, the 1800's?"

"Yes. I was a con man in my day, and quite good at it, I must say."

"Married?"

His expression was grim. "No. Sadly, I never realized that dream."

"Then you were in love?"

"Yes. Her name was Angelique Knightsbride. She was the daughter of a wealthy department store owner."

"What happened?"

"My career was exposed by someone with a vendetta against me. After Angelique learned the truth as to how I made my living, I received a letter explaining she was to be married to another man."

Arianne felt the pain of his loss and realized there was more to Shylock than she'd thought. He wasn't a shallow, self-centered jerk.

"So how did you...die?"

"I went to prison for killing a man who'd prostituted his daughter. I felt I'd done the community a great service. The authorities didn't share my vision. Murder is murder. It was at Newgate Prison, even before my trial, that I suffered my final disgrace. Drunken prisoners raped and murdered me for the sport of it."

"But how did that bring you to my father?"

"I'd never been judged or punished for my deeds and thus my soul went to purgatory where I would never experience peace, or hell. Then came your father."

Arianne hung her head. Perhaps she'd been too harsh on her personal ghost. He was suffering just as she was. They both wanted their freedom.

His voice cut her thoughts. "And that is my story. Please understand, I'm not here for your pity. I'm here to bring you back to your parents. It is your rightful place."

The old Shylock was back.

"You're only looking out for yourself, Shylock. A con man at his best. Get out. I'm not in the mood for your twisted advice and pathetic pleas. I will never return to Romania and never become what my parents expect of me."

He moved toward her. Arianne met his gaze, never wavering as he lifted her chin to look into her eyes. His gloved fingers seemed to hold no temperature at all.

"I know your thoughts, my dear. You have your own doubts and desires. How long can you possibly fight them?"

She pushed his hand away. "Till I return your dandy-ass to my father once and for all. You know, Shylock, you're just like anything else in this world that eventually outlives its usefulness. One day my father will grow tired of you and send you back where you came from, where you'll never persecute another man's daughter."

Shylock winced briefly as though she'd struck him. Was it pain she saw? A sudden memory? His expression smoldered under a lasting stare as his image slowly faded.

His voice was a whisper, "Nor a man's son." Then he was gone.

CHAPTER 10

Emelia left Daegon's lair in the caverns after delivering his evening kill once more. *Allegiance*, she'd learned, meant trading her service as a vampire for training. It was more than loyalty; it had become a pact between them. It was a small price for learning the ways of her new life and building the powers that would enable her to find her children. Surely, after twenty-one years she was almost ready.

Daegon had not shirked his part and had spent countless nights with her, instructing and correcting her. *"Unless you want to starve, you must believe that timing is everything. There is a way to hunt and a proper way to kill. These things you must learn."*

And learn she did. Night after night, they hunted together, slipping among the mortal population undetected until it was too late and a victim would fall. She soon mastered the art of stealth motion, and was able to move so quietly even the candle flames did not quiver. Her kills were quick and smooth, mercifully taking the prey before they could succumb to overwhelming panic.

"You must be quick and never allow their hearts to race too long, or blood will be wasted when you enter them," Daegon had warned.

Her powers of flying, invisibility, and speed improved beyond even Daegon's expectations and he behaved like a proud parent over a child's accomplishments. Yet, his tutelage had come with a price, as she brought his prey like sacrificial offerings. How long, she wondered, before she would command the night as the coven-master, with nothing to fear but the light of day.

"And what of that?" she had asked her mentor. "What power does the sun hold over us?"

He studied her for a moment, as if she'd asked the impossible. Then he said, "It represents the light of God. It exposes a vampire for what he really is and forces him to face his own evil, which ultimately destroys him."

"Then that is all there is to fear?" she asked.

A tired sigh escaped him as he pulled back his hood. "There is something else, for which you are not ready."

"What is it, Daegon? I want to know."

"In time, you will come to understand that your immortality is limited because of your physical presence. You *can* die."

"What is it?" she repeated. "Tell me."

He closed his eyes briefly and started, "It is the Jen-Ku you must fear. They are the reason many of us feel trapped in this place. Only a few are able to get passed them or survive an attack."

"Who are they? How will I know them?" she asked.

"Who or what they are isn't important, but you will know them to be like no other human."

"I don't understand. What gives them so much power?"

"They are a prestigious priest sect that broke from the church hundreds of years ago. They are a considerable force against the vampire."

"How can a priest kill?"

"Ah, you're wise to question this. Since the church does not recognize vampires, it cannot deal with what they call the *walking dead*. It cannot condone murder, even in the name of God, and therefore claims no association with the Jen-Ku."

Emelia frowned. "Why are they so feared?"

"A Jen-Ku priest is highly trained in the martial arts and they have developed many powers, some equal to the vampire, including the ability to cloak their thoughts. The Jen-Ku weapon of choice is a curved dagger formed to cut out the vampire's heart with speed and accuracy. It is written, they will not cease until all vampires are extinguished from the earth. If you encounter one, you will be unable to get into their mind, and that is your cue to flee."

"But how is it your coven has survived in the caverns all these years?"

"I am the primary defender, and they do not attack us here. Still, we have lost many to them."

"Is that what happened to Jerrick?"

"Yes. The poor fool wouldn't listen to me and came to find an ambush."

Emelia recalled hunting that particular evening with Daegon, when they'd come upon a coven member writhing on the ground. Jerrick's chest had been sliced open, his heart missing from its protective cavity. Daegon ordered her to stay with Jerrick and hurried off into the forest seeking the killer.

She cradled the vampire, but was helpless as he clung to her, his body jerking in spasmodic rhythms as he choked on thick, blackened blood. Eyes wide in terror, Jerrick's gaze fixed on her, never releasing until his head fell back into her lap. She watched in horror as his skin tightened against his bones until she thought it would tear apart. Finally, it turned black like badly burned meat and shriveled to dust.

She forced the memory away as she made her way back home and listened closely for any unusual sounds nearby. She heard only forest animals along the ground and hurried on. The sky had turned from deep black to purple. The sun would soon rise. Sadness gripped her as she felt without hope. She longed for the day she would be powerful enough to overcome the Jen-Ku, and her only fear would be the sun's light on her darkened soul. For on that glorious day, she would leave this place to fulfill her promise and her heart's empty void to find her children at last.

DESTINY'S CALL

PART II
Dark Destiny

DESTINY'S CALL

CHAPTER 11

Chicago, Present

Harriet Gross wriggled her arthritic toes inside fuzzy pink slippers as she sat on the side of the hospital bed. This was the first time in weeks she'd been able to get up by herself and go to the bathroom. She swore there was a permanent bedpan etching on her behind.

She scuffed along the smooth floor tiles pushing her I.V. pole with one hand as she held her open-backed gown closed. Inside the bathroom, she checked her appearance in the mirror. Sunken blue eyes rested in hollowed sockets against a yellow-gray complexion. Tiny sprigs of white hair resembled sporadic weed patches sprouting from her bald scalp. The chemotherapy had had its way with her body, and she decided she'd seen healthier looking holocaust victims. But there was hope—hope like never before.

When she'd been diagnosed with leukemia, the prognosis had been grim. No one, including Harriet, ever expected to live over a year—let alone be cured. When Dr. Brewster approached her about an experimental procedure involving DNA exchange, she'd said yes immediately. What did she have to lose except the cancer? Her husband, George, and daughter, Sally, had tried to talk her out of it, arguing at least some time together was better than none. They reminded her that if the treatment failed or went wrong, she could die within days. Harriet had decided to take the chance.

Sally reluctantly obliged as the DNA donor, and Harriet was moved to the intensive care unit prior to the process to insure a more secluded environment from the press. Even staff members had no idea what was about to happen.

The morning of the procedure, she'd been prepped, drugged, and allowed to see her family before being wheeled into the operating suite. Although she'd floated in and out of twilight sleep, she recalled Dr. Brewster's pleasant blue eyes above a white mask and his reassuring words, "I'm ready to kick leukemia's ass, care to join me?"

An hour later, she'd awakened in recovery and felt no different than before. The wait began. That was almost two weeks ago. Since then, she'd had more tests than ever. She'd been probed, prodded, and poked like a piece of oven meat. It had been emotionally draining, physically exhausting and yet spiritually uplifting with the daily hope she held in her heart.

Harriet's energy and blood count levels were slowly returning to normal, and she'd gladly said good-bye to her excruciating bone pain. Gone were the night sweats and sleeplessness. Erased from her routine were the countless times a day she'd pressed the PCA, or patient controlled analgesic pump, attached to a port inside her chest. It seemed to her Dr. Brewster's plan was a success.

She checked her teeth in the mirror and smiled. No bleeding gums. "Hmm. At this rate, I'll be back in a bikini by June and will need a weekly hair appointment again. Who knows? Maybe that younger DNA will even give me back my sex drive!" Happy tears flooded her eyes at the thought of having a normal life again. With the tests results due back tomorrow, she had only one more day to wait for a miracle.

* * *

Inside the large cathedral, aromas of incense rode the sound of chimes as altar candles cried tears of the whitest wax. Red-cushioned, oak pews hugged either side of the long aisle, beside the stained glass windows that displayed landmark biblical scenes. The immense pipe organ stretched hollow fingers toward the ceiling as if in praise, while its great symphonic lungs rumbled the communion hymn.

Parishioners lined the way to the altar, some standing quietly meditating on their own dark thoughts, others chatting softly to one another, but all had come to together for the common purpose of hope and the promise of forgiveness.

Dr. Arianne Brasov bowed her head to finish a prayer before making her way to the front to receive communion. She stared at the statue of Christ on the cross until someone nudged her to move ahead. For six years, she'd prayed for a miracle, for some sort of sign that she would be healed. *How long, Lord? Am I wasting my time here?*

She knew it was probably a sin to be here; yet, she realized hope hides fear and common sense from the person who needs it most. She gathered her courage and moved closer to Father Jonah as he offered communion. His white robe was bright against the soft yellow lights above the altar, and he held the surreal look of a glowing saint. How she loved him.

When she'd first arrived in Chicago, she'd been alone and scared. Father Jonah had come to her rescue. He'd prayed with her and had listened to her hopes for the work she was starting at the Research Center. She was living a dream come true, and yet she could not confess the entire truth. The past was catching up fast and not even God could save her if it did.

Communion wine trickled down Arianne's throat like warm blood.

"Body of Christ..." Father Jonah's voice echoed throughout the cathedral as the communion procession continued.

She looked away from the silver cross that hung about his neck, and became locked with the young priest's gaze. His mournful expression called to her. Unreadable, it spoke volumes. Her naked soul stretched before him and she stifled a cry as his lingering stare branded her with Hell's fire. It seared her to the core and she broke from the line, nearly colliding with an elderly woman wearing too much perfume and a sweet smile.

The woman's crooked index finger pointed to a spot on Arianne's blouse. "Peroxide is the best way to get *that* out."

Arianne frowned at the bright red blotch of communion wine.

"Best hurry home before the stain sets, dearie." The woman waddled on toward the next row of pews.

Arianne closed her eyes and felt the same haunting presence she'd felt when she'd entered St. Victor's Church. The unwelcome aura was a warning to turn her away. She grabbed her coat and purse and hurried toward the large ornate doors. Her steps quickened through the entryway past statues wearing fixed, penetrating stares.

"Go. Hurry," one whispered.

Her breath caught when she heard the dead saints suddenly scream, "Get out! Leave this place before it's too late!"

She pushed the heavy door open and rushed outside. Her heels descended the marble steps at a staccato pace. An icy gush of Chicago air filled her lungs as she turned her face to the skies. The frigid winter sun did nothing to warm her frozen soul. Arianne rushed from the sanctity of God's house unaware she was being followed.

Traffic din blared as she pressed ahead, but it did not drown the saint's wails in the wind. She buried her face in her scarf and hurried on.

Suddenly she was yanked to an awkward stop, and found herself looking up into eyes of stone.

"Arianne." The familiar voice was ancient and heavy.

For a brief moment, her heart ached with pity, pity that quickly turned to anger as she recalled her stalker's evil intent. With gritted teeth, she spat his name. "Shylock. I should have known." She jerked her arm free and stepped off the curb.

He fell into step beside her, his voice much calmer now behind a dark smile. "Why do you torture yourself? You can never hope to be pure." Was it sarcasm or warning in his voice?

"Get away!" She picked up her pace.

"You cannot escape your heritage."

She dodged a slew of oncoming pedestrians and pressed ahead. "In God's house even a whore can be made clean. Why not me?"

Shylock's expression was incredulous. "Because *she* has only taken the seed not the blood!"

Arianne stopped. A lifetime of heartache and guilt ripped through her thin defense. She slapped his cheek hard.

Shylock only smiled down at her. "Was that for me or your father?"

She slapped him again, this time harder.

His smile grew weary. "For Mother?"

Before she could raise her hand once more, she stubbornly met his gaze. What was she doing?

"Go to hell." She pushed him out of her way and disappeared into the crowd.

He looked after her and frowned. "Too late."

* * *

Brasov, Romania, Present

As the sun sets behind the Transylvanian Alps, the shutters and shades of the small town in its foothills quickly draw closed with locks intact. The children playing hard on the streets and yards carrying the sweet smell of dirt and sweat are called in for the night, away from their imaginations and into the reality of a safe home. For thirty years it has been this way—for eternity it will always be.

Tourists roam the streets freely with their guidebooks and cameras in tow, completely unaware of the well-founded fear of the locals. The night terrors that have cursed the area for years are explained as legend or ghost story for tourism purposes, but the discovery of hundreds of bloody corpses over the years cannot be passed off so easily.

Those who have seen it for themselves and have lived to tell about it, recount the sight of a beautiful woman with flowing blonde hair, riding recklessly on a red horse. Her white dress appears fluorescent in the darkness—a fleeting streak of light against the moonlit night. It is only when she stops that fear spreads like fire in a parched desolate forest. Some say her screams can be heard for miles and echo over the Alps—a heartsick banshee cry, perhaps in response to her own pain or fear. It is for this she is known as the *horse demon*...

* * *

Dusk enveloped the small graveyard where Emelia knelt beside the tombstone that bore her name and epitaph. Vladimir's rested next to it, covered with dried leaves and bits of gravel, which she gently brushed away. The sky slipped into the twilight hues of purple and gray, summoning her nocturnal hunger. It was time to hunt.

She kept her head lowered to give the somber impression of one deep in mourning at a loved one's grave. She knew there would soon be a passerby who would come near enough to comfort her. She could see it in her mind like a gypsy's prediction in a crystal ball. This she had learned from Daegon.

For many years, she'd remained loyal to the coven-master in return for his tutelage in the ways and powers of the vampire. Her frequent visits to the coven lair had upset Vladimir. He'd told her Daegon was of the highest evil and not to be trusted. But her powers had grown and surpassed her husband's. His mistrust of Daegon had cost him, and he would never be considered for coven-master, should something happen to Daegon. Emelia had proven herself worthy of this title, yet she cared nothing for the position. Her desire was only for her children.

While she held hope of seeing them again, she knew the circumstances would be quite different now, for they were grown. It was her goal to find and bring them to their own potential as spirits of the night—as vampire. The Von Tirgov name would live forever and they would rule a coven of their own.

Arianne held the most promise for this plan, for according to Daegon, she was half mortal and half vampire. *"All that is needed, is her first kill to become full vampire. Surely, she could be persuaded by you, Emelia, as her beautiful, immortal mother."*

She knew she must build her powers to enable her to leave Romania without fear of destruction. Vladimir's plan to convince Arianne to return by using Shylock was a waste of time. He'd failed every attempt to bring her daughter home and she wished her husband would join her in the effort to find a way to leave Romania. Once they were in America, she was sure the task would not take long and she and her children would rule the darkness.

Emelia's senses were magnified by a sudden presence. Dramatically crossing herself to show her grief, she bent her head as in prayer. The figure shuffled quietly toward her, the steps muffled in the dew-sodden grass. A brief smile formed at the success of her ploy. Who can resist the grieving widow?

She felt her nerves bristle when a hand rested gently on her shoulder. Her comforter was a priest. Had he been just any priest, a simple man of the faith, she would have entertained no fear, and in seconds his soul would have been released to the heavenly Trinity. But Daegon had taught her well. Unable to penetrate this man's thoughts, she knew he was a Jen-Ku.

Emelia played along and hoped to maintain his belief he was comforting a widow. Suddenly, she detected the pungent adrenaline aroma that signaled his readiness to fight. He knew what she was.

She thrust upward and sailed over his head, landing behind him. Crouched and ready, her fangs descended into place. Only one of them would leave this graveyard of their own accord. Emelia vowed it would be her.

The priest turned quickly and dropped into a roll, avoiding her kick. He drew his dagger from the belt around his tunic.

Emelia leapt high onto the thickest branch of a nearby tree. To her amazement, the priest followed.

He balanced easily on the lower branch; his voice was a coarse growl. "You cannot escape the Jen-Ku."

Emelia lunged. "Escape is for cowards."

His strength was more than she'd anticipated and with one swift turn, he held her immobile against the tree's trunk. "I release you to hell!" he called and thrust the blade into her chest, pinning her to the tree.

Her dress grew sticky with ebony blood. She summoned her strength and clutched the priest's throat. His eyes bulged wide and he released the dagger in order to fight her vice-like grip.

She raised him high above her head. "Hell is for tourists. Try living in *my* world."

With that, she brought his throat to her parted lips and sunk her fangs deep as she drank. His piercing screams cut through the night.

Finally, she threw him from the tree and watched him hurdle to the ground. She grabbed the dagger's pommel and jerked it from of her chest. Immediately the fire inside ceased and she saw the wound heal in the moon's pale light.

Emelia jumped from her perch and seized the priest by his hair to finish him. With his blood running freely from her mouth, she pressed her open lips to his and forced him to drink his own blood, commingled with her saliva. He would now join her in the curse he so vehemently despised. He would be hunted by his own kind.

As the priest lay before her, his eyes wide with the wonder and great fear she'd felt upon her own dark birth, she smiled in triumph. "Welcome to your new life."

With new blood flowing through her, she felt the heat of strength rise once more. She knew she had used her powers well. Tonight she'd proven her readiness for the challenge that awaited her. After thirty years of patiently learning and waiting, the time had come for her to find her children. The Jen-Ku no longer held any power over her.

CHAPTER 12

"Damn it! We're so close." Dr. Arianne Brasov pitched the white blouse she carried across the desk to her boss.

Dr. Fred Brewster held it up with a questioning look. "Really, Annie, I was under the impression ours was strictly a working relationship. Should I toss you my trousers?"

"Don't *Annie* me. You're the only one who can get away with that silly name. And no, I don't want to see your lily-white ass, but I *do* want you to look at this stain on my blouse and tell me what you think."

He frowned over the top of his bifocals and gently rubbed the red blotch. "Looks like blood, but then I'm only a hematologist. What do I know?"

"Exactly! How could that wine have turned to blood?"

He took a closer look. "Where did the stain come from?"

"A sloppy communion at St. Victor's. Why?"

"That could explain it." He examined it closer.

"I was afraid you'd say that. Guess I suspected it all along."

"Let's test it to be sure. Could be a reaction against the material that makes it *appear* to be blood."

Arianne gave her mentor a loving look. "Nice try. But we both know what it is and why. This curse is killing me, Fred. I can't live with this treacherous secret much longer. Sooner or later, someone is bound to find out what I am."

Fred's expression darkened. "Everyone has demons, Annie. We all have a baleful side better left shielded. But yours can be erased." He made his way around the desk and took her hands into his own. "Look. You're right. We *are* close. And we'll keep looking until we find a way to make your blood normal again. Don't get discouraged, we have time to find your cure."

Arianne felt her eyes begin to burn. God, how she hated to cry. "Was I *ever* normal, Fred?"

"Of course, you were. Before your mother was bitten, you were a happy little fetus, waiting to start your life. But then the unthinkable happened and your mother became a vampire. Unfortunately, you shared her blood, but only part of it. You had normal blood cells, Annie, and they can be that way again. We just have to find a safe way to cleanse the bad cells. Be patient a little longer."

Arianne picked up her blouse again and shook her head. "If we don't find a cure soon, my parents will find a way to take me back to the dark side forever. I can't let that happen. I'd take my own life."

"Annie, don't talk like that. We'll figure it out, I promise. Our work here is extremely innovative. I'm convinced DNA is the key to unlocking every disease and deformity in the universe. When those results come back on Mrs. Gross today, we'll know if we're on the right track. It will prove our theory on sectioning out and replacing DNA. All we need is one cure for the green light. Once that happens, we can start the process for your cure. But as I've said before, we need to find a donor with clean DNA, preferably from a family member."

"I know my Aunt Mira will do it."

"Yes, but we need a back-up in case it doesn't work. Matching can be a tricky thing."

"There's no one. My only relatives are vampires."

"We still have time, Annie. I promise you we'll find a way. But I won't rush the process. It has to be perfected, otherwise it could kill you."

Suddenly the office door swung open with a brief knock. A lab technician entered in a white lab smock and smug expression. His tone failed to reflect sincerity.

"Sorry to intrude, Dr. Brewster, but I have those results you were looking for." The tech's gaze fell on the stained blouse in Arianne's hands. "Looks like blood, Dr. Brasov. You should try peroxide."

Chills chased up her spine. "Yes, I've heard that somewhere."

Fred was clearly annoyed by his employee's rude intrusion. "Roger, Dr. Brasov and I were having a private discussion. I would appreciate a better attempt at knocking next time."

The tech shrugged and offered a weak smile. "Sorry, boss. Guess I was just excited about the news and wanted to be the first to congratulate you."

Fred glanced at Arianne before asking, "Congratulate me for what?"

"Well, Dr. Brewster, the results are in on Mrs. Gross. Everyone's goin' wild in the lab. It looks like you've discovered a cure for leukemia."

* * *

Von Tirgov Castle, Romania

Shylock felt his master's summons well before he found himself at the castle. The Chicago park bench where he'd been sitting and watching the ice skaters circle the pond became fluid beneath him and the scene began to fade. A great force drew him slowly into a consuming gray shadow that brought him to Von Tirgov Castle.

He passed through walls of stone and into the library where he stared at the dancing flames of the fireplace. *How long must I wait for peace? When will my ravaged soul be allowed to submerge in blissful, eternal slumber?*

If only Vladimir could feel my pain. His expression turned dark at the reality. He knew his evil past had mapped his future. After all, a bastard child turned con man didn't really deserve paradise. Surely, God could absolve his sin and at least allow his soul to rest—no longer lingering in limbo or playing slave to a hell-bound master.

He broke his stare from the flames and swallowed the hurt and anger he harbored. In the end, he doubted Vladimir would truly free him, and in perfect irony, *he* would be the victim of a con game.

Suddenly his attention was drawn to the awkward bending of the fireplace flames. A great gush of wind snuffed out the blaze and fanned a sooty cloud across the room. Shylock raised an arm to cover his face from the ashes and heard his master's voice.

"You fool!" Vladimir thundered.

Shylock dropped to one knee and bent his head. "Master."

"Where is my daughter? I do not feel her presence." The vampire moved across the room away from Shylock and the cooling logs ignited once more.

Shylock watched his master cautiously. Vladimir's face glowed against the yellow light.

"Master, it is a difficult task. Arianne is not willing to come and share your life. Instead she desires freedom from the family's curse."

Vladimir turned on him. "That can never be! She is half vampire and now that she's grown, she's in danger of the Jen-Ku. Arianne must return to the safety of our castle before it is too late!"

Shylock waited for the wrath to fall. Surely, Vladimir would send him back to purgatory now that he'd failed. He was surprised to hear the sudden calm in his master's voice.

"Do not allow her to think that way. Now, I understand why she doesn't come. You have failed me and ultimately yourself. You speak of freedom for my daughter, but don't you see your own freedom lies with Arianne? When you accomplish your task, I will give you eternal rest and final peace. Not before! If you are wise, you will make her see the truth."

A movement in the doorway drew Vladimir's attention. "Emelia. Come in."

Shylock watched her glide across the room to greet her husband. She planted a tender kiss upon his cheek and leaned against him. "Darling? Will you retire soon? The sun will rise before long."

Vladimir brushed a lock of blonde hair from her neck. "Soon, my dear. I'm instructing Shylock about Arianne."

Emelia's gaze turned cold. Her exposed fangs glistened as she hissed at him. "What good is he, Vladimir? He has proven useless in the endeavor. Surely there is another way? Our daughter is in danger. Every day pushes her further from us and closer to the fate that will destroy her. Why do you have patience with this fool?"

She placed both hands gently to Vladimir's face. "Don't force me to spend eternity without my children."

Shylock turned away, afraid his anger would show. Too often, he entertained the fantasy of watching the shocked expression on her pale oval face as he wrenched her blackened heart from her chest and exposed it to the sun's light. He smiled now at the thought of the cold dark liquid pouring from her chest while she fought for another breath.

Vladimir's voice pierced the dream. "Shylock, my wife is just in her concern. We've been patient long enough. If you do not bring Arianne before the next full moon, you will indeed spend eternity in purgatory."

He dropped to his knees. "No, Master. You promised. You promised me freedom! I will do anything for you. I beg more time!" He cowered at the vampire's anger.

"Before the next full moon or I will return you to the gray abyss where I found you!"

Shylock slowly raised his head to find he was alone. Fireplace embers were dying now, along with his hope. As his body grew transparent to leave the castle and return to Arianne, he knew what he must do. This time he would not fail.

CHAPTER 13

Arianne greeted the condo security guard as she made her way to the lobby elevators. The elderly black man offered a smile from behind the large desk as smooth jazz played from the small radio beside the phone. Arianne was convinced Rhorman Tines had been part of the blue prints when the condominiums were built. She couldn't recall a time when he hadn't kept his vigil over the building and she felt a sense of security when she came home late at night. Nothing got passed Rhorman.

She pushed the elevator button and longed for a hot shower and a cool glass of wine. Her feet ached, her stomach growled and the events of the day chased themselves inside her brain like naughty two-year-olds. She entered the luxurious mirrored elevator and grimaced at her reflection. Her hair stood at attention thanks to the "Windy City," and complimented the shadows under insomniac eyes. She leaned her head back and felt her stomach go briefly weightless as it back-talked from nutritional neglect. The past few days had not been kind to her work schedule or her hopes. The wine stain on her blouse had tested positive as blood and confirmed her suspicion that her cursed soul had no business in church, let alone taking communion. It was just another reminder she would never be clean—never see a cure.

To add sunshine to the paradise of her day, she'd lost her best friend and co-worker to fame. Dr. Brewster's discovery had proven how fickle life could be. The medical community had prayed for a leukemia cure for too long. Then boom, it happened. But the joy she'd anticipated was absent, replaced by fear and resentment. Guilt clutched her stomach when she realized how selfish she was being. This miracle had taken away the one man on the planet who possessed the genius to save her. Their work together to find the cure for her dark secret was temporarily on hold, for Fred had been catapulted from behind the microscope and into the spotlight. No more midnight sessions at the lab testing and examining all options. Her mentor was more likely to be spending his evenings talking with late night talk show hosts on the subject of slide staining techniques. Her hope was slowly dying.

She opened her condo door and found herself smiling for the first time all day. "Come here, baby."

A low-pitched howl filled the spacious entryway as the sixty-pound wolf made his way toward her, ears lowered. Arianne bent to embrace him. "Destiny, what's wrong? You look like you've been naughty. Did you chew up another bra?" The wolf licked her chin and howled once more.

She buried her head in the animal's white fur and held him close. "You're the only thing right in my life, even if you *were* a gift from my parents."

Two years before, she'd moved to Chicago, far enough from Indiana to spread her wings and close enough to home and Aunt Mira. For the first time, she had her own apartment, utilities in her name and some second-hand furniture. Although her schedule had been hectic, it should have been the best time in her life as the new Dr. Brasov, but she had labeled one day in particular, the worst day of her life.

Finally settled with her medical credentials in order and a positive outlook, she'd landed a job in the emergency room at a large Chicago hospital. The first month had proven to be tough with sixteen-hour shifts and meals on the run. Yet, she felt good about herself and the work she did—everything from controlling midnight fevers to successful heart codes. Her tainted past was slowly fading into the forgotten shadows and she held the hope that if she buried herself in the work she loved, her pain would eventually die and wash away. Then it happened.

The emergency room door burst open as a young woman in a faded bathrobe rushed inside. "Help me! Somebody help!"

In her arms was a frail, bony child of about eight, in pink and white Barbie pajamas. The child's bare feet were gray and her left arm dangled over her mother's like a flaccid dishtowel. Arianne's heart hammered. She knew in her heart it was too late. Tears soaked the mother's cheeks as she helplessly offered the little girl to Arianne. As she cradled the child, she heard the woman whisper, "Please, save my baby."

Behind the curtain, everyone realized the child had been dead for quite some time, apparently passing in her sleep. Her bald head showed the signs of post-chemo, peach-fuzz growth. As she examined the child's ravaged, emaciated body, Arianne felt a strange overpowering burning in her soul. There was nothing more she could do for the little girl, yet she continued to poke and prod. Why, she wondered? What had gone wrong? How could this be prevented from happening to someone else? Before long, she felt a gentle tug on her sleeve. It was one of the nurses.

"Dr. Brasov, we really need to call it," she said softly. "The mother is waiting."

Arianne closed her eyes to clear her mind. What would she say to the mother—the hope for a cancer cure is right around the corner, but medical science hasn't come quite far enough to save your daughter? Later, as she held the grieving woman in her arms, she knew she'd turned a major corner in her career. She decided to become a soldier in the war against cancer as a researcher.

When she reached her apartment that evening, she inserted the key, and had stopped when a low whine came from inside. She listened carefully and jumped back when something scratched at the door. Before she could run for her neighbor's across the hall, she heard a mournful wail, as if in distress. Fear cast aside, she slowly opened the door to find two, wide brown eyes staring up at her surrounded by thick white fur. How had the pup gotten in, she wondered?

A low growl followed by a high-pitched howl commanded her attention. She picked him up and he nuzzled her neck. The sweet puppy scent filled her senses and she felt a sudden rush of release and comfort after her horrific day. Her heart abruptly tumbled from its high spot when she noticed the red rose on the kitchen table, beside it a folded note. The animal licked her chin as she read it.

Dearest Arianne,

Your parents have sent you the wolf pup as a token of their love and for your pleasure and protection. They do love you and wish for you to embrace your destiny.

Shylock

For the first time in her life, she felt a strange bond with the parents she'd never met. She wished in her heart she could accept their love. Shylock's words caught her attention as she reread the last line...*embrace your destiny*. She held the wolf up to her face and looked into its eyes. "I think that's a wonderful idea, probably the only one Shylock has ever had. I will embrace my destiny, and that is what I will call you."

She smiled at the memory now as she made her way to the kitchen with Destiny following close behind. The flashing light of the answering machine briefly caught her attention. Her stomach clenched. What now? She decided to wait until she'd eaten and continued into the kitchen.

"Come on," she called to the animal. "I'm sure you're as hungry as I am and if I don't get something to eat soon, I'll be howling right along with you."

Blinded by the kitchen light, she blinked hard in disbelief. A single long stemmed red rose lay upon the counter.

"Damn," she whispered under her breath.

"Indeed." The familiar deep voice echoed in the kitchen.

She whirled around ready for a fight. "How many times must I warn you to stay out of my home?"

Shylock brushed passed her. "As many times as you wish. It will do you no good." He uncorked a bottle of burgundy and poured a glass for her. "I'm here to stay. Drink?"

She snatched the glass from his hand and threw it against the wall. The shattering sound felt good to her bleeding emotions. She wanted to smash another. A long splintered shared glistened on the floor and she grabbed it. Her voice was barely a whisper as she pinned him against the sink.

"Now you listen to me, you useless, black-hearted sack of worms. Tell my father I want no part of his blood-sucking family reunion. I will not come to him, now or ever. He is wasting his time and *your* talent as a dark conscience."

Shylock cocked his head and looked down at her. He raised an eyebrow and grinned. "My, you *are* a tough little vampiress. Why don't you cut me and see if I bleed? Perhaps that's just the push you need to see the error of your ways." He clutched her wrist and eased the shard toward his throat. "Go ahead, Arianne, take the blood. It is your destiny."

Before the glass could pierce his skin, there was a low, seething growl behind them. Arianne sensed what was coming and quickly jumped aside. The wolf lunged, knocking Shylock to the floor.

Arianne stood nearby watching. "No, Shylock. *That's* my Destiny and apparently, yours, too."

As the wolf ripped another piece of his shirt away, Arianne smiled and snapped her fingers. "Heel."

The wolf immediately stopped the attack and came to her side.

The unwelcome spirit got up and adjusted what was left of his shirt. "You don't understand the implications of your actions. When your father released me from purgatory, I owed him my very existence. He is my master and I will do as he asks. Do not underestimate my worth or power. For although I do his bidding, I am not without a will of my own."

Arianne held Destiny's collar tight. "Is that a threat?"

"Merely fact, my dear. You don't realize I also have the ability to help you."

"Help me what—go to hell with you and my parents?"

"Hardly. You're achieving that all by yourself. But there is a way for us to both achieve our goals."

Arianne couldn't turn away. His eyes stared through her; his words enticed her soul. Was it possible that her dark conscience could actually be the one thing to save her?

Before she could ask, she saw his features fading, but his parting words stayed with her like a haunting melody.

"There is a way, Arianne. All is not lost."

CHAPTER 14

Across town, Lieutenant David Spears trudged up the narrow staircase of the Windhaven Apartments and noted the rancid cigar odor before he reached the second floor. The gut-wrenching smell meant only one thing—the Chief was on the scene.

What the hell's he doing here?

A uniformed officer greeted David at the top of the stairs, his radio cutting in and out with a static voice. "How's it going?"

David shook his head. "I love my job, Petrie. I love my job." The steps creaked under his weight as he slid a hand along the wobbly railing. "Is that incense I smell?"

The officer rolled his eyes. "No. That's just the chief's *no-sense* cigar."

David passed several officers in the hallway and an older woman in curlers, wearing a tattered winter robe. An apartment door stood open near the end of the hall and exposed a circus of people inside from cops to forensics. In the center ring of the chaos stood ringmaster, Chief Jessie "Mags" Magnus, puffing away on a bite-size stogie.

" 'Bout damn time you got here, Spears. Your beeper need new batteries?"

"I couldn't find the apartment in the fog of cigar smoke," David replied as he continued passed his superior toward the crime scene. To his annoyance, Mags followed.

"Yeah, well, you better make your little comments while you can. After twenty-five years, I've about had all the fun I can take.

Retirement's lookin' pretty good right now."

David ignored the man's idle threat—the same one he always reserved for stressful days or the only comeback after a good zinger by one of his staff members.

"How'd you get here so fast, Mags?"

"I was down at O'Riley's downing a few brews when the call came in. Figured I was close by. What the hell."

David nodded. "So, what do we have?"

"Single male, about twenty-five, found after neighbors downstairs heard a bunch of noise and called the landlady."

"That her outside in the robe?" David entered the small bedroom with Mags on his heels.

"Yup. Wait till you see this, Spears. It's quite creative."

David moved inside the small master bedroom and into the bathroom to find the victim on his knees, his head wedged inside the toilet. A black leather dress belt had been tightened around his neck, cutting into the skin.

"Who is he?" David asked.

"His name if Paul Bently. The landlady says he's employed at the Research Center as some sort of lab tech or something."

The detective bent and searched the floor for clues. "How long ago did this happen?"

"The call came in about ten with complaints of excessive noise."

"I'll need to talk with the tenants," David stood. "Any sign of forced entry?"

"Nope. No visible footprints either."

"Maybe he took his shoes off," David teased.

"How thoughtful. But doesn't that strike you as a little odd? With all the crappy slush outside, this guy comes waltzing in here across the fansie-pansie white carpet and doesn't leave a smudge?"

"We'll see what prints come up. We may not need his feet."

"Whoever he is, he's not too bright, coming in here at night with all the other tenants at home. Anyone could have seen him leave."

"When it comes to murder, you don't always need to be smart, just lucky."

Mags moved out of the way to let an evidence technician by. David started to follow, then stooped to inspect what looked like a tiny paper fragment stuck on the nail head of the doorway threshold. He called the tech over. "You'll want to bag this."

Not smart, just lucky.

* * *

"Dr. Brasov?"

Arianne jumped at the unexpected interruption. When she swung around on her stool, she saw a sandy-haired man with tan, rugged features. Cop, she labeled, and turned her attention back to the microscope. "What can I do for you, Officer?"

Out of the corner of her eye, she saw him move beside her as she continued to count platelets on the slide.

"I was going to introduce myself properly, but you've proven to be a psychic. There's probably no need to tell you my name." The man crossed his arms over his chest.

Arianne straightened and silently reprimanded herself for being such a bitch. When you stay up all night with your dark conscience, it can do terrible things to your manners. She smiled and shook hands with him. "Touché. Can we start over?"

His lop-sided grin said it all. "Sure."

His hand was warm and caressed hers firmly. Arianne cleared her throat. "Uh, and *you* are?"

"Detective David Spears, Homicide. Can I ask you a few questions about Paul Bently?"

"Ah, that was you on my answering machine last night."

"Yes."

"Sorry I didn't get back to you. I got in late and forgot to check my messages."

"No problem."

Arianne frowned. "Is Paul in trouble?"

"Yes, I'm afraid so. Paul was murdered last night in his apartment."

"Oh, my God. I can't believe it. Why?" She suddenly felt cold all over.

"That's what I'm trying to find out, but more importantly, *who*."

"If there's anything I can do Detective Spears, please let me know."

"Please call me David." He leaned against the counter. "Actually I'd like to know if you have any ideas about who might want him dead. You know the usual scuttlebutt around the workplace. Was he having any problems?"

"What kind of problems?"

"Gambling, drugs, a bad break-up recently?"

Arianne thought a moment. "I really didn't know him that well. The lab techs kind of hang around together and leave us doctors out of it."

"I see." He glanced around the spacious lab, his attention drawn to the microscope. "So this is the famous lab. Nice."

"Yes. This is Dr. Brewster's lab. Small, but effective. Actually, we all work together, but he's in charge. The discovery was his and we're all very excited for him."

"Pardon my observation, Dr. Brasov, but you don't sound all that enthused."

She forced a smile. "Do I give that impression? I don't mean to. We worked closely on other projects and he's been a mentor to me. This is the miracle we've prayed for and, frankly, it couldn't have happened to a more deserving person. I suppose I kind of miss him now that he's been thrown into the limelight."

David nodded. "Well, all that Hollywood stuff fades pretty quickly when another hot media ticket shows up. He'll be back in the lab sooner than you think."

Arianne smiled. She hadn't thought of it that way. After all, she knew Fred wouldn't be able to keep away from his work for too long. He loved what he did more than anything.

"I think you may be right. Finding a cure is just the beginning. We still have a lot of work to do."

The lab door swung open and Arianne looked up to see one of the lab techs coming in.

"Good morning, Jimmy. I'd like you to meet Detective David Spears."

The two men shook hands as Jimmy teased, "What did you do, Dr. Brasov?"

David's glance made her uneasy. There was something about him that made him easy to talk to. Too easy.

"Don't get your hopes up, Jimmy. I'm not going anywhere. Detective Spears is looking for some information on Paul Bently."

Jimmy shrugged his wide shoulders. "What's up with Paul?"

David straightened. "I'm sorry to tell you this, but he was killed last night."

"No way. What happened?"

Arianne watched David's expression change. Gone were the easy smile and warm glances. He was back to business. "He was murdered."

Jimmy swallowed hard, his large brown eyes wide. "Murdered? I can't believe it. Who'd do something like that to Paul? He was the nicest guy here."

"I'm sure he was, but not everyone felt that way. Have you heard anything lately that might indicate he was in some sort of trouble?"

Jimmy ran a pudgy hand through his short hair. "Not really. But he was kind of quiet. Never said much about his personal life."

"How well did you know him?"

"Not too well. He hung around with other guys from the lab, but I'm not into camping and all that. I wish I could help you."

"Thanks, anyway, Jimmy." David turned to Arianne. "I'll need a list of all the lab employees, and I want to speak with each of them."

"Sure. Whatever you need." She turned to Jimmy. "Could you get the employee roster for the Detective?"

"I'll be right back."

David's expression softened as he said, "Thanks for your help, Dr. Brasov."

Arianne felt her cheeks grow warm at his smile. She hadn't blushed since college. What was happening to her? "Please call me Arianne."

Their gazes locked briefly before he turned to follow Jimmy. She wanted to call him back, then realized how foolish that was. They'd just met. How could she possibly know anything about him? Dr. Brewster's wise advice came to mind. *"Arianne, sometimes when our minds can't make sense of something, our hearts have to do the serious thinking for us and come up with the real answers."*

Right now, her heart told her David Spears might be a person worth trusting.

CHAPTER 15

That night, Arianne awoke drenched. The nightstand clock showed it was only midnight. She braced herself and knew what was next. The coming of the full moon always triggered violent physical attacks, barely controlled by any medication. At the advice of Dr. Brewster, she used Demerol to ease some of the pain.

She fumbled in the drawer and found the small leather bag that contained the syringe and ampoule. The body aches were nearly at their peak and she quickly injected herself.

Destiny whined on the other side of the bedroom door as she bolted it shut. He, too, seemed to know what was about to happen. "Be a good boy and go lay down," she called.

Before the last words were out, she doubled over in pain and hobbled to the bed. She crawled under the covers and gripped them tight against her. Suddenly her blood grew cold and her teeth began to chatter. She was freezing and no amount of blankets would keep her warm.

Hot tears flowed down icy cheeks as she shivered violently in bed. How much more could she take? Each attack seemed to grow more dangerous than the last. Through her blurred vision, she thought she saw a dark shadow in the corner by the dresser.

"Shylock?" she whispered.

Another round of shakes gripped her and she squeezed her eyes shut. She could hear Destiny scratching at the door, desperately trying to get in. After a few seconds, the shaking ceased.

Arianne laid her head back against the back of the bed and took a cleansing breath. The pain was already beginning to break through the painkiller. Next time she would have to use a higher dose. Her body was on fire now and she stripped off her gown and saw her skin pink with heat. Naked before the mirror, she took in the view of tousled ebony hair and bloodshot, animal-like eyes. Her open mouth exposed pearly white fangs that glistened against the lamplight.

She pushed herself from the dresser and rushed for the door. The knob was slippery in her hand and she groped at it clumsily. The door wouldn't open. She yanked hard and shook it without success. Arianne threw her head back and screamed as she repeatedly thrust her shoulder against it. Then the shadow she'd seen a moment ago, moved out of the corner, and Shylock stood before her.

"You know what to do. End your torture and become complete. Be whole."

Her gaze followed Shylock as if in a trance. The pain was easing and she told herself to fight.

As she stood before the mirror again, he commanded, "Look at yourself! You are Arianne Von Tirgov—heiress to your father's empire. Go! Take your victim and be done! Do not deny yourself any longer."

With that, the bolt on the door flew open, giving her freedom. She could feel her strength return and felt her head begin to clear. Her fangs glistened as she hissed at the dark-haired vampire before her and she fought the desire to suckle warm human blood. The longing threatened to overpower her, but she focused on Fred's encouraging words. *"I promise you we'll find a way."*

She heard her phone in the living room and the answering machine pick up. How she wanted to answer and hear a human voice. She needed to keep a clear head. Instead, she stiffened as Shylock caressed her shoulders from behind. There was something comforting in his touch, like a brother tending to a younger sister. He remained silent and his eyes would not meet hers in the mirror. As she lost consciousness, she felt the gentle way he allowed her to sink to the floor.

She awoke in the fetal position a short time later, alone.

* * *

Emelia closed her eyes as her silken gown shimmered down her bare skin and fell to the floor. She viewed herself and smiled. After all these years, her body had not aged. Immortality. Forever beautiful.

How she wanted to share these gifts with her defiant, strong-willed daughter. Arianne, however, saw it as a curse. It would be impossible for her to take her rightful place as a Von Tirgov unless she was convinced otherwise. Emelia smiled. Soon that would change.

As her powers developed more fully, she would approach Daegon for his help. The Jen-Ku were very powerful, but he knew their ways. There had to be a safe way out of the homeland. Her heart was light for the first time in years in the hope soon she would find her daughter and quite possibly Michael as well. Tonight was a celebration at her triumph over the Jen-Ku priest and the impending end to the pain she and Vladimir had shared for too long.

The golden candlelight gave her skin a pale, buttery glow. Suddenly there was a presence behind her and Vladimir's mouth trailed her exposed neck. She turned to face him and felt him harden against her, as she pressed close.

"Emelia," he whispered, "I would give you the world."

She nuzzled his neck. "I only want my children."

A deep, sadness showed in his eyes as he caressed her face. "I cannot force Arianne to come."

"Then she will come willingly."

"I will find a way," he promised as they moved toward the large canopy bed.

"I already have, my darling. I already have."

*   *   *

Arianne approached the altar cautiously. It was the first time she recalled seeing it barren. Only a long white cloth covered the top—no candles, no incense, no offering. The cathedral was vacant and she continued closer to the altar, up the three familiar steps to the place where Father Jonah usually stood for communion. The air was heavy and smelled of mildew and burnt candles. A sudden chill gripped her bones at the dampness, enveloping her like a death shroud.

Where was Father Jonah? She needed his gentle guidance and warm acceptance now. The desire to be healed and cleansed bordered on obsession, and she wondered if it were possible at all. Guilt welled inside at the thought of the curse she dared bring into God's holy house—like Satan crashing a baptism.

A quiet sob choked her as she fell to her knees before the altar. She only wanted to be cleansed. Was this too much for God, she wondered? As her body shook with heavy sobs, she felt a warm hand rest lightly on her shoulder. She raised her tear-stained face, and saw Father Jonah's reassuring smile.

"Why are you crying, Arianne?"

"Father, I'm so dirty. I can never be free. Even God has turned His face from me."

He helped her up without a reply, and stroked her cheek as he motioned for her to lie upon the altar.

Puzzled by his request, she asked, "Father, are you sure?"

His only reply was a nod and a brief smile.

On the altar, she laid back, arms to her sides, never taking her gaze from him. As he began to pray over her with his arms raised, she closed her eyes. She trusted her priest. He was one of the few.

Suddenly, his voice became hoarse, as though he were being choked. She opened her eyes and cried out at the sight before her. The priest's eyes were shiny black and shaped like those of a snake. His face had drained of its color, turning grayish-white. She watched in horror as he leaned closer and barred piercing white fangs. She struggled to get up, but he held her down in a vice grip. A primal scream rose from her soul as his fangs plunged deep into her neck.

Still fighting his grasp, the smell of blood reached her and she realized it was her own. As the warm liquid trickled to her chest, the sound of ringing bells grew louder. She felt her life slipping slowly away. Again the mass bells chimed through the cathedral until she faded.

Ringgg. Arianne's eyes opened. She still felt the clutches of her vivid nightmare as she tore herself from its aura. The chiming in her dream had been the doorbell. She grabbed her robe and headed for the living room as it rang once more. She glanced through the door's viewer and saw David Spears. Shaking herself from the dream's lingering effects, she let him in.

His rugged features were more pronounced by the circles under his eyes and stubble of facial hair. Apparently Detective Spears was getting even less sleep than she was. He projected a magnetism that drew her, and she wondered if it stemmed from his confidence, cockiness, or that he simply made her feel safe.

The warm smile she recalled from their first meeting was absent. Today he was strictly business.

"Dr. Brasov."

"Good morning, Detective. It's a bit early for cloak-n-dagger, don't you think?" Her smile faded when his failed to appear.

"Arianne. Can I come in?"

"Sure. Is something wrong?"

She closed the door behind him, and motioned for him to sit on the couch. He remained standing. Suddenly, Destiny bounded in from the bedroom to greet their visitor. To Arianne's surprise, David never moved as the sixty-pound wolf came at him. Instead, he stooped and gave Destiny a brief, friendly rubdown. Satisfied, Destiny moved on to the kitchen, sniffing for scraps.

David pinched the bridge of his nose and stood. "I don't know how to tell you this, so I'll just say it."

Arianne felt her knees weaken.

"Fred Brewster is dead."

It didn't register. She knew David had spoken, but the words didn't make sense.

"What did you say?"

"I'm sorry, Arianne. Dr. Brewster is dead."

Arianne sat on the sofa arm and closed her eyes. "Oh, God. It can't be." Suddenly, she began to shiver. "What happened?"

"That's the really tough part. He was murdered." David moved closer and rested a hand on her shoulder. "It happened at the lab."

"The lab? But how? Who?"

"I was hoping you might be able to tell me. Is there anyone you can think of who would want him dead?"

Arianne felt like she was on automatic pilot as she headed for the kitchen. Perhaps this was all part of her nightmare. If she went about her routine, it would end like all silly bad dreams—abruptly and happily-ever-after. Her hands shook as she reached for the coffee can in the cupboard. Suddenly she found it hard to see clearly passed the tears.

"Coffee?" she heard herself asking.

David raised an eyebrow as if to question her actions. She ignored his look, and filled the coffee maker with water, trying to collect her thoughts. None if this was going away. The reality hurt deep. Fred Brewster, her best friend, confidante, mentor and, most of all, father figure, was gone.

She glanced toward the ceiling for answers she didn't have and turned to David. "I'm sorry you have to see me this way. Usually I'm quite cool under pressure. But this has shaken my world. Fred was family."

His eyes expressed empathy. "I can understand. That's why it's important for you to try and recall anything, any detail, no matter how small."

Arianne let the fresh brewed coffee aroma fill her senses. How many pots of coffee had she and Fred shared over the years? "Strong java promotes a quick mind," had been their motto. Right now clear thinking was in order.

"I can't think of anyone who would hurt Fred. Everyone at the lab loved him."

"Not everyone. Keep trying."

She filled their mugs and shook her head. "How was Fred killed?"

David winced as he took a sip from his mug. "Are you *sure* you want to know?"

"Look, I'm a doctor. It's not as if I've never seen or heard unpleasant details before. If I'm going to offer my help, I think I should know everything."

"He had some serious chemical burns on his face, hands, and throat..." His voice trailed off.

Her heart pounded and she moved in front of him. "And? What aren't you telling me?"

He cupped her shoulders. "Apparently he didn't die quick enough for the killer, because the offender stabbed him in the heart."

Arianne fought nausea as she pictured the brutal scene. A wave of anger shot though her. Could it have been Shylock?

David broke her train of thought. "What? You thought of something?"

"No. I wish I could help, but none of this makes sense. Fred was the kindest, gentlest, and most intelligent man I've ever known. The only thing I can come up with is jealousy."

"Jealousy?" David frowned.

"Yes. I know it sounds sick, but he found the key to a leukemia cure. Do you know how many prominent, dedicated people have worked on that for countless years? I would hope that everyone who's ever worked or hoped for a cure would be happy and grateful to Fred, but right now it's the only idea I can come up with."

"I don't know about jealousy, but maybe something just as sick. Who would stand to lose over a cure like that?"

Before she could answer, David's pager went off. With a quick check of the message, he said, "I'm sorry, but I have to go. Will you be all right?"

Arianne nodded and followed him to the door. She caught a glimpse of her answering machine's flashing light. The phone had rung the night before during her attack.

David turned back with his hand on the doorknob. "Keep this locked to be on the safe side. I don't want to scare you, but if these murders have something to do with the lab, we don't know the connection yet."

As the door closed behind him, she pushed the play button on the machine. Chills raced down her arms at the familiar voice.

"Annie, this is Fred. Call me ASAP. It's important. I've found a vital piece to your cure. I should be here for a while yet, if you can get back to me." With that, the message cut off.

CHAPTER 16

David pulled out of Arianne's condo parking lot and headed toward the station. Traffic was unusually light and he replayed his visit with Arianne, in part for the case and partly for pleasure. Her tousled long hair and throaty voice told him he'd awakened her. It was an enticing look. He also recalled her shocked, painful expression at the news of Dr. Brewster's death. He'd wanted to hold her close and protect her from the hurt, but had maintained the necessary professional attitude instead. With two murders from the same lab, he needed to see all of the facts without clouded judgment, especially if it meant suspecting the beautiful doctor.

He'd done his homework and according to background information, Arianne was thirty years old and never married. She'd worked with Dr. Brewster for three years and had never been in trouble with the law—not even a parking ticket. She had no family in the area, but there was an aunt in Indiana. The records weren't clear, but his information showed, she had been born in Romania and had been brought to America after her parents' deaths. Consequently, her aunt raised her, putting her through college and med school with a sizeable inheritance from her parents.

As far as he could tell, she'd lived a relatively normal life until her boss had found a leukemia cure and was murdered. So far, she wasn't really a suspect, but she couldn't be completely ruled out, either. If Arianne was keeping any dark secrets, he hadn't found them.

Think, David, he told himself. Who would want lab personnel

dead? It must have something to do with the recent discovery. Whoever the killer was, they seemed to have a definite plan. Forensics had found no unusual prints in Paul Bently's apartment. The guy probably knew enough to wear gloves. Lab gloves? Easy enough to obtain. Now Dr. Brewster brutally murdered in his own lab—again, no forced entry, and David bet they probably wouldn't find any prints except for the employees'. *Unless the murderer is an employee.*

At a red light, he pushed on the CD player and let his thoughts ride the music. The possibility of it being an employee put the whole lab in danger until they could find him. Or her. This could easily turn into a serial killing of the worst kind—a vendetta. Considering this option, he realized the next likely target might be Arianne, turning her from a possible suspect to potential victim.

* * *

Forensics had never been David's favorite pastime. Unfortunately, autopsies came with the territory if you were a homicide detective. David glanced away from the body before him, and focused on the beautiful coroner, Dr. Barbara Gainor, who'd made it perfectly clear long ago, she wasn't interested in anything but a professional relationship with him. *"Can't blame a guy for trying,"* he'd told her.

Since then, they'd become friends in the gruesome world of murder. David rationalized that since his last relationship had ended bitterly, he wasn't ready for another showdown. Perhaps that was true. Maybe not. Deep in the night, when his spirits sunk low, alone in his empty apartment, loneliness seeped in like dampness into arthritic bones.

A sudden, *snap*, shook him from his thoughts as Dr. Gainor stripped off her rubber gloves and tossed them into the garbage. "What's wrong with you, Spears? You look a little pale." She slipped off her mask and began washing her hands in the deep metal sink.

David shed his own mask as she dried off and walked into her small office.

"Coffee?" She asked pouring two cups.

"You're brilliant," he said, accepting the steaming cup.

She plopped down into the high-backed office chair and leaned back. "Ah, another great performance by Dr. Gainor." Her grin faded as David sat down.

"Yeah. Bravo. Now let's hear the review." David stretched out on the couch and closed his eyes.

"Jeez, Spears, you look like you're next. Sit up, will you?"

He remained prone, and propped his hands behind his head for a pillow. "Yeah, you'd like to see me naked."

"Believe me, the only way I'd do that is if you *were* dead."

He sat up. "What a way to go. Can we just get on with it?"

She frowned and propped her feet on her desk. "Okay, Spears. I can see you're into one of your dark, brooding moods. Just the facts, ma'am?"

David nodded. "Something like that."

She pulled out a small notepad from her desk, writing as she spoke. "Well, mechanism of death is a slashed heart. The burns on his face, hands, and down his throat were from hydrochloric acid."

David wasn't surprised. "We figured it was something like that. Based on the fluid spill over the counter, it looks like he was doused with the acid in the lab, then was dragged or he crawled, to his office where he was stabbed."

Barbara thought a moment and then said, "Chances are, he was nearly dead when he was stabbed. HCL is toxic if ingested or inhaled."

"We found an interesting smudged footprint at he scene as well. Looks like the guy slipped in the acid." David leaned forward taking another sip of coffee.

"Then you might want to look for burns on potential suspects." Barbara sat back in her chair.

David shook his head. There had to be more. "What else can you tell me?"

"The weapon wasn't your average knife. The wound shape seems to indicate some sort of curved blade, almost claw-like. Standard slashings aren't this clean and precise. It seems the killer was a professional. He came equipped with the right tool for the job."

"A professional?" David put down his cup and rose to pace. After a third return in front of her desk, he shook his head. "None of this adds up. Brewster was just a dedicated doctor spending long hours in his lab. He wasn't into anything that called for a hit."

Barbara sipped her coffee then set it aside. "His recent celebrity status might have played a part. There are many sickos out there taking in the world from the big screen in their living room. You can't rule that out."

"Right. But just how many of them carry miniature sickles?"

Barbara rested her chin onto her palm. "Looks like you've got a crime to solve, Spears. I can only do so much of your job for you." She tore off the top page of the notepad, and handed it to him.

"What's this?"

"A script for a little something to counter your dark mood. You're taking life way too serious."

He shook his head and ripped it in half. "Just say no remember?"

"Listen, David. Don't let this whole thing get to you. I mean, it's your job, not your life. There's a difference."

David stared at her a moment. He knew she was right, he'd learned that lesson the hard way. It wasn't that easy. "I know, Barbara. Thanks for caring." He let the silence between them settle before asking. "Anything else unusual about the good doctor?"

"Nope."

"What about a Dr. Arianne Brasov? Ring any bells?"

"Oh, yeah. As a hematologist/oncologist, she's currently working, or was working with Dr. Brewster in cancer research. She was his right hand. You should see her."

"I've already talked to her."

Barbara grinned. "Why don't you see her again?"

"What are you smiling about?"

"I don't know why I didn't think of this before. I know her personally. You two might just hit it off."

David held up his palms. "No way. Not interested."

"Why not?"

"Forget it." He shook his head.

Barbara tapped her pencil on the desk in an annoying rhythm. Finally, she said softly, "It's Diane isn't it?"

A familiar ache clenched his heart. It had been two years and her name could still pull him back to a time when he'd never been happier, and consequently more miserable. A faded dream now, he wished Barbara wouldn't have brought it up.

"Spears, you have to move on. She wasn't the one."

"Why? Because I couldn't spend a little less time with corpses and more time with someone warm and alive?"

"That's why she left you, but not the reason it wouldn't have worked."

Barbara had a way of needling a person until she finally drove her point home like a javelin. This was one of those times. David tried to deflect her direction. "It doesn't matter. Like you said, 'She wasn't the one.' Let's move on."

Not easily diverted, Barbara leveled him with a knowing smile. "You *have* to see Arianne again."

"Why?"

"Because she might have the missing link you need to solve this murder."

* * *

Guilt.

Arianne added it to her list of attributes. She squinted in the Research Center's darkened hallway. The streetlights outside cast an eerie blue glow through the windows down the hall. She had just enough light to see the keyhole of the lab's entrance. Her hand shook as she inserted the key. Yellow police tape coiled at her feet like a snake. It had *accidentally* fallen to the floor.

She wished David were here, even though he'd probably never allow her into the lab. It was a crime scene now, not her place of employment. She shouldn't be here and would most likely be arrested if they caught her. How could she explain her reasons for breaking in? The truth was the murder victim had left vital information about her cure. Yes, tell the world the research she and Fred had worked on for so long had not just been a cancer cure. Many late night hours had pertained to the search to make her own blood normal and rid her of the vampire DNA. Now a possible cure lay somewhere behind a barrier of police tape. Screw the guilt.

She turned the key, heard the familiar click of the open lock, and went inside. A cold shiver passed through her at the thought of what had happened here. The silhouette of tables and lab equipment seemed foreboding against the darkness of the room. If she turned on the lights, they would be seen from the outside. Slowly, she made her way to Fred's office in the dark.

She knew she should have called David back this morning when she'd played Fred's message. It might be crucial evidence. But that would have led to more questions—questions she didn't want to answer. Not yet. Her trust in Fred had been complete. She'd been able to share her darkest secrets and confide in him without fear. Now she was alone. Trusting David would take a while, if it ever happened at all. Although she felt he could be trusted, he was the detective in this murder investigation, and right now she didn't know just how deep his loyalties to the department ran. It was too soon to let down her guard.

Inside Fred's office, she closed the door and switched on the small desk lamp. The cramped room contained no outside window so even if the building was under surveillance, they'd never see the light.

She gasped at the sight and closed her eyes. A chalk body image of Fred's last moments lay etched out on the floor behind the desk where he'd crawled for the phone. The reality of what had taken place hit her. She felt like a voyeur, intruding on the very personal experience of death. Was she being selfish? In her endeavor to find a cure, had she become so callous that she could trample over a chalked bodyline without remorse?

Tears spilled onto her cheeks as she remembered Fred. He'd always supported her ideas, offering fatherly encouragements and advice along the way. What would Fred say now, she wondered?

She wiped the tears from her face and sighed. He would tell her to stop blubbering and get to work. A smile formed as she recalled one of his favorite sayings, "Self-preservation can be a noble profession."

Although he'd used it in reference to pathogens whose strains had survived the test of time, the rule seemed to apply here, too.

She removed several large volumes of medical reference books from the bookcase, and saw the small safe. Apparently, the police hadn't gotten this far. Maybe they never would. Who would suspect a prominent research doctor would keep a safe hidden in his office? Fred had made sure she'd had the combination, just in case. She shivered when she considered he suspected something like this might happen.

Right-left-right. The tumblers clicked into place. Arianne stopped. She thought she heard a door close. After a long pause, she shook off the paranoia. Thankfully, this would be the end of her career in breaking and entering. She didn't have the nerve for it.

She opened the safe and reached inside to pull out the contents. Most of it was familiar to her—cancer study documents and research findings, a set of slides, and his chili recipe that he'd thrown into the mix as a joke. Fred made the best chili she'd ever eaten, but he'd adamantly refused to give up the recipe, warning her that then he'd have to kill her. The irony made her nauseous.

Arianne rifled through the last of the papers, and spied a manila envelope with her name on it. ANNIE. No one called her that except him. She wouldn't allow it. Her fingers trembled as she tore it open and looked over the documents inside. They were medical records for her mother, Emelia Von Tirgov. Typed in Romanian, she struggled to recall what would have been her native tongue had she remained in her birthplace. Still, her Aunt Mira had made sure she'd learned enough of the language to get by in the event she ever returned there.

A yellow receipt sailed leaf-like to the floor. Apparently, Fred had paid to have the documents translated. The records had come from her mother's physician's office, stating medical history, including pregnancies. Arianne's eyes widened as she read the Para/Gravida numbers stating how many times Emelia had conceived and how many of those ended in a viable birth.

Two. She read it again. Although her Romanian was a bit rusty, she knew the number two when she saw it. It had to be a mistake. She was an only child.

She read further and confirmed her mother had indeed conceived twice and had taken both pregnancies to term. Had her sibling died? Why hadn't Aunt Mira mentioned it?

The other document was a hospital birth record for Emelia, which stated her mother had given birth to a baby boy two years prior to Arianne. The record confirmed it had been a viable birth without complications. Arianne had a brother. A pink post-it note contained Fred's familiar scrawl: *Annie, here's the link we need for the donor DNA—your brother is the best match!*

A sudden noise behind caused her to turn. David Spears leaned casually against the file cabinet near the door. His arms remained crossed as he offered a hint of a smile. "Find everything okay, *Inspector*?"

Keep cool, she told herself. She shoved the papers back inside the envelope and turned to face him. "I just needed to pick up a few things. I thought as long as the lab is closed for now, I could at least get some paperwork done."

He frowned and glanced at the envelope. "You're a terrible liar. What's that?"

She tossed it casually onto the desk. "Nothing important, really. Just some slide information that needs cataloging."

He moved toward the desk and reached for it. "Then you won't mind if I borrow it for the investigation?"

Arianne's hand slammed down on top of it, pinning it to the desk.

His hand covered hers as he leaned close. "Mind if I take a look?"

Her cheeks grew hot, partly from her attempt at lying, but mainly, over the nearness of his body. She looked and saw his facial hair had been shaved and his skin smelled of mild spice cologne.

His hand remained on hers, gently but firmly in place. He wasn't going anywhere. He was ready to go the distance in this showdown. At this rate, they might stand here all night. Perhaps it was time to trust someone. Most likely, she didn't have a choice.

She met his stare, and finally gave. "Okay, you win. But I hope you've had your caffeine quota for the day, because you're going to need an alert mind to take in what I'm about to tell you."

David's expression softened but never wavered. "I'm listening."

CHAPTER 17

David threw his Camaro into drive and headed toward the coroner's office while Metallica's music pounded the dashboard. This was the first morning in days he'd awakened to his alarm instead of the phone. Maybe things were getting back to normal.

Nodding rhythmically to the music...*and the dirt still stains me...so wash me until I'm clean,* he knew normal was out of the question. He'd never believed in voodoo or the bogeyman, but after hearing Arianne's explanation about her past, he felt the rug pulled out from under his convictions. He recalled her pained expression, and considered her place in the medical field, there was no reason for her to lie. He knew it was the truth.

...so hold me until it sleeps.

He'd been amazed at how calmly she'd described her situation. It was simply a matter of fact to her. But hearing words like vampire and curse, seemed strange coming from the very normal, well-educated doctor.

She'd explained that her mother's vampire husband had bitten her while she was pregnant with Arianne. Because mother and child share blood, Arianne had become infected with her mother's tainted DNA, thus making her a victim without being bitten. Arianne was only half vampire and needed to take her first prey in order to come full circle and join her parents in their unholy reign.

She'd explained that after her parent's *deaths*, she'd been taken away from her home in Romania. Kidnapped. Her mother's sister, Mira

Brasov, had risked her life to save her. She was brought to America, far from the possibility of consummating the horrific plan to make her full vampire. Her life had been relatively normal until her twenty-first birthday—that was when she'd met Shylock.

It was at this point in the confession David had looked around Fred's cramped lab office for something stronger than rubbing alcohol. As a homicide detective, he'd seen and heard many far-fetched and frightening things, but this topped them all. If anyone else had tried to serve this to him, he'd have had them committed. He hoped it wouldn't come to that with Dr. Brasov.

He'd found nothing more than a roll of breath mints on the desk and nodded for her to continue. "Who's this Shylock character?"

After a long moment, Arianne started. "Technically, he doesn't even exist. I tend to view him as a recurring bad dream. You know, something that affects you because you see it, but no one else can share it with you because it isn't a tangible thing?"

She sat on Fred's desk with the manila envelope conveniently tucked under her rump. "Shylock is my dark conscience, sent by my father to encourage me to take my place as heir to the Von Tirgov empire, or curse, depending on how you look at it."

David frowned. "But your name is Brasov."

She smiled. "Very perceptive, Sherlock. My birth name was Von Tirgov, but my aunt changed it. Anyway, Shylock first appeared to me when I turned twenty-one and has been around ever since."

David straightened, adjusting his gun holster. "And you believe you're part vampire?"

"Yes. As a medical student, I tested my own blood, and even studied it under a microscope. It's not normal. Fred is the only one who knew. We were working together for a cure."

"So, where are your parents now?"

"In Romania. They still reside in their castle. They can't leave their homeland or they risk destruction. That's why Shylock is so important. He's their only link to me. They want me back and no act is too desperate for them to achieve their goal."

After much persuasion, Arianne had reluctantly turned over the envelope with Fred's findings, revealing she had a brother she never knew about. After a brief crash course in DNA, he'd learned why Arianne had risked breaking into the lab to find what Dr. Brewster had left for her.

If Arianne was insane, it was the best cover since Ted Bundy. She came off extremely credible. If she wasn't crazy, the world of homicide had just taken a sickening twist.

David pulled into the coroner parking lot, still trying to digest Arianne's story. It couldn't be. Could it? Vampires were the last explanation he'd expected to hear from her. It would take some doing to accept her story, if ever. Right now, he needed to concentrate on the investigation.

* * *

Arianne tugged at her navy skirt as she sat in her car in front of Shay's Funeral Home. She'd parked behind the faded, gray-bricked building to avoid the mass of media vans and visitor cars on the street. Tapping a polished fingernail against the steering wheel, she checked her watch again. Only five minutes later than before. Although she'd arrived early for Fred's funeral, the parking lot was already filled. It had turned into a media frenzy. The world was in shock over the murder of the man who'd discovered a leukemia cure. The journalistic angles for a murder motive were diverse—from jealousy in the medical field to pharmaceutical companies standing to lose too much over a cure of this magnitude.

Arianne didn't care about that; she only wanted the person caught. So far, they had no suspect, no leads, and no justice. Tears threatened her mascara as she thought about how unfair this world could be. Fred didn't deserve to die. He was a nice guy doing his job. Heroes, she'd learned, didn't ride off into the sunset in white hats; they sunk into cold darkness with their hearts slashed.

She closed her eyes to shake the vision from her mind. Suddenly she sensed she wasn't alone. With her eyes still shut, she gritted her teeth. "Why now, Shylock?"

He sighed. "I'm not without compassion, Arianne. I realize how much Fred meant to you. After all, he was your last hope."

Hot anger temporarily replaced her grief. "And *I'm* not without supporters, Shylock. Fred's death won't be in vain. His work will continue as a tribute. The entire lab will work day and night if necessary. We'll never stop."

His lips twisted into a knowing smile. "Ah, but your motives are not selfless, my dear. I know you were working together on a cure for your own tainted blood. You cannot play the victim with me."

"I'm no victim, but Fred was. And you've certainly sealed your fate, my friend, because I know *you* killed him."

Shylock's expression was incredulous. "Why would I bother to kill him?"

Arianne's wrist trembled with contained anger as she checked the time once more. "Because he was helping me and had found a way. You couldn't abide that could you? You selfish, immoral bastard!"

He gripped her arm as she reached for the door. "Arianne, wait. I swear to you I didn't do it."

She'd never heard remorse in his voice before. Was it simply more manipulation?

Shylock continued, "Killing Dr. Brewster is not the answer to my dilemma, if anything it only makes the situation worse. Alienating you won't help, you already distrust me." He held up a hand and added, "And rightfully so. But you don't understand. There are many things you do not know, things that you *should* know. I can help you, if only you'd let me."

Arianne had him right where she wanted him, after so many years, she was going to expose the most damning evidence ever and permanently wipe the cock-sure grin from his lips. "I already know I have a brother."

She stared solidly at his attempt to maintain a stone expression, noting with satisfaction the slight widening of his eyes at her statement. Before he could reply, she spotted Detective Spears going into the side entrance of the funeral home. She opened the car door and quipped, "Don't wait up."

CHAPTER 18

The funeral home's spacious foyer was filled to capacity as people waited in line to enter the visitation room. The scent of fresh flowers and stale perfume hung in the air like a smothering cloud. Arianne removed her coat and searched for David in the line ahead. His tailored navy suit and fresh haircut projected a sympathetic, reserved look. Detective Spears appeared to be off duty. She watched him scan the crowd and nod at her in recognition. Her cheeks warmed as he made his way toward her.

"How're you doing?" he asked quietly, touching her arm.

"I've been better." She felt his warmth through her blazer sleeve.

"Are you alone?"

"Yes, I came early, but it really didn't do much good. Looks like the press camped out overnight."

"Yeah, well it's their job to be annoying. Kind of like detectives." He smiled.

"Well, right now I don't find you annoying. I'm glad to have someone to talk to."

"Isn't anyone here from the lab?"

"So far I haven't seen anyone. They're probably waiting until the media clears." She moved ahead with the line, then asked, "Are you here on business?"

"I'm *always* on duty," he stated matter-of-factly, glancing around the room. "But I'm also concerned about you."

"Why?"

"If Paul and Fred were in danger, you could be, too. We still don't have a motive and since you two worked so closely together, we can't rule you out as a possible target."

"That means everyone in the lab could be in danger."

"Right, but you were closest to Fred, practically partners. You know everything Fred did about the DNA procedure. If they went to the trouble of killing him, you might be next. You need to watch yourself."

"Is this related to the cure?"

"We don't know, but until then it's a possibility."

As the line inched on, Arianne saw their destination against the far wall. Huge floral arrangements on metal stands lined the room with photos of Fred placed randomly between them. She noticed two women with enough family resemblance to assume they were siblings, standing at the end of the receiving line beside the elegant gold urn housing Fred's cremated remains.

"Those two must be Fred's nieces." She nodded toward them.

"His only family," David stated, leaning close.

Arianne whispered, "Yes. His sister died a few years ago. He only spoke of her girls a couple of times. I'm not sure they were very close."

"Not very. The one on the left is Ana and the taller blonde is Sharon. Both thirty-something, married with kids, and live in the Chicago area. Neither of them can remember the last time they saw or even spoke with their Uncle Fred."

Arianne smiled. "You've done your homework, Detective. Very impressive."

"Not really. We still don't have a suspect. But I have a feeling it won't be long."

Before she could press David further, she found herself in front of Fred's nieces.

A limp hand clasped hers as the tall blonde said, "Hello. I'm Sharon and this is my sister, Ana."

Arianne's eyes brimmed as she offered her condolences, all the while feeling she was the one in need of sympathy. Both women were impeccably dressed, accessorized with heavy gold jewelry and perfect make-up. Not a tear-smudge of mascara or eyeliner to be found.

"I'm Arianne Brasov, Fred's associate at the lab."

The sisters glanced at one another. Sharon took Arianne's hands into her own. "You must be devastated. Working with him every day like that, I'm sure you two were very close."

Arianne found she couldn't speak as sobs choked her throat. Tears trailed one another down her cheeks as she tried to regain her composure. The large urn gleamed brightly under the yellow, overhead floodlights, reminding her that this was the very last moment she'd be this close to Fred again. She felt as though her chest might explode. Then, she felt David's firm grasp around her waist, pulling her close to lean on him. He nodded to both women, briefly shaking hands.

Recognition lit their faces as Ana blushed. "Ah, Detective Spears, how nice of you to come."

"I'm very sorry for your loss." He held onto Arianne. "If there's anything I or the department can do, please don't hesitate to call."

Ana rested a hand on his arm. "Please, Detective, find whoever did this."

Moving on, Arianne was aware of David's remaining support around her waist. It brought a surprising amount of comfort to her, like an old friend come to the rescue. For the first time in days, she'd allowed her broken heart and shattered spirit to grieve at no expense. It felt good to let someone else be strong. She was tired of the fight.

After the service ended, Arianne walked with David to her car. She was relieved to see it was empty. A bitter wind picked up, and she buried her chin into her coat as her eyes teared against its icy blast. Perhaps the healing could begin now.

Her car lights blinked at the keyless remote. "Hurry, get in," she told David.

Inside, they treasured the warmth as tiny white wisps chugged from their lips. Arianne started the car, blasting the heater. "God, it's cold. I can't feel my fingers." She laughed.

David shook his head. "Why do we live here? Cold, rain, or snow most of the year, or windy and one hundred degree temps the rest."

Arianne felt her fingers begin to thaw. "Because it's the greatest city in the world."

He cocked his head at her, furrowing both brows. She saw the little boy David had been years ago, making a sour face. He'd never shown this side before.

"I mean it!" She laughed.

"Well, it's not so great for a homicide detective sometimes."

"No, I don't suppose it is."

Wiping a small patch of condensation from the passenger window, he watched the media caravan departing. "I guess being a doctor has its drawbacks as well."

"At times. Research is more tedious, but just as rewarding. I still see our patients and monitor their progress. I really love what I do."

He turned back to her. "I'm still concerned for your safety."

"Don't worry about me, David. I'm a lot tougher than I look, and a bit wiser. I know when to duck and right now looks like a real good time."

"What do you mean?"

"I think it's time I plan a trip home."

CHAPTER 19

Arianne closed her eyes against the satin spray of shower water, allowing the warmth to release her tensions. She recalled her conversation with David from the day before at the funeral, and smiled. His emerald eyes flashed at the news of her plan to return home. Apparently, he'd interpreted home as Romania. His expression still haunted her. Had she seen fear or pain beyond his usual calm demeanor?

After explaining "home" was Indiana to visit her Aunt Mira, he'd seemed to relax. But then it was *her* smile that faded when he'd responded.

"I'll go with you," he'd said matter-of-factly.

How could four little words create such chaos? Her mouth went dry and her palms began to sweat. She felt the roller coaster of feelings as surprise, fear, and finally panic set in as he stared at her. Holding the reins on it all, she managed a calm grin. "You will not."

He rested a hand on her arm. "I told you I'm concerned for your safety because admit it or not, you're involved. You're too close."

"I don't need a babysitter. Besides, how can you just pick up and leave?"

"Believe it or not, detectives do get days off. I look at it as moonlighting."

"Moonlighting?"

"As your bodyguard."

She couldn't wipe the smile from her face now as she lathered up.

A bodyguard?

Her mind quickly shot to the movie about the relationship between a singer and her guardian. How would it feel to hold David close? What would it take her to let go and trust? She needed that now but knew it could never be, not while she carried the curse within. The risk was too great that she could give in to the evil longing and take the life of someone close. As her monthly attacks grew stronger, she feared something inside was changing, evolving. If she didn't find the cure soon, it was only a matter of time before the bolted bedroom door wouldn't hold her.

Suddenly, the soap shot out of her hands and landed at her feet with a heavy thud. Before she could pick it up, a light-headed sensation filled her and she watched the soap begin to rise. Trance-like, her gaze remained focused on the pink disk as it levitated and finally reached her palm. The feeling subsided as she stared in disbelief. Her scientific mind told her it couldn't have happened, but her spirit of adventure pushed through the logic, excited to have tapped into something new. The fact that she'd just moved an object with her mind didn't frighten her. Instead, she found it felt natural and right, not the least bit strange. It confirmed her belief that she was quickly progressing in a paranormal state.

Arianne rinsed off, and finished getting ready just in time to hear the door buzzer. She checked the viewer and smiled.

"I'll be right there." She called and fixed her gaze on the door's dead bolt, concentrating. In seconds, the thumb-turn gave a solid click as it unlocked in obedience.

Arianne felt strangely powerful and in control for the first time in her life. Perhaps the ability to overcome the deadly obstacle in her life could be found within, after all.

She opened the door and watched David enter wearing faded blue jeans, a navy blue hooded sweatshirt, and the sexiest grin he'd ever offered.

"Good morning," he said. "Ready to go?"

She pulled the towel from her damp hair. "Yup. Just about."

David's familiar spice cologne wafted passed as he went to greet Destiny. "Hey big guy. It's perfect dog sledding weather out there. Lots of snow."

Destiny howled softly at his new friend and licked the underside of David's chin.

Arianne grinned. "Sorry, Detective. Destiny isn't a sled dog. In fact, he's not a dog at all. He's one hundred percent wolf."

David's hand froze over Destiny's head. "Wolf?"

Arianne continued towel-drying her hair. "Yes. A gift from my parents for companionship as well as protection. Most people make the same mistake and assume he's a Husky. I never correct them."

"Probably just as well," he cautiously rubbed the wolf's side. "Your parents have strange taste in gift-giving. I won't even ask about birthdays."

She headed toward the bedroom. "I'll just be a minute. We're all packed and ready to go."

"We?"

"Uh-huh. Don't worry. Destiny's a light packer."

David smiled. "He won't have a problem with me coming along?"

"Not as long as you behave," she said, closing the door behind her.

* * *

David was surprised when Arianne insisted they drive her car because of Destiny's shedding.

"He's used to riding in my car; it's familiar to him," she explained.

Before David could object, Destiny jumped in and lay down across the back seat.

David shrugged. "Okay, but I offered. Wouldn't you like to kick back and relax while I drive?"

"Nope. Driving *is* relaxing. I probably should have been a trucker."

After loading the car, they headed for Lake Shore Drive. As they approached, David motioned toward the choppy waters of Lake Michigan. "Do you like the water?"

Arianne nodded. "Swim like a fish, but I was a late bloomer. I didn't learn until high school, when it was mandatory for graduation. How about you?"

"I could live on the water." He grinned. "I keep my boat in Monroe Harbor. We'll have to go sailing some time."

"I've never been on a sail boat and couldn't tell starboard from port. But I'd be happy to soak up the sun, Captain." After a moment she asked, "What's your boat's name?"

"Winds-O-Change."

Arianne brushed a lock of hair from her face. "Let me guess. The winds are always changing here in Chicago."

"They don't call it the windy city for nothing. But that's not the reason for the name. I've always loved sailing because it relaxes me.

After my parents died five years ago, it was my only source of comfort. I named my rig the Winds-O-Change because life is always changing, either good or bad. Things never stay the same and we have to ride the waves, so to speak."

David watched Arianne's expression grow dark, and he regretted his cryptic words. After losing Fred, she probably didn't want to hear about rolling with the punches; instead she most likely needed a comforting hug, or a shoulder to cry on. He hoped to offer that shoulder.

Her soft voice broke his thoughts. "I'm so sorry you lost your parents. How did it happen?"

"Car accident on their way back from Florida. They hit a patch of black ice a couple hours from home. It seems like yesterday." He watched the waves beating the shore for a moment. "I'm sorry to bring up such a sore topic. I know you're still hurting over Fred. It was bad timing on my part; sometimes I just don't think."

Her warm smile returned as they headed south. "I disagree, David. You think rather deeply for someone caught up in such a brutal career."

They drove in silence past a large baseball stadium as he considered her comment. He'd never thought about his job as brutal. The violence was just part of the job. He had to admit it could be a little tough on sleep sometimes, especially when a case wouldn't come together. Still, losing shut-eye was easier than waking in the dark, drenched in sweat, and trying to erase the vivid images of your parents' deaths. Guilt stilled plagued him at the thought of it.

His father's disappointment and brief sigh had been audible through the crackly phone line the day before their trip five years before...

"Are you sure you can't make it, David? Your mother has really been looking forward to it."

David's cell phone gave another warning beep, signaling a low battery.

He cursed the device and tried to explain. "Dad, I just can't get away. There's been a break in the case and I need to keep close by. Tell Mom I love her, and I promise to make it up to her."

"It's not just that, son...I was counting on you to help with the driving. Florida's quite a haul and my legs cramp sometimes. Besides, I'm not as sharp behind the wheel as I used to be."

"Next time, Dad. For sure. It's just this case—"

Beep—Beep.

Nothing. The phone died then—and his parents seven days later on an icy stretch of highway returning home. No more broken promises, only a broken heart.

David severed his train of thought and wondered if Arianne had noticed. He was relieved to see her glance back at Destiny, and then ask, "What made you choose homicide?"

"It chose *me*," he said honestly. "The opportunity arose and I was ready for a change. It wasn't a life-long goal or anything."

"Then why do you stay?"

"My incredible stubborn streak. I don't give up easily."

"You sound like me. Once I start something, I have to see it through till the end. It's almost obsessive."

"Like finding a cancer cure?"

She nodded. "Yes. There's still so much work to do, especially after finding the missing link. Fred's work isn't finished, and I intend to keep working as though he were right beside me."

"Even if it means risking your life?"

"My life's already at risk and so are others if I can't correct my DNA. My reasons aren't purely selfish. Like I said, I have to see it through till the end, whatever that may be."

David rode in silence, wondering just how far she'd have to take it. Wherever it was, he would go the distance as well. His stubborn streak wouldn't have it any other way.

CHAPTER 20

The block long, blacktop driveway stretched down the center of Mira's snow covered yard like a zipper on a sweater. Her petite white house perched on top of a hill over two full acres, and seemed to stare with black shutter eyes. She knew her aunt wouldn't mind the visit and extra guest. When she'd telephoned to tell her she was coming home for the weekend, and bringing David, Mira sounded ecstatic. Although Mira kept busy running the bakery, Arianne wondered if she ever felt lonely living by herself. For reasons unknown, her aunt had never married.

Arianne felt her heart race as she cut the engine. Home at last. "Welcome to St. John." She beamed a smile his way. "Home to some of the friendliest people in the world and the best home-cooked meals you'll ever taste—from Aunt Mira's kitchen, of course."

Destiny was pacing the back seat, whining in anticipation.

"Come on, baby," she called, getting out.

"Coming," David teased.

As soon as they reached the front door, it opened wide. Mira stood inside waiting for a hug.

"It's so good to see you. Come in, come in," she motioned, shutting the door behind them. Mira stooped to welcome Destiny as the wolf howled his own greetings. Finally, she straightened to meet David. "And you must be Detective Spears. How nice to meet you."

"Please, call me David," he said.

Arianne sighed, feeling immediately at ease. As Aunt Mira took

David's arm and led him to the living room, Arianne lagged behind taking in the kitchen aromas of fresh baked bread and possibly a cherry pie. She closed her eyes to allow the feelings of safe harbor and solace to sink in deep.

She heard Aunt Mira chatter in the other room as Destiny lapped heartily from his water bowl. She smiled as the thought of rescuing David from her aunt's conversational clutches came and went. Let him have the full tour. Maybe next time he'd think twice about forcing his protection on her, when the greatest danger at Mira's was gaining five pounds.

Arianne buttered a generous slice of warm bread and was just about to take a bite when she heard laughter. "This is Arianne in the fountain at the zoo…"

She dropped the tasty treat onto the counter and headed for the living room. It wasn't David who needed saving, it was her pride. "Aunt Mira? Don't show him that picture!"

David didn't appear to be a distraught captive as he sat beside her aunt on the couch. In fact, he looked quite pleased being privy to Arianne's naked baby photo.

Arianne felt her cheeks grow hot under his quizzical expression. She reached for the photo album. "Give me that thing before I have to move out of state from embarrassment."

David diverted her grasp, holding tight to the book. "Ah..ah..ah…not so fast, Dr. Brasov. I believe there's a law against indecent exposure."

Arms crossed, foot tapping the carpet, Arianne tried to look mad. "You'll learn the meaning of indecent if you don't put away those pictures, Detective." She couldn't stop a smile from forming as Aunt Mira stood.

"Why don't we have lunch? There's a pot of my famous vegetable soup on the stove just waiting."

David offered the photo album to Mira, saying, "Sounds good to me," then turned to Arianne, "How about you, Ms. Godiva?"

* * *

After lunch, they relaxed before a roaring fireplace, sipping brandy and chatting. As the liquor and crackling flames lulled her into a near-trance, Arianne recalled the true reason for her visit. She had a brother, and many questions.

She set her snifter aside and straightened. "Aunt Mira?"

Her aunt looked away from the flames. "Yes, dear?"

"There's something I need to ask you about."

"What's that?"

Arianne glanced at David, then back at Mira. This was the hardest question she'd ever asked.

David leaned forward, taking on the detective role. "It has to do with Fred Brewster's murder, Ms. Brasov."

Mira paled as her eyes grew wide. "I don't understand. What could I possibly know about it, except it was a horrible tragedy for all of us." She turned to Arianne, her expression tender. "I know how you loved him, dear. He was like a father to you."

Arianne swallowed hard at the painful truth of Mira's words. "You see, Fred left me some documents I found after he was killed."

"What kind of documents?" Mira picked imaginary lint from her skirt.

"Aunt Mira, I know about my brother."

Mira briefly closed her eyes, as if to block out the truth of the situation. After a few moments, she spoke quietly, "I knew I couldn't keep it from you forever. Trouble is there just never seemed to be a good time to tell you." She glanced down at her hands as they twisted in her lap. "I'm sorry you had to find out this way."

"Why didn't you tell me?" Arianne fought her tears.

"There was no good reason for you to know. When you were younger, I felt it might put you in danger because you'd try to find him. Then as the years went on, I just couldn't find the words."

"But he's my brother, my flesh and blood. Why did you give him up?"

Her aunt's voice grew strong now as she replied, "He is not all your flesh and blood. There are *differences*." Her nervous glance toward David told Arianne she was referring to the curse.

David cut in. "Arianne has told me everything, Mira. You don't have to be afraid; I'm here to help. You see, we have reason to believe Fred's murder is related to another death in the area. If this is true, Arianne could be in danger. It's important we know as many details as possible. I promise you, her background is for my ears only."

Mira drained her brandy glass, and leaned back. "All right. I pray to God you don't hate me for what I'm about to tell you because everything I did was for you and Michael's protection."

Arianne nodded for her to go on. "I could never hate you. I just want the truth."

As her aunt described the events leading up to the abduction, Arianne tried hard to draw up memories of a little blond, curly-haired, blue-eyed toddler called Michael. It seemed no such memory existed. Surely somewhere deep in her subconscious she should see him peering into her crib, possibly tickling her or offering a pacifier. Her heart ached to find him.

"That day at the orphanage," Mira continued as if reliving it over again, "I was introduced to Father Martin and Sister Gwen. They took to Michael right away. Of course, who wouldn't have loved him with his big blue eyes and those golden curls? Michael was only two, but he could say quite a few words in Romanian and English, too. He certainly charmed the priest."

She turned to Arianne. "Your mother saw to the language training. Regardless of how things turned out, she was a dedicated, loving parent. She had high hopes for the two of you and that's why she wanted you both to know English and Romanian. She loved you so much."

David encouraged Mira to continue.

She nodded and went on. "After a brief tour of the facilities where Michael would stay, it was time to say good-bye." Her voice broke, but she pushed on. "I held him close, and tried not to cry. Then I set him down and Sister Gwen led him away by the hand to play with a group of toddlers across the room. I stayed for some time, just standing there watching with a million questions running through my head. Was this the right thing to do? Would he really be all right? How safe were the both of you if I kept you together? Finally, I knew there was no other way. Michael glanced my way and waved. When he went back to playing, I left. I never saw him again."

Arianne met David's somber look, barely maintaining her composure. "But why did you believe we were in danger together?"

"I felt your parents would stop at nothing to find you and get you back. I thought if you were separated, they would have a harder time tracking you. We moved shortly after coming to the U.S., actually we moved several times. I thought if I could save one of you from them, it would be the right thing. It was a painful, desperate time in my life. But looking back, I have no regrets. In my heart, I feel I did the right thing, but I pray for your forgiveness."

Arianne went to Mira, holding her close as the tears came. "There's nothing to forgive. You did everything for our safety. It couldn't have been easy."

She brushed the hair from her aunt's face. Mira was her mother in so many ways. "Now it's time we find him. Only this time you don't have to be alone, we'll find him together."

* * *

That evening, Mira retired early, leaving Arianne and David to themselves before the fire. As the embers glowed beneath the flames, Arianne snuggled close inside her winter robe. The day's events chased each other in her mind while David double-checked doors and windows. His sidearm remained on the coffee table, adding to her uneasiness. Was she really in danger? If so, would a gun be enough to save her?

Once again, her thoughts returned to the supernatural powers she seemed to possess. For now, it was better kept to herself. Looking back, she realized the past several months had been filled with strange, unexplained occurrences that proved something within her was changing. There had been times when she was running late and couldn't find her car keys, and they'd suddenly drop to the floor from where they'd been. Or the incident when she'd swerved to avoid hitting a deer with her car and had landed in a ditch. With each try, her wheels only seemed to sink deeper into the mud. Finally, she'd resigned herself to the fact she'd need a tow truck and lots of hot chocolate as the temperatures plummeted.

While she waited for assistance, she closed her eyes, and tried to remain calm. She felt a slight jerk of the car's rear as the vehicle slowly rolled forward and out of the gully. The ability to move objects with her mind was growing. None of the medical books in the world could explain her symptoms, and she could only guess what these sudden changes might mean.

David sat beside her on the couch, apparently satisfied the house was secure. His arm rested along the back, inches from her shoulder. She stifled a yawn, feeling her body unwinding from fatigue and spiraling into drowsiness.

With her eyes closed, she asked him, "Can I get personal?"

"Excuse me?" surprise sounded in his voice.

She grinned. "Why aren't you married?"

"I didn't see *that* one coming," he admitted. "I guess I'll have to go with the cliché that, I haven't met the right person, yet."

She nodded. Her eyelids felt like bricks. "I see. Do you date?"

"Occasionally. How about you?"

She allowed the truth to surface. "Only in my dreams, David. Until I find the cure, I can't afford to get serious with anyone. It just wouldn't be fair to either of us."

She watched his expression change, as he seemed to move to another place in time. Finally, she asked, "Are you okay? Did I offend you?"

His smile returned. "No. I'm fine. Just thinking about what you said."

"Don't quote me. I'm not thinking straight right now."

He leaned closer. "It made perfect sense."

"What?"

"About being fair."

She stared into the fireplace. "Right. Give and take and all that. One day I hope to share it."

"Me, too."

"Sleepy?" David's voice was quiet.

She nodded, laying her head back.

"Why don't you go on to bed? I'll stay up for a while, maybe catch the news."

She grinned. "You're not kidding me, David. You're still playing the bodyguard role. But I'm telling you there's nothing to be concerned about."

"Maybe."

"Trust me. Go to bed. Aunt Mira has already turned down your covers. I wouldn't be surprised to find a couple of wrapped mint chocolates on your pillow."

"She likes me," David stated proudly. "Most women do."

Arianne rolled her eyes. "Oh, here we go. Better watch yourself going into the bedroom, your head might get stuck in the doorway."

"I'll keep that in mind." His fingers toyed with a strand of her hair. "Would you like me to tuck you in?"

Longing stirred within her like a warm wave rushing the shore. Yes, she *would* like him to tuck her in, and hold her tight until the demons left. Perhaps one day it could be. Her hand closed gently over his on her shoulder as she met his gaze. "Thanks for the offer, and for being here with me. But you're right, I should get some sleep, and so should you." She allowed her grasp to linger briefly before letting go. Some other time, she told herself.

*　　*　　*

That night, Arianne fell asleep right away, her body and soul exhausted from the emotional roller coaster of the past week. At least now, she had a fit for some of the jagged puzzle pieces of her life. Mira's confirmation about Michael had given her a certain amount of peace. Closure was a better remedy than sleep aids any day, she decided as she drifted off. Later, she would regret the sleep she'd longed for, for it did not bring the rest of a sound slumber, but rather the fitful thrashing of chaos as her mind peered through the darkened window of a haunted past.

Another pillow sailed to the floor as Arianne raced toward the little boy before her.

"Michael, come back!" She called as he ran deeper into the fog. "I can't see you, come back!"

Briefly, she stopped, out of breath and shivering from the cold. Suddenly she heard a sharp cry ahead and she hurried into the murky haze.

"Michael?" The hairs on her arms raised in alarm as she continued forward. The air tasted acrid and felt charged with danger. Carefully she moved, listening for the slightest sound. A tall shadow only a couple of feet ahead froze in the fog. She stepped closer, and her heart crumbled as she saw a child's limp body on the ground. The dark figure above her moved swiftly, with an arm raised to strike. The curved blade of a dagger sliced at her chest as she jumped back. When she fell to the ground, the shadow moved over her, its black eyes snake-like through the thick mist. She screamed in anticipation of the dagger's thrust.

"Arianne. Wake up!" David's voice awoke her.

She squinted against the sudden light and fought the nightmare's effects. "I'm okay," she said, her hands trembling.

"What happened?" David sat on the bed.

"Just a bad dream, I guess."

"Are you sure?"

She followed David's glance around her bedroom. The yellow window sheers hung in shreds from their rod and a small wicker chair lay on its side. The dresser was in shambles with overturned bottles of nail polish and perfume. Arianne stared in disbelief as reality struck her—she'd done this in her sleep. "Looks like you locked the doors for nothing, David. It's not what's outside we need to fear, it's what's on the inside trying to get out."

CHAPTER 21

Bright winter sunlight splayed through Arianne's frayed bedroom curtains, no longer effective in shutting out light. Arianne forced herself up after a fitful night of restless sleep following her nightmare. She dressed in her favorite faded jeans and red pullover and knelt on the floor, picking up the contents of the dresser top. How could she have created such havoc without knowing it? Could her powers really be that strong? A movement in the doorway made her jump. Who or what was she expecting? Aunt Mira leaned against the door jamb wrapped in her robe, holding a cup of coffee. Her smile spoke the heartfelt, comforting words she didn't say.

Arianne looked around the room. "Sorry about the curtains. You know I'll replace them."

"Don't be too hard on yourself, Arianne. It wasn't your fault."

She arranged the last few items on the dresser. "It's not my fault, but I'm still responsible."

"It was just a nightmare—"

"Just a nightmare?" Arianne cut her off. "Look at this place and tell me you honestly believe that."

"You've been under a lot of stress lately, with Fred's murder and that damn Shylock hounding you. It's no wonder you're sleepwalking."

Arianne realized Mira still didn't understand what was happening. She moved to the window and glanced out over the whiteness of the vast yard, trying to find the words. "I wasn't sleepwalking, Aunt Mira. Lately, there has been an increase of strange occurrences. Weird, supernatural things have been a part of my whole life, but recently they've been happening more often and with greater intensity. Something is changing inside me. My abilities are growing stronger. I'm afraid of what it might mean."

Mira sipped her coffee as if buying a chance to take it all in. Finally, she nodded. "I was afraid something like this might happen. Truthfully, I don't know what it means It could be nothing or it could be everything. You need to find out, Arianne."

"But how? Who would know, other than Shylock? And he'll simply tell me to go see my father."

Mira sighed. "I've protected you as long as I can, but this is beyond my grasp. It could mean your life."

"What are you saying?" She felt Mira's soothing palm against her cheek.

Mira said softly, "Perhaps it is time to meet your parents."

* * *

That afternoon, Arianne dressed in layers and laced up her boots. David watched from the kitchen as she pulled on her gloves.

"And where are *you* going, Nanook?"

She zipped her coat and headed for the back door. "I need some fresh air to clear my head. Care to come?"

"We're right behind you," he said, grabbing his coat.

"Who's *we*?"

"Never leave home without it," he said, patting his holstered gun.

The snow crunched under their feet, as they headed toward the small stretch of woods behind Mira's property. Arianne felt the tension begin to ease as crisp air filled her lungs and her legs moved along the familiar terrain. She'd spent countless hours hiking, and sitting under the huge weeping willow at the edge of Mira's yard during her teens. Somehow, her sessions with Old Man Willow had always calmed her when she'd needed it most. This was one of those times. Aunt Mira's words echoed through her mind against the traipsing sound of her boots.

"Perhaps it is time to meet your parents."

The words cut her to the quick. Did she really want her to meet the very people responsible for all the pain and hardship in both their lives? How could her aunt say such a thing?

Guilt flooded her as she came to terms with her most honest, inner feelings. She did wonder about her mother and father. There were even times when she'd envisioned seeing them for the first time. What would they say? What would she do? Could there ever be a bond between them?

Now it looked as though her greatest fear might become reality in order to save her life. There was no way to know what the increase in her powers meant or just how far they might go, without contacting her parents. Either way, it could mean her destruction.

She moved up a steep incline, and thrust her walking stick into the thick snow. A quick backward glance confirmed David was having no problem keeping up. His sandy brown hair blew gently in the winter breeze and his green eyes sparkled against the surrounding whiteness of snow. She forced her thoughts on climbing the snow hill.

He caught her glance and said, "I'm right behind you."

"It's beautiful out here this time of year. I've hiked all over the country, but this is by far the most captivating during the winter." Suddenly, Arianne's stick slipped on the ground, causing her to lose her balance. She landed face forward, and slid back down toward David like a seal on its belly. Before she'd gone very far, a firm grip stopped her momentum and she looked up to see him grinning at her.

Cradled in his arms at the bottom of hill, she felt her breath catch as he leaned close.

"You're right," he said softly, "the scene *is* captivating."

With that, he touched his lips to hers, tenderly exploring as she allowed his warmth to fill her.

Her heart bounded as she let go and took in pleasure and acceptance for the first time in her life. It felt natural to give and receive on such an intimate level and something stirred deep within, filling her with strength and courage like never before. She knew the time had come for her to stop fearing her past and face her future head on.

As David pulled back, she saw the tenderness linger in his expression while he stroked her cheek with his finger.

Finally, he broke the spell, eyeing the slope before them. "Ready to try again?"

His words held more meaning for her than he knew. "Let's go."

When they reached the top of the hill, they stopped to catch their breath. Arianne was aware of David's arm brushing against hers and of something else. The hairs on her neck bristled. She closed her eyes briefly and felt a slight sensation of vertigo pass. Suddenly she caught an unfamiliar scent. It was close by.

Her hearing seemed greatly magnified. She was aware of David's breaths and the faint sound of his heartbeat.

He stood nearby. "What's wrong?"

She shook the sensation away, and pressed a gloved index finger to her lips.

He cocked his head in question, and followed her lead, mouthing, "What?"

The still silence echoed. It was *too* quiet. She could see David felt it as well, his eyes narrowed, meticulously scanning the area. Nothing. Barren trees jutted from the solid white ground under a blue sky. It was the perfect day.

The scent was gone now and Arianne started forward with David by her side. They trudged on in silence into the last group of dense trees. Her tension eased as they went along.

After a while, David asked, "What did you see back there?"

"Nothing, really. It's what I felt and what I could smell."

"Smell?"

"It's hard to explain. First, I sensed something, and then there was this incredibly strong odor. It put me on guard, as if something dangerous was close by."

"I felt it, too, but apparently not as intensely as you did."

Arianne stopped to explain. "I realize what I've asked you to believe about me is overwhelming. Actually, you've accepted it pretty well, unless you're a good actor." She glanced around and continued, "My life has never been *normal*, but I've always had certain abilities, I guess you'd say they border on paranormal. They're becoming sharper, more developed lately and I don't know why."

"What do you think is happening? Any ideas?"

"I'm only guessing, but I'd say it has something to do with my DNA. These powers have been triggered and most likely, there's nothing I can do about it, much like someone growing old. It's in the genes."

"So you're saying it's a natural progression of some sort."

"Something like that, but since my particular circumstances aren't documented in any medical reference, it's impossible to say."

"How can I help?"

Suddenly a branch cracked and David was slammed to the ground. Arianne stood stunned as a man in black pinned him. David appeared helpless as the man straddled him. Before Arianne could react, David cut into the man's arms at the elbows with both hands, breaking the grip and forcing the attacker to roll to the side.

David jumped to his feet in a karate stance, awaiting the assailant's next move.

"Arianne, run!" David commanded.

Frozen, she stood fixed in place.

"Do it!" he yelled.

With that, the man somersaulted through the icy snow in an attempt to knock David off his feet. Ready this time, David avoided the attack, countering with a few moves of his own. The two seemed to be equally matched, and they circled one another in defense.

Finally, the man spoke. "My name is Mandari and I'm here to warn you. You are in grave danger, my friend."

David continued to watch him carefully. "You haven't proved it to *me*."

"It is not *me* you should fear. Leave Arianne to me in order to save your mortal soul!"

Suddenly he turned toward Arianne, pulling a curved dagger from a hidden sheath under his tunic. She saw the blade gleaming against the sun, as he raised it over her chest.

She heard David yell, "No!" as he drew his gun.

Fierceness erupted deep inside her. Everything moved in slow motion. The blade was inches from her skin. She grabbed the attacker's wrist and jerked his arm sideways. His unexpected thrust-kick sent her sailing backwards and onto the ground. Shots rang out and she quickly rolled out of range. As David fired once more, she watched in awe as the man jumped high and landed solidly on a tree branch.

He warned. "You cannot escape the Jen-Ku."

David held his aim, never blinking. "Jen-who?"

A bright flash of fire exploded in the tree and he was gone, leaving only smoke and the smell of sulfur behind.

* * *

That afternoon, Arianne slammed her condo door as she dropped her luggage to the floor. She pitched her keys onto the end table. "Shylock!"

Before she'd gone two steps, she heard him answer, "*This* is certainly a first; you summoning *me*?" His arrogant tone made her want to smash something. She fingered the rim of a nearby vase. Her upper lip curled at the sight of him relaxing in her living room.

She rounded the couch and knocked his feet from the coffee table. "Don't get excited. This isn't a social call."

"What? No tea and crumpets?"

"What the hell is a Jen-Ku?" She enjoyed the brief glimmer of shock in his expression. "Why didn't you warn me?"

"Warn you?" He arched an eyebrow. "Whatever for? You are not yet a vampire."

"Well, tell that to the guy who attacked me this morning. Just who are the Jen-Ku? And why was I attacked?"

Shylock pressed his fingertips together, forming a steeple under his chin, his eyes closed, as if in deep thought before he spoke. "Hundreds of years ago, there were a group of priests who broke from the church over a disagreement about the destruction of vampires. They felt if priests were allowed to perform exorcisms to cast out demons, they should have the right to destroy the walking dead. The church disagreed. Eventually, they formed their own sect, and began traveling the country in search of vampires."

"This guy was no ordinary priest. He had martial arts training and some pretty impressive moves. I thought priests were kind, gentle, and forgiving!"

Shylock shrugged. "Like I said, they broke from the church. The Jen-Ku *are* kind and gentle as long as you're not a vampire. They feel they are doing a service to God. They've developed powers of their own, similar to the vampire."

"So why me, Shylock? How could they possibly know about my past?"

"The Jen-Ku are very powerful and are everywhere. They're worldwide. Now that they've found you, you can never rest. It is important you mature in your abilities; it could save your life. The one thing you must avoid is the Jen-Ku dagger."

"That curved knife?"

"It is more than that. The only way to truly kill a vampire is to cut out the heart and expose it to the sun's light. It will burn to ashes in seconds, eliminating the vampire's pump—or life source—if you will. Once this is accomplished, the vampire dies a very slow, excruciating death. That is why the Jen-Ku dagger is curved; it cuts out the heart quickly and completely."

Arianne closed her eyes, and allowed Shylock's words to sink in. Finally, she said, "So where's your 'just-come-home-where-you'll-be-safe' speech, Shylock?"

He offered no reply.

"Are you growing tired of the job or have you conceded defeat?"

Arianne suggested.

"Hardly," he said. "Arianne, accept it or not, you and I are very much alike. We're both searching to be cleansed for deeds that are not our fault. We long for the forgiveness of a God who has seemingly turned his back, yet watches and judges our every thought and action. It is the cruelest form of deceit, to offer hope where there is none."

She'd never heard him speak this way. But then, she'd never given him the chance. His words sliced her spiritual safety net, yet captured her feelings fully. Through it all, however, she couldn't accept his deduction about hope. "Ah. That is where you and I differ. Where you have lost all expectations for good, I rely on my faith, which is surer than hope."

"Perhaps. Please don't disregard my warning. You must use the gifts given for self-preservation. It is the only way."

Eyeing him cautiously, she asked, "Why are you helping me? You're risking your freedom."

His chuckle softened his dark demeanor, making him almost pleasant against the shadows now hovering as the sun set. "You didn't know me in the old days. I have always been a risk taker; my very income depended on it. It was when I chose to do the right thing that my luck soured."

"So why the change of heart?"

"Let's just say the battle is already lost, I am but one more casualty. For me, it is not a matter of faith, nor hope, but of honor."

"I suppose the old adage 'honor among thieves' applies here. After all, you've stolen a piece of my life, or at least kept it from me."

"Ah. You're referring to your brother. You're mistaken. It was your beloved aunt who stole him from you."

"It doesn't matter, Shylock. I'm going to find him. I don't care how long it takes, or what I have to do."

He nodded. "Or, you can eliminate all the trouble and I can simply take you to him."

CHAPTER 22

A crumpled Pepsi can sailed across David's path on his way to his desk, and landed in a nearby wastebasket. The police station was chaotic, but he barely noticed, as he dodged his co-workers and several people waiting to file legal complaints in the crowded room. After this morning's festivities in the woods behind Mira's, he felt he had one more piece to fit the puzzle—trouble is, he had no idea what puzzle the piece fit.

Just who or what is a Jen-Ku and why does it mean trouble for Arianne, he wondered? He recalled the silence between them as they made their way back from the hike. Neither had seemed to know what to say. *He* sure didn't. How had he missed his shot? No one was that fast. However, up until a week ago, vampires only existed in fiction, he reminded himself. The world was changing fast since he'd met Arianne. He had a feeling it would change a lot more before it was over.

The taste of their first kiss hadn't faded before they'd had to fight for their lives. It was a battle he welcomed if it would free her from the pain. It was turning into a see-saw—for every upside, there came a quick downslide.

Stopping at his desk, he spotted several post-it messages stuck to the computer monitor. The first one was a reminder from Bill Sanders that David owed him fifty bucks. Garbage. He tossed it in the waste can. The next was a lengthy illegible scrawl, which he also threw away. The last one caught his attention.

Spears-
Results on acid for Fred Brewster—Splatter pattern consistent with accidental spill.

He reread it, realizing its meaning. Dr. Brewster hadn't been intentionally doused with acid; there'd been an accident first. He'd been murdered afterward. But why kill someone who's already dying? See-saw.

He shoved aside several small stacks of paperwork. Right now, he needed to find out about the Jen-Ku and what they wanted with Arianne. While the computer world did not fascinate him, he had befriended the Internet. It was like a telephone to the world, where all you have to do is ask. He typed in the unfamiliar name, and wondered if he'd spelled it correctly. Suddenly the screen displayed numerous sites about the elusive priesthood.

He clicked on one promising history and status, and watched a black background cover his screen and form red letters.

JEN-KU
"In His Service"

He scanned down and read bits and pieces. "Oh, my God. This is unbelievable."

As the search continued, he realized why Arianne had been attacked, and why she was in more danger than he'd thought. Their goal to eliminate all vampires was clear.

"That's why they're coming for her; they know her secret."

The phone rang, jarring his train of thought. "Spears," he answered, cradling the receiver between his shoulder and ear.

"David?" Arianne asked.

"Yeah, what's up? You okay?" He clicked print, and watched the paper feed through the printer.

"I'm fine. Are you busy right now?"

"No, why?"

"I need to go to church."

* * *

David's black Camaro pulled next to the curb. Arianne got in before he could put it in park. "Thanks for coming. I didn't know how credible I sounded on the phone."

David pulled into traffic. "So you're in need of a little salvation, huh?"

She buckled her seat belt with a sound click. "Yes."

"All right. What's this about? You said something about seeing Father Jonah?"

"Yes, but that isn't his name. It's Michael."

David's eyebrows shot up. "As in...your brother?"

"Yes. Father Jonah St. Paul is Michael Von Tirgov. My own flesh and blood."

"You got connections with the Feds?" He grinned then added, "Who told you this?"

"My dark conscience." She shook her head, still finding it hard to believe.

"Shylock told you?"

"Yes."

"And you believe him?"

"Yes. That's the strange part, David. I do. No strings attached. No ploy to get me home to Romania. For the first time since I've know him, I feel I can trust him."

"How did he find Michael?"

"He's known his whereabouts for years, never letting on to my parents."

"But why?"

"Because Michael is a priest."

"So?"

"Shylock may be a lot of things, but one thing he has is a deep fear of God. If my parents had known, they would've sent him to Michael just as they did to me, and Shylock wanted no part of that."

"So why tell you now? There's got to be an angle in it for him somewhere."

"He said something about the battle already being lost and he's just another casualty. I don't know, but it sounds like Shylock has a dark conscience of his own."

As the car slowed, Arianne fought the wave of butterflies in her stomach. The stoic steeple stood above the brick building that was St. Victor's Church. Wide concrete steps ascended to the large ornate wooden doors, welcoming the masses. Her brother was inside.

"Are you okay?" David's hand touched hers.

"Yes, I'm ready."

Inside, David stayed beside her as they moved down the long aisle. Before the altar, they stopped, unsure of which way to go. Then, as if in answer to her prayer, the choice was made as a friendly voice beckoned them to the left. Father Jonah stood in his familiar dark clothing and pastoral collar. A silver cross hung from around his neck, glistening against the soft yellow ceiling lights.

Arianne closed her eyes trying to summon all of the calm and courage she could find. How could she ever find the words? *God, give me courage,* she prayed, and then felt David beside her, touching her arm.

They followed the priest to the back office. David stayed right behind her.

Father Jonah's tone was tender and as welcoming as always. "Arianne, it's so good to see you. And who is this?" he extended a hand to David.

Arianne made the necessary introductions with a dry mouth and trembling voice. It was getting harder to maintain her composure. She looked at his eyes and saw the shape of her own, the curve of his chin and even the way he carried himself. After all, of the times she'd received communion from him, looking into his face, she wondered how she could have missed the resemblance.

"Please, sit," he offered. "Now, what can I do for you two?"

She wanted to speak, but the words caught tight in her throat. Her legs shook as she took a seat before the desk. She knew he was staring at her but she couldn't do anything but tremble. Then she heard David explain.

"Father Jonah, Arianne has come today, with some news. Good news."

"Really? Well, I'd love to hear it. But frankly, I've never seen you this quiet, Arianne. Are you all right?"

Her voice sounded tight. "Father, please listen and promise you won't stop me until I've finished."

A look of concern crossed his face. "Of course."

"At the age of two you were brought from Romania to the U.S. and given up to an orphanage."

The priest's eyes went wide, and the color drained from his face. He sat down, in silence.

Arianne continued. "The woman who brought you there was your aunt, Mira Brasov, sister to your mother, Emelia Von Tirgov."

His voice was a mere whisper, "How do you know this?"

"Your aunt wasn't alone with you when she brought you from Romania. I was with her. I am your sister." Arianne closed her eyes briefly now that the truth was out.

"My sister?" His eyes brimmed with tears over a growing smile. "I have a sister." He moved around the desk to meet her.

Arianne rushed to him, catching him in a warm embrace. At this moment, he was not Father Jonah, her priest and soul's shepherd. He was Michael. She buried her face in his neck, like a sister would to her big brother. She held his hands to her face, and knew Shylock had told the truth.

After all of the heartache, all of the chaos in her life, she was not alone. Now another shared her past, her blood and possibly her life to come. Filled with closure, she realized new doors were opening, some pleasant, some overflowing with pain. They would go through them together.

He drew back without letting go. "I can't believe this. It's truly God's miracle! How did you find this out?"

Arianne glanced toward David, then back at her brother. "*That's* the hard part, Fath…, I mean, Michael."

He paused, smiling. "The nuns used to call me that. It's been a long time."

Arianne nodded. "Why did you change your name?"

"When I was old enough, I decided to adopt the name of the orphanage that took me in, and loved me enough to raise me. As for 'Jonah,' he's one of my favorite Bible characters. You see, he was lost and tossed about by life when God intervened to straighten him out. I guess I really identify with that. But how is it your name is Brasov?"

"Aunt Mira gave me her name to keep things less complicated."

"I don't see what's so complicated about a woman taking in her dead sister's child as her own. Still, I suppose it raised fewer questions that way."

"Something like that." She realized there was so much he needed to know, a lifetime full of truths and secrets.

Taking her hands, he asked, "Tell me, how did our parents die?"

The answer wasn't easy, but looking into his honest, searching eyes, she could not lie, not only to a priest, but also to her precious brother who deserved to know the truth. Finally, she said, "They didn't."

CHAPTER 23

Emelia fingered the edge of her bedroom desk, deep in thought. Everything seemed to be in order; her plan was falling into place. She double-checked the windows to insure total darkness as she waited for Vladimir to return from his hunt. The sun would rise soon.

Daegon startled her from behind. "Your absence has been untimely." He tossed her passport aside. "Do you plan an extended tour?"

Emelia met his icy stare. "Are you a soldier of the President's Securitate? Do you police my every move?" She could feel the anger smoldering beneath his smile.

"I've missed you. You've not visited the caverns lately."

"You mean I haven't been bringing your fatted, tender kill. Have you forgotten how to hunt after all my years of service?"

"Is that what you think, Emelia? That I've tolerated your ignorance and clumsy demonstrations of my tutelage so I could feed? Haven't I made good on my promise to instruct you in the ways of the vampire and bring you to your full potential?"

"Yes, and it proved useful in fighting the Jen-Ku priest. *He* is now the prey."

"It gave you great pleasure, I'm sure." He gestured toward the ticket on the desk. "Why a plane? You've no need of one; you're a vampire."

"Daegon, you surprise me. You taught me to be wary of the Jen-Ku. Traveling as a mortal will bring no attention to me. It's safer that way."

"Wise, indeed." Daegon stood to pace, his boots treading over the elegant carpet. "Still, I have doubts for your safety. I don't believe you are ready."

"That's what you want me to believe. But it's a lie, isn't it? The truth is I've been ready for years. In your pathetic manipulation to keep me as your slave, you led me to think there was so much more to learn." She stretched out her arms dramatically and went on. "Oh, the great coven-master, Daegon, holds all the answers, dispensing them like treats to a pet for good behavior. When *will* I be ready? After it's too late to find my children?"

Her dissertation did not appear to move him. Instead, he continued pacing, with his hands behind his back. "The student is never greater than the master."

"You aren't my master. I'm not a coven member. We had a deal, that's all."

In a flash, he was across the room, gripping her by the throat. His words slithered from under a sneer, "And I kept...my...word."

She broke his hold with one hand, and stepped aside. "Then our time together is finished."

"I see. You feel secure in your knowledge as a vampire. Yet, do you know what will happen—what is probably already happening to your daughter?"

Emelia stopped, feeling fear for the first time in thirty years.

Daegon continued, "I will gladly tell you. If Arianne does not take her first kill and become vampire soon, she will start to deteriorate. Her teeth must pierce the skin of another to break the seal of mortality, or she will rot like a corpse from the inside out! It will start slowly, progressing at a more rapid rate as time goes on. Eventually, she will die an excruciating death sending her soul to eternal purgatory. Being half mortal and half immortal, she cannot enter heaven or hell. You can't have it both ways."

Emelia held her rage. "Why didn't you tell me this before?"

"I knew you would foolishly rush off to her, risking yourself and all others of our kind to exposure. By now, of course, I'm sure your abilities will get you safely passed the Jen-Ku. You should make it in time for her funeral. After all, she never made it to yours."

"You heartless bastard!"

"So I've been told. Your husband gave me that impression when he refused to join me years ago. I believe it was shortly before your unfortunate *accident*."

Daegon's evil plan lay before her. He'd sought revenge against

Vladimir's refusal by causing her fall that night. Not only had he taken her life, but now Arianne's was in danger as well. She'd been a fool, duped into serving the equivalent of Satan's brother. Fury welled inside—a fiery consumption bent on release.

He rose to leave. "If you'll excuse me, I'd best leave before the daylight." Then turning he said, "Oh, it *is* true that I could have released you years ago, actually before your training even started. You see, in order to make you my equal, all you needed was a taste of my blood." His satisfied smile lingered after his words.

"Then I shall have it!" she said, rushing him.

His cape rose and fell in graceful folds as he avoided her charge with ease. He raised his arm, and she was suddenly lifted and thrown backwards. She slammed hard against the wall and slid to the floor. When Daegon turned to go, she grabbed the Jen-Ku dagger she'd taken from the priest.

With a forceful leap, she landed in front of him. "I want you to see this coming," she spat, thrusting the blade into his chest.

Holding him in a tight embrace, she forced him back onto the bed, as the door burst open and Olga called, "What's happening in here?"

Emelia sliced Daegon's chest wide, cracking open his rib cage like an eggshell. The dagger's curved blade sliced through his chest, and she brought out his heart. It spurted blood across the bed as she yanked it from its cavity.

"Olga! Take it," Emelia commanded, holding out the shiny muscle.

The frightened woman stood frozen in the doorway with eyes wide.

Daegon struggled beneath Emelia's grip and lifted her upward.

Emelia screamed. "Do it, Olga! Redeem yourself for the loss of my children!"

Olga reached with trembling hands and took the bloody heart.

"Now go quickly with it, outside. Expose it to the sun until it turns to ashes. Go!"

The woman rushed from the room, leaving Emelia with Daegon. His arms weakened and Emelia fell on top of him, blood splashing onto her cheeks. His face was gray, and all of the warmth drained from his wax-like body. He gasped for air as his lungs gurgled and dark pungent, fluid bubbled from his lips. His eyes tried to hold her gaze then rolled back inside his head.

Emelia pushed herself off, and watched his face sink into hollow sockets of bone beneath. His fangs remained a vivid reminder of his legacy of death. Blackened, necrotic fingers protruded from the sleeves under his velvet cloak like brittle twigs, and his large ruby ring hung loosely against the bed's coverlet. The blood of his last victim had ceased flowing. Daegon was dead.

Vladimir stood in the doorway. "It's over. Olga has returned with the ashes. You're free."

"Come with me," she pleaded. "Together we can bring back our children."

"The risk is too great. You mustn't go. I don't believe our combined powers are enough to survive the priesthood. We will find another way."

"I wish I could share your confidence, but my heart tells me different. I leave tonight."

* * *

The airport page called once more as the check-in line moved slowly. "Flight 101 to London, now boarding."

Emelia placed her ticket on the counter and watched the pulse beating in the attendant's throat. "What a beautiful young woman you are," she said in an old woman's voice.

The woman blushed and offered a gracious, "Thank you," before handing Emelia back her ticket packet.

Emelia shuffled toward the gate with hunched shoulders, and kept her gaze on the floor ahead. Her hair, now the color of gray paste, lay neatly coiled in a bun under a pink cotton naframa, the head covering of choice for an elderly Romanian woman. A beige, knee-length coat almost met the top of her clumsy black boots.

When she boarded the plane, a stewardess assisted her in finding her seat, offering a pillow and blanket for the long night flight. "Pleasant dreams, Mrs. Covasna."

"Please, call me Olga."

Seated beside her, she smiled at the handsome young man fastening his seat belt.

"Can't be too careful," he said. "Have you flown before?"

She smiled, looking into his clear blue eyes. "Yes, many times."

"I haven't. Truthfully, it makes me a bit nervous."

She patted his hand. "That's why I fly at night. If you go to sleep, it's over before you know it."

"The layover in London shouldn't add too much time to the trip. Is this your first time to America?"

Emelia fingered her locket, tracing the etched *B* with her fingernail. "Yes. I'm surprising my children with a visit."

DESTINY'S CALL

PART III

Final Redemption

CHAPTER 24

Michael's expression betrayed confusion as he sat in the office with David and Arianne. His voice, however, remained calm. "I don't understand."

"Michael, this is so hard. How do I explain a lifetime of lies and darkness?"

"Arianne, I'm a priest. I'm not afraid of the dark side. It goes with the job."

"Even if the other side is part of you? Even if it means that *I* am evil, too?"

"We're all sinners, I think the term *evil* is a bit harsh." Looking into her eyes, he added, "What happened to our parents?"

She glanced once at David, who nodded for her to go on.

"Well, let me back-track a little so it will make more sense, if that's possible. You and I were kidnapped by our Aunt Mira and brought to America."

"Kidnapped? How can that be? She had custody."

"Yes, legally, she did. That's why she was able to give you up to the orphanage."

Storms passed over Michael's eyes, and she could feel his pain. The deep void he felt spread through Arianne like poison, making her wise to the sorrow of hell itself. She waited for the sensation to pass, and continued. "Mira had no choice but to separate us, it was for our own safety. You see she knew our parents would eventually come for us."

"But they died."

"No, Michael, they only died to this life. They were reborn to the other side as vampires."

If she'd expected an explosive reaction with waving hands and a head shaking in denial, she would have been disappointed. Her life experience had taught her to expect nothing, and always be ready for the unexpected. This proved to be one of those times. Her brother simply sighed with closed eyes, and remained motionless, as if in prayer. Finally he spoke, tears threatening to spill onto his fair, freckled cheeks.

"All my life, I've known there was something...unholy about me, I guess, for lack of a better word. It's gotten to the point where recently I've considered leaving the priesthood. But now, you've given me the answer."

"Michael, you're not unholy. You're clean. It's just our parents and myself who are unclean."

"You?"

"Our mother was bitten when she was pregnant with me. We shared the same blood, and therefore, when I was born I was only half mortal." She felt him draw away from her, not in the physical sense, but emotionally, as if she were a threat. "Please don't hate me. I've never taken the blood—that is the one thing I must do to become full vampire. It is what our parents desire most. But I would die before taking a life."

"This is too incredible." He raised his hands. "I'm not calling you a liar; it's just so much to believe."

Arianne sighed, deciding what she must do.

"Maybe this will help you accept the horrible truth." She felt her jaws moving to accommodate the fangs. A strange feeling filled her, seeping into her bones, and settling into the core of her being. She opened her mouth wide, and exposed her fangs, closing her eyes to the look of horror she knew they would bring.

After several seconds, she turned away, taking a deep breath. She felt Michael's consoling arm wrap around her waist to pull her close. She allowed his acceptance and tender touch of forgiveness that opened the door to a hopeful future. She held him tight as her fangs slowly receded and she felt whole again.

Her gaze fell on David, and she was surprised to see him offer a nod of encouragement. If this display of truth didn't send him running, nothing would.

She turned back to Michael. "There is hope for me. There is a way to be rid of this curse."

"God's love will forgive. You are still His child."

"I believe that, I really do. But I'm talking about something else. It's the medical procedure Fred Brewster used to cure cancer. There is every reason to believe it will work on me. All I need is a DNA donor—someone who's DNA is closely related but clean. I'm asking for your help Michael."

"Of course, I'll help. Now that I know what the fight is, I can prepare for battle, a battle we will not lose."

"All I need is a blood sample. It won't take long."

"We'll do it today. The sooner the better to end this pain."

"I'm afraid this in only the beginning. Our parents will never stop searching for us. You need to understand there is still a risk. I'm afraid we will never be safe until they are destroyed."

David leaned forward. "They aren't your only concern. A Jen-Ku priest attacked us. Do you know anything about them?"

Michael's forehead creased as he paced in the small office. "Good Lord help us."

"That bad, huh?"

"Yes, David, *that bad*. From what I've learned of them, they're looked upon as evil. Since the church doesn't recognize vampires as real, it condemns their actions, believing they kill innocent people for the sake of their cause. They are extremely dangerous because they feel justified in their endeavors. Until now, I too, simply considered them a dying breed of misled zealots."

"Believe me, Father, there was nothing misleading about the hits I took. He was right on target. Never thought I'd have to fight a priest."

"Be careful, David. They aren't just priests. They're more like a SWAT team."

"SWAT members don't fly—this guy did."

"Fly?"

"More like one helluva leap that landed him on a tree branch."

"That makes sense. They train constantly for battle to be able to match the vampire's strength. After hundreds of years, they've probably almost mastered the powers needed to defeat their foe, yet they lack one thing."

"What's that?"

"God's will. They fight in His name, but without His approval or direction. Nowhere in the Bible does it mention vampires or condoning murder for that reason. 'Vengeance is mine, saith the Lord,' but they've taken His battle for their own. My advice is to keep as far away from them as you can."

Arianne shook her head. "It doesn't make sense. Why me? I'm not full vampire and I don't kill."

"They must know you're part vampire and that's all they need to know," Michael said.

"But how?"

"They're world-wide and very powerful. I'm sure they have their ways of tracing vampire lineage. One thing you must remember is, once you're their target, they will not stop until they've destroyed you."

* * *

Later that afternoon, Arianne flipped the patient chart closed with a sound snap. She couldn't contain her smile. Harriet Gross's lab work was probably better than half of the nurses' on the oncology unit, and definitely better than her own. Fred's cure remained sure.

Sandy Jergins, one of the staff nurses, sat at the station between Arianne and a tall stack of charts. A blonde bob-cut framed her baby-doll face, sparkling blue eyes and a warm, genuine smile that as far as Arianne could recall was always present. Oncology, she knew was a tough field, where patients frequently deteriorated and passed just when they seem to be responding. She knew the day-to-day care of cancer patients could take its toll on staff members, offering the highest burnout and employee turnover in the hospital. Arianne admired Sandy's courage and envied her emotional stamina.

Sandy offered a bright smile behind tired eyes. "Any new orders on Harriet?"

Arianne shook her head. "Nope. She seems to be doing great. How does she seem to you?"

"Well, her vitals remain stable, no temp, excellent appetite—"

Arianne held up her hands. "Whoa. I know all that, I just read her chart. But tell me what you *really* see."

Sandy arched a perfectly shaped eyebrow, and toyed with the red stethoscope around her neck. "Ahh…you want my expert prognosis." She chuckled.

"Right." Arianne smiled.

"Dr. Brasov, Harriet will probably go home before Christmas, happy and just as sassy as she was before her cancer. Unless something unforeseen happens, I'd bet my next paycheck that *that* little lady will be sipping Mai-Tai's on the beach next summer—her cancer a distant memory."

Arianne thought a moment then asked, "Your whole check, huh?"

"And believe me, Dr. Brasov, there'll be lots of overtime on that puppy."

* * *

Arianne knocked briefly before entering Harriet's room. She heard the television dishing the familiar fare of popular talk shows. Harriet's voice broke in over the tearful whining of one of the show's guests. "Don't be such a ninny! Leave the fool and get on with your life!"

Arianne stifled a grin, and peeked around the corner. "Harriet? May I come in?"

The woman's expression brightened and she abruptly turned off the TV "Dr. Brasov! What a pleasant surprise," then cautiously added, "You're not here with any bad news, are you?"

"Of course not."

"Good. Then come and sit down." She patted a spot on the bed. "I want to show you these." She pulled out several magazines from the bedside table. Each one had several pages folded over as markers.

"I want your honest opinion, Doctor. Do you like any of these for me?"

As Arianne considered the hairstyle photos, Harriet continued, "I just thought…well, you know, I've been given a second chance, a new life. Why not a new hairstyle to go with it?"

"I understand, Harriet," Arianne said, browsing over the pages. She pointed to one. "Well, definitely *not* this one."

"What? Too chic? Too young?"

"Too cutsie."

"What about that one?" Harriet pointed.

"Harriet, you're sixty, not one hundred and sixty."

"No, but now, thanks to Dr. Brewster and you, I will live to my normal life expectancy." She took Arianne's hands into her own. "I want you to know how sorry I am about Dr. Brewster. The news was devastating to me and, of course, everyone who knew him, but most of all I'm sure you feel like you've lost a very good friend."

Arianne took a deep breath, trying to keep her composure. The woman's well-intended words cut deep, re-opening her healing wounds. "Thank you, Harriet. I promise you his work will continue. He would want it that way."

"That's good to hear, because so many will benefit from it."

"Now, let's talk about you. How are you doing?"

Harriet's blue eyes glistened. "Fantastic. No pain, no fever, no night sweats, or spending countless hours in the john being sick. *And* I have energy to spare. Frankly, I can't wait to get out of here."

"That's really up to your oncologist, Dr. Harris, but I'll certainly put in a good word for you."

"Oh, would you? My daughter has been asking about it, you know, with the holidays coming and all. I guess we're all just a bit anxious."

"Well, your lab results are normal, there's no sign of cancer anywhere, and you look terrific. Frankly, I can't see why Dr. Harris would be opposed to making discharge plans."

"Soon?"

Arianne smiled. "I'd say, probably for Christmas."

* * *

As Arianne headed for her car in the hospital parking garage, she checked her watch. She was running late, again. She pressed the keyless remote, and saw her car lights flash once. There was less than an hour to get home, and get ready for her date with David, a seemingly impossible order considering city rush-hour traffic. Her hand shook as she slipped the key into the ignition. Perhaps a testimony to pre-date jitters.

Why not? She was entitled to a few butterflies—hell, maybe a whole field of them, after remaining out of the dating game for so long. Loneliness crept in during the most inopportune moments in life, such as Christmas or birthdays, and always reminded her that the risk of a date blooming into something more was just too high. Until she found a cure, she'd decided long ago, it would be wise to avoid potentially serious relationships.

Somehow though, David was different. He knew the secret, understood it—at least he pretended to, and realized the risk. What harm could there be in Chinese food and a movie, after all, they'd already shared a kiss.

Her hand gave another jolty twitch when she turned the heater up full blast.

"When's the last time you ate, *Doctor*?" she questioned herself as the car warmed up.

She checked the visor mirror, and saw two blood-shot blue eyes set against the washed out pallor of her skin. A stray lock of ebony hair hung like a limp ribbon across her forehead, with the rest of her hair slipping from the ponytail holder.

"I need a makeover, and before seven o'clock," she said to her reflection.

She pulled out of the garage, and squinted against the brightness of oncoming traffic. The headlights were surrounded by hazy halos, making it hard to focus on the road. It was difficult to judge distance and she nearly rear-ended the car in front of her carrying two small children in the back.

"What's going on? Don't tell me I need glasses."

Breathing deep, she tried to stay calm. *It isn't that much further. Just drive slow.*

YONK! A car sped around her as the driver offered a special salute.

"Hmmm. I saw *that* as plain as day." She chuckled.

Suddenly, her vision spun out of control. Her foot hit the brakes and she heard several horns blast behind her. She squeezed her eyelids shut for a moment, and was relieved to see everything right itself. Slowly she continued to the red light, and decided to check her messages. When she reached for her cell phone, she saw two phones. A quick glance out the windshield confirmed everything appeared in twos.

She rubbed her eyes but nothing changed. She looked out over the city street and the double vision remained. The light changed, but she didn't move. She had no choice but to wait until her vision cleared.

Once again, a barrage of horns blared from behind, and her nerves tightened. Tremors shook her hand as she pushed the hazard light button and prepared to be the cause of a major traffic delay only ten minutes from her home.

"What's happening to me!" she cried.

CHAPTER 25

O'Hare International Airport. Labeled one of the largest and busiest airfields in the world, it remains secure in the fact that no matter how many come after it, O'Hare is unique; it *is* Chicago. Hardly noticed among the harried passengers was a tall man, wearing a business suit with a gray silk tie who passed the customs area on his way to the bar. He took a seat on a stool, and ordered a club soda, double lime. His watchful almond-shaped eyes scanned the terminals, slowly, methodically. In such a busy place, it could be easy to miss the person you seek, he decided. Moreover, it could be deadly.

He took a sip of his drink, and set it down as the young woman beside him nearly fell into his lap.

"Oh...excuse me," she slurred. "I'm so sorry. Guess it's a bit early for a Manhattan, huh?" Her smudged lipstick created a lop-sided smile. "By the way, what time is it?"

The man looked up at the clock. "Six-thirty, miss."

"That's Ms. but you can call me Ginny," she said, offering a handshake. "Looks like I have plenty of time before my flight." She drained her glass and motioned to the bartender for another. "So, what's your name?"

"John," he lied.

"Well, John, where are you headed?"

"I'm waiting for someone." He took another sip and turned his attention to the small television huddled in the far corner above Johnny Walker's colorful family.

"Lucky gal," Ginny commented, watching the television anchor.

"...with no leads in the murder of Dr. Fred Brewster..." the pretty blonde was saying.

The murdered man's picture remained on the screen as the broadcast continued.

Ginny nodded toward the TV "Now that's a real shame. Who would want the guy dead? I mean, he discovered the cure for cancer. He's one of the good guys!"

The man closed his eyes briefly, and tried to shut out the vivid scenes flashing through his mind—visions of the doctor's last moments...

The lab door had been open as he entered from the darkened hallway in the Research Center. As he moved passed a long worktable, he realized someone was still inside. He noticed an overturned beaker on the counter top, its contents splattered and dripping onto the floor. A muffled cry came from across the lab, and he stepped around the mess, and headed toward a room in the back.

The small office was empty, containing only a cluttered desk with paperwork strewn across the top and several manila folders. Framed diplomas, certificates, and a photo of an older man with a young woman, hung on the paneled wall.

Suddenly the swivel chair moved and someone moaned. He rounded the desk, and saw the man from the photo, lying on the floor. Blood soaked his shirt from the gaping wound over his heart. His eyes were wide in terror as he lay gasping for air. The victim's face had been badly burned and his left eye was a muddled mass of jelly.

Then he recognized him as the doctor who'd found the cure for leukemia—the man working with Dr. Arianne Brasov. Helplessly, Dr. Brewster pulled at the man's trouser leg, his expression pleading. The man bent down close, but saw it was too late for the good doctor.

Ginny's voice suddenly interrupted. "Hey, can I buy you a drink?"

"No, thank you," he said, still feeling the emotion of the memory.

"Are you okay? You're looking a little pale."

He forced a smile. "I'm fine."

"Well, I sure don't know what the world is coming to when we murder our own."

"The balance between good and evil has truly shifted."

She stared at him a moment. "Brother, that's deep. You a philosopher or something?"

"Hardly. I'm simply an observer, hoping for justice."

Ginny played with the ice in her drink as if looking for a reply.

The television newscaster continued with another prominent story. "A local Chicago priest is still being held without bond for alleged molestation of two teen boys."

As the arrest footage ran, Ginny perked up again. "See that? A priest held for sex crimes! I think you're right about that good and evil shift. Can you imagine a priest doing that?"

He felt the muscles in his jaw tighten as he watched the man being led away in handcuffs. His pulse quickened, heated in anger at the thought.

Ginny shook her head. "Well, I don't care what he did, that's still no way to treat a priest."

The man stood suddenly and tossed several bills onto the bar.

Ginny spun around on her bar stool. "Hey! Where're you going? Was it something I said?"

He never turned back, and made his way through the crowd. Ms. Ginny might be a little flirtatious and a lot drunk, but she was right about one thing—that was no way to treat a priest.

* * *

David greeted the condo security guard as he headed for the elevators. "Hey, Rhorman, how's it going?"

"Evenin'. I guess I'm doin' all right. Dr. B's expecting you, said she had to hurry before you got here."

David frowned. "How long ago was that?"

"Oh, about fifteen minutes ago. She came racing in here like somethin' was chasing her, looking kind of frazzled."

"Thanks, Rhorman. I'll take my time."

"Have a good evening."

The older man's knowing smile spoke volumes. David figured he'd probably seen it all. When you're privy to the comings and goings of a building full of people, you have the best seat in the house. David felt the security guard's gaze follow him all the way to the elevators.

He was surprised when Arianne answered the door right away. She looked far from frazzled in a cowl-neck sweater and form-fitting faded jeans.

"Come on in. I'll just be a minute," she said on her way into the bedroom.

Destiny picked up the conversation then with a low howl as he bounded over to greet David. He gave the wolf a hearty rubdown, and the animal playfully buried his head into David's side, nearly knocking him over.

"You're a lot friendlier than you look."

"Gee, thanks." Arianne came into the living room, struggling to get her watch fastened.

"You," David moved to help her, "are beautiful." Up close, he saw something was wrong. Her eyes didn't quite meet his when he drew close as she turned her head to check her collar in the hall mirror. Her smile seemed forced and nervous. She was hiding something.

The clasp slid into place. "There you go," he said and held on to her hand. It was ice cold.

"Thanks," she said looking uncomfortable.

"Arianne, is something wrong?"

"Wrong? No. Why?"

"You seem distracted. Are you sure you want to go out tonight?"

"Absolutely," she smiled, and gently pulled back her hand. "Ready?"

David crossed his arms over his chest. "You're not going to tell me, are you?"

"Tell you what?"

"Something happened, I can see it. Don't hide. I'm here for you."

She sighed and rested her trembling fingertips on his sleeve. "I know that, David, and I appreciate it. It's nothing really, just a rough day followed by heavy traffic. You know how it is."

He knew. But he didn't believe that was the problem. Digging for answers as a detective had taught him to read people, and as far as he could see, Arianne's story was a tall tale. Reluctantly, he let it go with a nod, "I've had a few of those days, myself. Personally, I recommend a scary movie followed by some kung pao."

"Sounds like the treatment of choice."

*   *   *

The movie had all the right effects in just the right places, and David was surprised when Arianne clutched his arm. As time went on, he pulled her to him and they snuggled close. When the movie ended, they headed to Chinatown for spicy authentic food. Afterward, they hurried from the cold, to David's apartment.

"Very nice," Arianne said, pulling off her gloves inside. She wandered passed the small foyer and into the spacious living room to study the wall art above the long oak curio table. She stopped at each picture, seemingly fascinated.

"Care for a drink?" he asked.

"Sure. What do you have?"

"Fully stocked bar, coffee, tea or—"

She shot him a look that dared him to say it. "Blackberry brandy on the rocks will do."

"You got it." He pulled out a glass. "Hey, what's so interesting over there? It's not the Art Museum."

"Well, Detective, I would think you already know the best way to find out what someone is all about is to check the books they read and the art on their walls."

"I must have missed that in Homicide 101." He handed her the drink. "Here's to crime solving as an art form."

They toasted and he offered her a seat on the couch.

David sat beside her. "And what do my walls tell you about me?"

"You like the cold."

"That's it?" He cocked his head.

"Ice fishing and skiing? That's says cold to me."

"They're just photos of my annual trip with some guys from the station, and very easily replaced by photos of you in a bikini on my sailboat."

"It's nice to know I'd beat out a trout in a wall display."

David laughed. The old Arianne was back. "So what did I miss on *your* walls? If I recall, there was quite a selection of sketches, mostly of wooded areas, I believe."

"Very perceptive. You're a natural."

"Local artist?"

"Yes, they're mine."

"*You* sketched those?"

"Uh-huh. I always take a sketchpad on my hikes. It's so relaxing to climb a hill, capture the landscape, and then take it home with me."

"I bet you'd love sailing. There are some areas of the Lake Michigan shoreline that would make great sketches."

"Call me when the lake thaws." She set her glass down. "I like this place. How long have you been here?"

"A few years."

"What made you choose this side of the city?"

"It really wasn't my call. I had a...roommate."

"Oh," she said, taking a drink of her brandy. The silence that followed hung between them like a confessional partition.

David was reminded of Diane and all they'd meant to one another. They'd shared everything except the heartache. He was surprised to find that for the first time in two years the idea of talking about it didn't bother him. In fact, he wanted to.

"It was three years ago," he said. "I met Diane at a karate competition. She'd just taken first place in the women's division and I'd nabbed a first in the men's. A local newspaper photographer wanted a shot of the winners together."

"Love at first sight?" Arianne asked.

"*I* thought so. Anyway, we dated about a year before it fell apart. I was working on a tough case and had to put in many strange hours. It seemed my promise not to let work come before those I cared about had faded fast. I tried, I really did, but something always happened. It seemed there was a huge space between us, even when we were together."

"What happened?"

"Well, I came home one night to empty drawers and closets, and a note on the kitchen table. She'd set a single dinner place with a note explaining, this is how she'd eaten for too long and now I could do it in her stead."

"Ouch. That was cold."

"But well-deserved, and it woke me up. After my parents died, I never thought I'd lose sight of my own promise to put my family first. When Diane drove the point home, I realized I'd done it again. There won't be a third time." He held her gaze a moment before pulling her close.

Her lips were warm and tasted like brandy, so sweet and inviting.

He felt her lean close, and kiss him back deeply with tender passion, as her tongue explored. She filled his senses, yet he wanted more. As their embrace grew deeper, he felt a swell of desire.

"Do you want to stop?" he asked against her lips.

"No." She nuzzled his neck, and then pulled away slowly. "But we should."

David sat back, and ran a hand through his hair. Arianne's lips were rosy and puffed, and her dark hair tousled. He wanted to touch her again, but he knew she was right. It was too soon. There was too much at stake—at least from her point of view, and he respected that. If there was no cure for her, where would that leave them? He'd been through the excruciating pain of a broken heart over a relationship that was doomed; he didn't want Arianne to go through it, too.

Happy ending or not, he decided he would be there for her, holding on tight. If the dark side wanted her, they'd have to go through *him*.

CHAPTER 26

Michael removed his pastoral collaret, and laid it on the small wooden nightstand beside his bed. His neck felt bare without it, as if he were somehow exposed and vulnerable to the evil of this world. Like a soldier without a weapon.

He hung his priest's garments in the closet, and pulled out a pair of jeans, a gray flannel shirt, and tan loafers. He dressed quickly, feeling strange in the rugged texture of street clothes. One item remained, however, signifying his profession—a profession he may never return to. The silver cross dangled from a chain around his neck. *That*, he decided, would stay right where it was.

The small oval mirror on the wall reflected an image he barely recognized. He thought his long chin and wide eyes made him look like a cartoon character he'd watched as a child—a child in an orphanage with so many questions.

Who am I, and where did I come from, had been the main queries of his life, and until yesterday, there seemed to be no answers. Then suddenly, he had a sister and family roots, however twisted they might be. The incredible story Arianne had told hadn't seemed all that unbelievable at the time, and it wasn't until he'd retired for the night that strange shadows and thoughts had haunted him. He couldn't call them dreams exactly, for sleep never visited. They seemed to be whispers echoing into a faded void. And then he'd seen small wisps of light fleeting over his bed and disappearing before he could focus or make sense of them. Demons, he decided and got up to pray.

He closed his eyes into the solitude and safety of His Father's world, and felt the strange specters' presence lingering about like flies at a picnic. Michael knew he wasn't alone in the room. Finally, when he could concentrate no longer, he jumped up and denounced Satan and all of his principalities.

Alone in the dim light of his bedside lamp, he waited, frozen in silence. His eyes darted back and forth, looking for any sign that the brief, but forceful exorcism had worked. Silence. His heart pounded a fearful cadence. More silence. He sighed as the tension ebbed like a cleansing wave carrying beach debris out to sea. Perhaps it had all been his vivid imagination and lack of sound sleep, after all, Satan is a supreme strategist, knowing just when and where to strike.

Arianne's confirmation about his shaded past had certainly made him an easy target for the Dark Prince. Self-doubt loomed larger than any demon his mind could conjure, as the truth settled across his soul. His parents were vampires.

How could he remain a priest with the awful truth stretched out before him? His service to God seemed hypocritical to him now. On his knees, he asked for an answer, with his eyes fixed on the sorrowful face of Jesus on the crucifix above his bed.

"Show me the way, Lord, I am lost. I have served you with an open and glad heart, but I fear my service has been in vain."

He gasped as tears trickled down the cheeks of the ceramic Christ. He felt a quick tug on the back of his neck and his silver cross clattered to the floor. When he picked up the chain, it was still intact. Michael knew he had his answer.

The memories of the night before were still fresh as he latched his suitcase now and took a final look around. He was glad he'd started sabbatical proceedings long ago. It was as if he knew there was trouble ahead, yet no one could have predicted this.

His gaze fell warily on the crucifix above his bed. No tears. No demons present. He clutched the cross around his neck and gave it a tug to make sure the clasp would hold. It remained as solid as his decision to leave the only life he'd ever known for one he wasn't sure he wanted to know.

A brief knock disrupted his thoughts.

"Come in."

Father Joseph Paul closed the heavy wooden door behind him. His large watery eyes and fat puckered lips made him look like a fish waiting for a hook. He enfolded Michael into an embrace. "Just came to see you off."

Michael nodded, and avoided his eyes.

The rotund little man sauntered about Michael's cramped quarters, fingering books and unopened mail as he went. "When you came to me yesterday, I didn't get a chance to say what needed to be said. With the phone ringing every few minutes and my appointments showing up on time for a change, your sabbatical was the only thing we discussed. But, there are a few personal notes I'd like to share."

"Please have a seat," Michael offered as the man filtered passed the open closet, eyeing several boxes on the shelf.

"No, no. I think better on my feet, you know. And I know you're anxious to get going, so I'll try to keep this brief." He paced before Michael, his shoes offering an annoying squeak with every step. "I know you need some personal time and I'm not going to tell you how to use it, but please humor an old man and promise me you'll be careful."

Michael didn't understand. "Of course."

"There are many things outside the safety and seclusion of the church. Things of a non-human nature." The old man paused for emphasis.

Michael had already witnessed the very phenomenon in question and had news for Brother Joe—they're not just outside the gilded church gates.

Father Joseph continued. "If you do God's work long enough and keep your heart and mind open, you'll see a lot of unexplainable events. It's not that you'd never experience them anyway, in time all of us do, it's just that you'll be out there," he pointed a sausage-like index finger toward the window, "away from the fortress. I just want you to find your way back to us, that's all." He stopped pacing, frustration etched in the creases of his face. "Does any of this make sense?"

"It makes a lot of sense," Michael conceded. "More than you know. But trust me when I tell you, I am not afraid. I know Satan's foot soldiers are relentless and never weary. Perhaps it is the test of our faith, when we're bombarded with the evil things of the world, or maybe it's a lesson along the path of spiritual growth. Whichever it might be, I'm prepared to deal with it."

"I trust your faith, my brother. It has always been strong. And I pray for your safety by guardian angels until your return to us."

As Michael hugged Father Joseph good-bye, something caught his attention across the room. The ceramic cheeks of the Savior were wet with tears.

* * *

David snatched up the phone on the first ring and continued typing the report. "Homicide, Detective Spears."

A nervous voice came through the line, so low David strained above the department office din to hear.

"I know who did it," the woman confessed.

"I'm sorry, ma'am, you'll have to speak up."

Louder, she said, "I know who killed him."

"Killed who, ma'am?"

"Oh, of course, how silly of me. You probably have lots of murders in a city this size."

"Not a lot, but enough to keep earning a check. Now, who did you say the victim was?"

"Well, I saw it plain as day."

"You saw the murder?"

"Yes. That nice doctor, uh, Dr. Brewster, I believe his name was. He didn't even see it coming."

David straightened, and grabbed a pen and paper. "Yes, ma'am, go on."

"Well, the lab was empty, except for Dr. Brewster and the killer, but he didn't know it."

"Do you work at the Research Center?"

"No."

"I'm sorry, I didn't catch your name."

"Elleen O'Connor. That's two ll's and two ee's, if you're writing it down."

David paused, pen in hand, "Go on...Elleen."

"It was just so terrible. Dr. Brewster was hunched over working with beakers and test tubes, apparently so involved he didn't hear the man coming up behind him. Then the man dropped something, a small metal object, kind of like a key. It seemed to startle the doctor because he jumped back suddenly and overturned several bottles. The liquid from one of the jars sprayed him in the face. The other man just stood there watching poor Dr. Brewster suffer as he choked and fell to the floor. Then he followed the doctor as he crawled to an office and then...then, he stabbed him! It was horrible!"

David's heart thundered as his mind raced. Did he have a witness or an accomplice? She certainly had all of the details correct, right down to the more gruesome facts they hadn't released to the public. What was it Elleen really wanted?

"Ms. O'Connor, were you there that night?"

"Oh, heavens no, Detective."

"You said you saw it plain as day."

"Yes, in my dream last night."

David heard the toilet flush on his hopes for a break in the case. Elleen wasn't a witness *or* an accomplice; she was a nut.

"Thank you for the information, Ms. O'Connor. I'll keep that in mind."

"Aren't you going to take down my number?"

"That won't be necessary, ma'am."

"Oh, all right then. If I think of anything else, I'll call you."

"Thanks so much. Good-bye." He glanced across the way at George Johnson, a homicide vet of twenty years.

"They just keep gettin' weirder and weirder, don't they?" George sniffed.

David shook his head. "Said she knows who killed Fred Brewster."

"Yeah, and Jimmy Hoffa's in my basement freezer, next to a hundred and fifty pound Bambi from my last hunting trip."

Johnson's phone rang then, saving David from a reply, as he considered Elleen's psychic phenomenon. She'd said she'd seen it in a dream, but the details were so close there was no way she could have made them up. How did she know about the acid spill and the stabbing? One thing he'd never believed was the so-called police psychics who solved cases by *trancing out* on their living room couches. But then he hadn't always believed in real vampires, either.

"Hey, Spears," Chief Magnus called from his office. "A minute."

"Great," David mumbled, and headed for the command performance.

Mags was seated behind his desk, shuffling small stacks of paperwork from one side to the other, then back again for lack of space. He wore the uni-brow look; a clear indication the stressed-out Chief wasn't in the mood for bullshit.

"Have a seat, Spears."

David sat, and tried to appear relaxed but attentive. Before he could hoist an ankle onto his knee, Mags jumped him.

"What the hell's going on with the Brewster case? I got the Mayor ridin' me like a damn rodeo bull wanting it solved yesterday!"

David took a breath. His own frustrations were on the rise. "I'd be happy to deliver, the day *before* yesterday, if I had something to go on. Crime lab says the acid splatter had to be an accident, meaning he wasn't intentionally doused. But something went wrong from the time he spilled the acid, to the place where he was skewered like a shish kabob. No witnesses, no fingerprints and everyone has an alibi."

Mags pinned David with a stare. "I don't give a rat's ass about what we don't have. What's your gut tellin' you on this one?"

Now the Chief wanted *him* to play psychic. His thoughts drifted to Elleen's thorough description of the murder, and stuck on one point that made a lot of sense. She'd said something about a small metal object, like a key. A key to the lab, perhaps?

He watched Mags replace a damp hanky in his back pocket as he waited for a response.

David leaned forward. "I think it's someone from the lab, but all I have is a smudged footprint with no treads."

"Well, keep on it and I'll stall the Mayor if I can. I suggest you start drinking caffeinated coffee if you don't already, because this is going to take every waking hour you can afford."

As David left the office, he felt the old tensions grinding away in the pit of his stomach. More hours on the job meant less time with Arianne when she needed him most. With the killer still at large, she was in danger. That meant he needed to find the guy before he struck again. Although he couldn't afford to break his promise not to let work interfere with his personal relationships, this time he couldn't afford not to. He poured himself a cup of coffee, and winced at the first bitter taste. The standing joke was that department java could keep you up for days. Hopefully he wouldn't need much more than that.

CHAPTER 27

The fasten seatbelt signs lit up inside the jet on its approach to O'Hare airport. The lights were still dim as the stewardess made her way down the aisle with steaming hand towels on a large cart. Passengers stirred from their peaceful sleep, in preparation to land.

Emelia gazed out the window at the bright city lights of Chicago, amazed at the vast skyline and tall buildings. Her homeland was much different, yet the black drape of night fell the same over both, providing a protective backdrop for freedom to roam. The plane trip had cost her time, with the layover in London delaying her by another day in order to take a night flight. There had been a brief wait in the London airport when they'd discovered a dead baggage handler, but luckily; Emelia had made it to the hotel in time.

She checked her watch and saw the early morning hour offered more than enough time to get through customs and to her hotel before dawn. She'd already fed, although not as much as she needed. It would sustain her for one more day.

The stewardess reached over to awaken the man beside Emelia. His head was covered with the thin airline blanket. "Sir? We're getting ready to land."

Emelia pressed an index finger to her lips, and whispered. "He's exhausted. Please give him a few more minutes. I'll be sure to awaken him in time."

The attendant nodded in compliance, and offered Emelia a towel. A short intercom click preceded the cheery voice of the pilot, who offered greetings to Chicago and a brief weather report. His commentary was interrupted by the muffled voices of passengers fully awake and ready to feel American soil under their feet. As their excited chatter filled the cabin and the plane started its descent, Emelia heard faint whimpering across the aisle. Looking over, she saw a little girl of about seven, cuddling a tattered teddy bear. Some of its brown fur was missing in patches and one eye hung lower than the other one. Chocolate brown ringlets encircled the child's head, and clung to wet cheeks. Emelia saw Arianne as a child and ached to comfort her. An orange and blue button with the airline insignia clutched the girl's faded cotton blouse, which was an apparent hand-me-down by the length of the sleeves. The child was traveling alone. Another large tear dropped like a rose petal onto the girl's shirt as she buried her face into the bear's chest.

Emelia disregarded the seat belt warning, and made her way across the aisle. She sat beside her and smiled as she introduced herself. "Hello. My name is Olga. May I sit here?"

The child's eyes brightened and a small smile curled the corners of her rosebud lips. "This is Charlie." She held up the bear.

Emelia shook the toy's fuzzy arm. "Pleased to meet you, Charlie."

"And I'm Gretchen." The tears had all but disappeared.

"Nice to meet you, Gretchen. Are you by yourself?"

"Yes. My mama says I'm a big girl and can fly by myself."

"You *are* a big girl and so am I, but can I tell you a secret?"

Gretchen's eyes widened and she leaned close.

"I'm scared."

The girl pulled back. "You are?"

Emelia nodded.

Gretchen reached over and clasped Emelia's hand. "Don't be a'scared. You'll be okay. I've got you."

With that, the plane touched down with a gentle bounce, ending the long night. Emelia felt the warmth of Gretchen's small hand, entwined with her own. A fleeting thought of Michael at age two on a plane with Mira captured her memory and held. Is this how he'd held her sister's hand? Had he too, been frightened? Mira had caused a great deal of pain in her efforts to be a hero; for that, she could never forgive her. She'd stolen a lifetime of memories, taking them for herself. If only there was a way to get them back.

The child's voice cut in, "Charlie's not afraid anymore."

"He isn't?" Emelia smiled at Gretchen's eager nod. "Well, I'm very glad to hear that. I'm not either."

"Is your auntie meeting you in the airport?"

"No, dear. I'm by myself today."

Gretchen's eyebrows formed a stern V. "That's too bad," then smiling, "I get to see my sister soon."

"Me, too," Emelia smiled back. "Me, too."

*   *   *

The streets of Chicago were strangely alive for three in the morning, unlike the little town of Brasov. Emelia took in the grandeur of the city with its overpowering skyscrapers standing like fortresses against the shores of Lake Michigan. It appeared to be a sleeping giant in the night, covered by a dark blanket stretching for miles; its waves were tiny wrinkles in the vast coverlet. Emelia was in awe of the city her daughter had chosen as home, a city personified and alive by its very presence, yet not too formidable to master.

The cab pulled to the curb before the large hotel. Emelia paid quickly and headed inside as the hour grew late. In her room, she hung the Do Not Disturb sign on the door and closed the heavy draperies. She'd left the clerk with special instruction regarding her need for complete privacy during the day, and received his promise her wishes would indeed be heeded.

She looked around the spacious room, and marveled at its luxury and detail. From the coffee maker, to the vase of fresh flowers, it seemed American hospitality lacked nothing. She spied the telephone book beside the phone and thumbed through it, finding Brasov A MD, and the address of the Research Center. She traced the entry with her finger, almost in disbelief that she was truly here, so near to her daughter, yet no closer to her desire for reconciliation. Arriving undetected by the Jen-Ku was only half the battle. Now she must convince her headstrong daughter the legacy she shunned was rightfully hers.

The familiar hunger ached within as she set the book aside. The past two days travel were beginning to take their toll, and being unable to feed, as she needed, had made her weak and tired. As she undressed, she wondered if she truly wanted Arianne to go through this as well; the wanton desire for the warm, metallic taste to fill you each night and nearly going mad when no suitable kill could be found. As the remnants of Olga dropped to the floor, she looked in the full-length mirror and saw eternal youth. Yes, Arianne deserved her chance at a life without age or decay, even if there was a small price to pay.

If Daegon was right, Arianne had no choice; she would die if she didn't become a full vampire soon. How could she make her daughter believe that her motives were for Arianne's survival and not self-serving? The mother/daughter bond had withered before it had a chance to take hold, leaving only a faded shell of memories across the void of time. There had to be a way to reach her and gain her trust.

She settled beneath the heavily quilted black coverlet she'd made to shield from the light, and thought of little Gretchen's excited words, "I get to see my sister soon." As the sun rose, Emelia closed her eyes with the reassuring thought that *her* sister was the answer. It was time for Mira to undo the damage. This time the need for her sister's help would not be a request.

* * *

Fred Brewster's office looked like nothing bad had happened. Gone were the crime scene tape and chalk body drawing, leaving an eerie quiet among his personal effects. His nieces had no apparent interest in clearing out the office, and were already back home with their families. The painful fall-out had been left to somebody else. Arianne took down a framed photo from the paneled wall. Fred's smile stared back at her, his blue eyes bright and full of life. In the photo taken not more than a year before, her own face leaned close to his. One of the lab techs, Jimmy, had wanted to try out his new camera and had bribed them with a pizza for posing. Happy times emanated from their smiles.

She fought the urge to cry, and placed the framed photo in the box with the other things—a paperweight shaped like buttocks from a bowling buddy in proctology, two cigars each sporting a label announcing the birth of his niece's twins, and the original petri dish used to grow the first genetically *cured* cells for Harriet Gross. Empty and scrubbed clean, it lay on the desk, passing for an oversized monocle for a near-sighted Cyclops. Fred had planned to put it in a glass case at home as his bronzed baby shoe, of sorts. These things she would keep.

The rest of the office consisted of reference books she'd have moved to her office later, and files that would eventually go to the basement archives. It seemed ludicrous that a man's entire career came down to a few boxes of personal items crammed into a tiny office, when the mark he'd left on the world had been so much more. How she missed him in her life, both personal and professional. There weren't many people she could trust with her secret and now she needed someone more than ever. If the procedure was to work on her, she'd have to bring someone into confidence to do it. The process wasn't difficult, but timing was important or the precious clean cells would die. With Michael's donated DNA already forming new cells in the incubator, she needed to find someone soon. But who? She nearly dropped the ceramic butt as a sharp voice came from the doorway. "Hey, Dr. Brasov?"

She cradled the novelty in her palm and turned to see Roger Thomas. His glasses lay at a funny angle across the bridge of his nose and a shock of long black bang hung over one of the lenses. "You want me to put up those Alpha slides or what?"

Arianne recalled with amusement, Fred's summation of Roger as, "not the sharpest scalpel on the tray."

"Yes, Roger, that's fine." Her hands still trembled.

He turned to go. His lab smock hung off his shoulders like Herman Munster's coat, and a blue checkered shirttail stuck out of his pants. She shook her head. Fred would have had some sort of humorous comment, she was sure.

As she sat behind Fred's desk, she saw that her fingertips were a pale shade of gray and felt numb. Her toes, she recalled from her morning shower, were the same color. It seemed her body was turning against her, and destroying itself in small increments. She had run all the standard tests and had found nothing. It had to be her vampire blood with the tainted DNA. Based on the increasing severity of her symptoms, she was running out of time.

A brief knock called her attention to another lab tech, Jimmy.

"Excuse me, Dr. Brasov?"

Her smile was genuine at the sight of him. "Come in. What can I do for you?"

"I finished those slides you needed and I'll probably get the next set done tomorrow, unless you want me to stay?"

"No, Jimmy. Go on home. They can wait."

"Are you sure?"

"Yup. Now get out of here and go see that girlfriend of yours."

A crimson blush lit his round face. "I don't have a girlfriend, Dr. Brasov. No time."

Not wanting to pry, she simply nodded. "I see. Well, don't worry about the slides right now. But I might be needing some extra help next week when we get ready to do another procedure."

His brown eyes widened. "Really? Already?"

"Yes. The first one has been labeled a success with no signs of ill effects or rejection. The more procedures we do, the better we get. Soon Dr. Brewster's process will be routine."

"Is the patient another cancer victim?"

"I can't tell you that, Jimmy, but it's important that I can count on your help."

"Sure."

"I appreciate it, and so would Dr. Brewster."

The phone rang, and Jimmy gave a quick wave goodnight.

"Research, Dr. Brasov."

"Arianne, this is Michael."

Pleasant warmth filled her at the sound of her brother's voice. Although he'd been her priest long before she knew he was family, his demeanor always brought calm, no matter what the circumstances. He was born for the priesthood.

"Michael, how nice to hear from you." His silence alerted her. "Is everything all right?"

"Yes...and no."

"What is it?"

"I'm fine, actually, I feel a great sense of relief. But I need to see you."

"Of course. When?"

"Whenever you want me. My schedule is pretty clear at this point."

"How about seven tonight?"

"Sounds great." He paused then asked, "How are things with you?"

The simple question held deep undertones, more than just a form of automatic speech. Arianne loved him for asking, and for caring.

"Everything is going as planned." She glanced at her darkened fingertips. "Well, almost, anyway. But we should be ready by next week."

"Well, I'm here for you, completely."

"Thanks, big brother. But don't let me get in the way of your duties. I realize your boss is bigger than both of us, and I wouldn't want to get in the way."

A long pause preceded his confession. "I'm afraid that won't be a problem, Sis. I've left the church."

CHAPTER 28

Dr. Barbara Gainor winked at David through the cube of window in the examination suite's door. Her large dark eyes reminded him of a doe, only he couldn't picture a deer in surgical garb. As she finished the autopsy, she glanced up again, jerking her head toward her left shoulder in a "come here" motion. David rolled his eyes, and donned a gown from the shelf.

Her sultry voice sounded muffled from behind her mask. "Hey there, Spears. How's it going?" Not waiting for an answer she asked, "Want to hand me that bucket?"

Obliging, he didn't ask why. "What's *this* all about? You need my expert opinion?"

"Nope," she said, returning what looked like slippery raw meat back inside the body cavity. "But, I thought you might find this interesting, even though it's not a homicide."

"You're such a fun date, doctor."

Barbara's gloved index finger pointed to something. When David leaned closer he saw two small puncture wounds on the corpse's left inner wrist.

"See these?" she said.

"Yes. What's the deal? Snake bite?"

"I thought so at first, but that's not the only thing. This guy died of hypovolemic shock, not venom."

"So?"

"David, this is the cleanest autopsy I've ever done. There was hardly any blood. It was as if he'd been drained."

Her word choice grabbed his attention. "Drained?"

"Right. But get this, there wasn't any blood where he was found."

"And that was?"

"He was a passenger on a night flight from London to Chicago. Attendants verify he was alive and drinking like a fish during the flight, but when they landed, he was dead. No signs of distress that anyone can recall, and no blood."

"What about those puncture wounds?"

"He couldn't have bled out that much through those tiny holes, and if he had, there would be evidence of it." She stepped down to the man's open torso and continued her work. "He did have a bleeding ulcer, actually a pretty bad one, and I'm sure the drinking only aggravated it. But it didn't kill him."

"What's your call, Ump?" David checked the wounds once more. Two dark openings glistened under the bright surgical lamp. They were too large for a snakebite, but a seemingly perfect fit for a vampire.

"I'm calling it natural causes due to hypovolemic shock. It's the best I can do. It's definitely not murder. There's only one other thing I can think of that might explain some of the blood loss."

"What's that?"

"Vampires."

David dropped the dead man's hand, causing it to thud hard on the metal table.

"Don't look at me like that, Spears, you know they're out there. Every big city has its cult, even Chicago. They keep to themselves and are hard to find because it's run like an underground. But I've had a couple of them in here when they've overdone it."

David didn't know if he was relieved by her reference to the vampire community or disappointed. She was talking about *real people acting like vampires*, he was thinking about real ones.

He shook his head. "I don't get too many calls to that part of town, but I've heard it gets a little weird down there."

Barbara chuckled. "These people would make Bela Lugosi turn over in his grave, if he's still in it. They have what are called, 'donors,' who actually allow themselves to be cut and bled for the purpose of feeding their vampire friends."

"And you think that's what happened to this guy?"

"I think it's a possibility. I don't know anything about London vampires, but I'd guess they have them there, too."

"But how was this guy able to get on a plane and get drunk during the flight with all that blood loss?"

"Well, *that*, combined with his bleeding ulcer and dehydration from the alcohol, probably did him in."

"But we can't prove any of this."

"Not unless you can find the London vampire."

"Was it a direct flight?"

She covered the body with a sheet and shrugged. "Couldn't say. Why?"

"Just curious. Like you said, it's not a murder."

Side by side at the deep metal double sink, they scrubbed to the elbows. Barbara toweled off and headed for her office. David followed, with his mind shooting off in a hundred different directions—vampire wanna-be's draining their friends, or real vampires feeding in the night. Which is it?

Barbara's office smelled like disinfectant and fresh coffee, a strange, but familiar aroma on his frequent visits. He sat on the couch as she sprinkled fish food into the fifty-gallon tank beside him. The bubbling gurgle would have been comforting white noise in any other office, but here it reminded him of someone trying to breath through a slit throat.

"So, tell me, what brings your here, Spears?"

"How do you do it, Barbara? Looking at death, day after day, with no break in the cycle?"

"You came all the way across town to ask me that?" She sat behind her desk and began doodling on a pad of paper. "You just wasted time and gas because frankly I don't have an answer. It's like any job, after a while you just do it. Why so philosophical all of the sudden?"

"I admire you, that's all."

"I already told you, I won't date you. Speaking of which, how's Arianne?"

"Privileged info, Doc. Sorry. But I *will* tell you the prognosis is good."

"Uh-huh. Keep me posted, will you? Now what can I help you with?"

"Brewster. We found a sloppy footprint in the lab, no treads, as if it was smudged or something. Got any ideas?"

"Slippers? Footies?" Suddenly, she snapped her fingers. "Surgical booties!"

"You're a genius. See why I love you?"

"Why would the guy be wearing them? Even if he worked in the lab, they don't routinely wear foot coverings unless it's a special procedure."

"Well, in this case it was special, he was there to commit murder, and needed to cover his tracks. Literally."

*   *   *

As he rode the elevator to Arianne's floor, Michael took in his image reflected in the mirrored walls inside. It seemed a lost child stood before him. Beside him was a brown leather suitcase. Dark circles hung under his eyes and offered a glimpse of his future as an old man. Many changes were in store for him beyond that of aging, he was sure. He'd witnessed some of them already by the simple fact he wore street clothes. The security guard, R Tines, his name badge stated, had been professional and polite when directing him to the elevators, but without his priestly garments, Michael felt the coolness associated with a man "just doin' his job." There'd been no open door to the soul, no invitation to share another's life and deepest cares. He stood like any other man now.

He muttered a prayer for the lost, and found himself included. "...and I give myself unto thee, gracious Father, for Your purposes always."

The elevator gave a sudden jerk and the lights flickered off and on again as it continued on its ascent. He went on praying, "With the hope of forgiveness and cleansing for my unpardonable sins."

This time the elevator seemed to break from its cables. It dropped rapidly for several seconds before slamming to a sudden halt, knocking Michael to the floor. He remained on all fours, afraid to move. Finally, the motor gave a solid click and began to hum as the elevator rose steadily upward.

He got to his feet, and saw every button on the control panel was lit; yet it wasn't stopping. Then the lights went out completely. Two panel lights remained on resembling a pair of burning yellow eyes. Michael panicked as he groped blindly for the alarm. His stomach lurched as the elevator torpedoed upward. The grinding gears screamed a raucous wail down the shaft. The gleaming panel eyes narrowed in the darkness as the walls whispered, "Penance for the sins of the father...penance for the sins of the father..."

Faster and faster the cubicle sped. Michael dropped to the floor, and clutched his crucifix. G-forces pinned his face hard to the carpet. It felt damp against his skin and smelled like metal. A piercing screech filled his ears and the cab slammed to a sudden halt. He was pitched into the air like a toy ball, and landed with a severe thud. The terror stopped.

He lay prostrate with his arms stretched out like the ceramic Christ hanging from the crucifix in his bedroom. He lay there several seconds waiting for another jolt. The taste of warm blood filled his mouth and he knew he'd bitten his tongue. A sudden burst of bright light blinded him as the lights came on and he felt the elevator begin a slow, but steady movement upward. He cried out at the sight before him, as tears of fresh blood trailed down the mirrored walls, making their way to the floor. The carpet was soaked with the sanguine wetness that squished beneath his shoes. The front of his clothes was covered with blood and he swiped at a damp patch congealing on his cheek.

A pleasant *ping* sounded to announce the ride was over. Final destination. The doors slid open with a gentle *whoosh*, and remained apart without incident. Michael grabbed his suitcase and hurried out. He stood in the hallway and waited as the doors closed softly behind him. Legs trembling as he went, he made his way to Arianne's door, and wondered how he would explain his appearance. He prayed no one got on the elevator before security could be notified.

The eerie whisper haunted him. *"Penance for the sins of the father."* The sins of his *vampire* father, he realized. His service to the church was a slap in God's face and now he was paying the price.

He rang the buzzer, still searching for the right words. Latches clicked from behind the door and Arianne's warm smile welcomed him.

"Right on time," she said, stepping aside to allow him in.

He looked down at his clothes and stopped.

"What's wrong, Michael? Is everything all right?"

He touched his cheek that had been covered in blood moments ago and found it clean. No signs of blood anywhere.

Arianne pulled him inside and hugged him. "It's so good to see you. But I have to admit I'm not used to seeing you in regular clothes." She adjusted his shirt collar in a loving gesture and led him to the couch.

"Have a seat, big brother, while I put on a pot of coffee."

Shock replaced fear as he tried to understand what had happened. His clothes were fine, his face was fine, and he knew there was no point in calling security about the elevator because that was fine, too. Then he realized as he stood looking out of the balcony windows, that he'd received a warning. Whatever evil was stalking him, and quite possibly Arianne too, had sent a sound caution. Why? Was he getting too close to unlocking a truth better left hidden?

Arianne came into the living room carrying a silver tray with all the essentials for a quiet evening before the fireplace.

"Cream and sugar?" she asked.

"Please," he said, turning from the sliding patio doors. "I hope I haven't intruded by my sudden tenancy."

"Of course not. We have a lot of catching up to do. But I don't understand why you've left the church. Is it something I've told you about our past?"

Taking a seat beside her on the couch, he forced his thoughts from the elevator and explained. "Yes and no. I've been haunted by feelings of guilt and darkness ever since I became a priest. Until you came to me with the answers about my life, I never understood those feelings."

"Great. I come along, spill the beans and the next thing I know, you've left your calling."

"It was only a matter of time, Arianne." The warning flashed fresh in his mind.

She turned and took his hands in her own. "Listen, Michael, you can't give in to the darkness, believe me, I know. You have to fight. Whatever it is, we can overcome it together. It's the only way."

"I don't want to drag you down with me."

"That's not going to happen because we're not going to lose."

As the evening went on, they talked, catching up on lost moments, trying to bridge the void.

It was almost midnight when Arianne stifled a yawn. "Sorry. I'm a little tired, I guess."

"I didn't mean to keep you up this late. Why don't we call it a night? We have the rest of our lives to catch up. We're finally together again."

Outside, a fierce wind cut through the night, swirling into a wailing howl. Its unseen forces grazed the patio doors like long spirit-fingers clawing to gain entrance. Inside, Arianne and Michael said goodnight as they retired with the realization that the Von Tirgov children were together now as a force to be dealt with against the evil seeking them.

In the lobby far below, the elevator opened its wide mouth to allow Rhorman Tines out after finishing his building rounds. He stepped onto the white polished tiles, and continued down the hall toward the entrance, whistling *Blessed Assurance*, unaware his size elevens were leaving a sticky crimson trail behind him.

CHAPTER 29

Chicago's Michigan Avenue is a stretch alive with traffic, people, shops, and restaurants, especially two weeks before Christmas. Department stores such as Marshall Field's and Neimann Marcus spare no expense in their window displays of twinkling lights, brightly colored animated characters, and of course, their very best merchandise.

People bundled in layers of fashionable dyed wool and protective lip balm enjoy the carnival atmosphere right down to the crunch of snow under their heavy boots. The enticing aroma of roasted chestnuts drifted from a corner vendor and mixed with the magical notes of *White Christmas* dancing over the airwaves. They spiraled together, offered like a prayer to the night, and rose toward the fluorescent white moon above.

Emelia moved effortlessly through the damp night sky toward the warmth of the crowded streets below. Her long skirt flowed like a veil as she touched down between two buildings and started for the sidewalk. Already she detected a strong fluttering heartbeat above the din of the crowd that raised like a beacon above all the others. She fought severe hunger pains as she searched the long walk for the beckoning pulse. Tonight she must feed to quench the thirst within.

The music and laughter took on a warped twang as her ears rang with a hollow tinny sound. She'd let herself go too long without feeding—a deadly mistake for a vampire. Her limbs were stiff and it seemed a core of ice had settled deep within her. As the buzzing in her head grew steadily louder, she saw the prey that would save her.

The man looked like he'd been poured into the Santa suit, greatly testing the side seams. His plump cheeks crested the top edge of his fake, snow-white beard beneath bright blue eyes as he huffed out repeated *Ho-Ho-Ho's* across the sidewalk. The incessant *clanka-clanka* of his shiny gold hand bell, posed a twisted version of Quasimodo gone mad. Emelia clenched her jaw as the piercing sound echoed in her ears.

She deposited several coins into the red bucket suspended on a stand, and smiled at his hearty "thank-you." Their eyes met briefly, but it was long enough for her to entrance his mind. His arm continued the ringing motion of the bell and his seasonal mirth never broke its cadence, but his eyes were now void of their earlier clarity, and had turned into two pools of gray fog.

Several passersby dropped their meager contributions into the bucket, barely seeming to notice they'd received no acknowledgment. Emelia beckoned the fat little elf toward her with her mind, as she moved back toward the side of the tall building. She saw his thoughts far beneath his suspended trance.

His mind's eye had focused on a dilapidated easy-chair sitting in front of a living room television. She felt his longing to be in it, drinking a frosty beer. From there, he moved to a darkened upstairs hallway where he turned into a small bedroom. The walls were decorated with decals of famous Disney characters surrounding a bed dressed in a pink bed-ruffle. Beneath the soft cotton sheets, a little girl snuggled a baby-doll bedecked in a white nightie trimmed in red satin piping. The girl's matching gown lay bunched up above her thighs, and Emelia felt his arousal as he made his way toward the child. She shuddered as he climbed into the small twin bed and mounted the child, her eyes wide in silent cries.

Suddenly, panic seized the man as he stroked the girl's satin skin. Emelia saw the fantasy die in his mind as his subconscious broke through to the realization of what was happening to him now. She heard his hidden screams deep in his mind as he fought to bring himself out of the trance.

Sheltered between the buildings, she pressed against his flabby gut, and pinned him to the wall. His pulse pounded counter-cadence to the still ringing bell as she brushed the false beard aside. Her eyes penetrated his blank stare like lasers, and she heard a final shriek through the veil between his mind and physical being.

Her lips enfolded a tuft of throat as she plunged her fangs deep. She closed her eyes in relief as the life-sustaining fluid coursed over her tongue. She pulled harder at the open vein underneath, and suckled until the bell began to slow its clamor. She felt her strength return as her pain subsided, and finally released him, the bell now silent.

The night air felt cool on her face as she left him and flew over the skyline. Her heightened perception guided her like radar to the condominium complex she sought. The building was a shadowy edifice against the face of the night.

Emelia slowed as she passed several balconies decorated with Christmas displays of plastic Nativity scenes and garland entwined like hideous red and green snakes. She swooped down to a rather plain balcony and hovered over it. She was careful not to let her feet disturb the delicate snow coverage. The patio doors were framed by a single string of tiny white lights.

Emelia's throat tightened at the sudden appearance of a young woman in the window, wearing a long ivory gown of silk and lace. Her black hair fell across her shoulders, and her blue eyes scanned the balcony's view. This angel, an enigma of delicate beauty she realized, was Arianne.

"My daughter," she whispered, and moved quickly to the side where Arianne's gaze wouldn't find her. "How long I've waited for this moment."

As Arianne leaned close to the glass, she pressed a palm to it, and Emelia felt her heart ache to touch the beauty she and Vladimir had created. She moved toward the place where her daughter stood, and cloaked her image so as not to be seen. Daegon had taught her well. With only the windowpane between them, Emelia could see the rise and fall of Arianne's breaths, and the tender pulse beating in her throat. She pressed her own hand to the glass as if to feel her daughter's palm.

Fresh determination filled her at the sight of Arianne. Her goal to save her daughter by the promise of her destiny was stronger than ever before. "I will not lose you again, Arianne."

* * *

Beyond the deep shadows, the tender moment did not go undetected. Fear coiled inside of Shylock like a boa's grip and drained all hope for Arianne's safety. Her mother had found her at last. He saw Emelia turn away and take her airborne leave, and knew he'd been wise not to act. Arianne would be safe for now, but time grew short. He faded into the moonlight to pursue the dangerous course that could determine her very fate.

* * *

A grandfather clock chimed the hour behind its stately stature and decorated face. Moons and suns aligned within the circle of bold roman numerals behind the outstretched hands to signify the time. The triangular silhouette of Mira's Christmas tree stood as a silent sentry as if guarding the front room window. "...Not a creature was stirring."

Emelia's stealth movement through the house went unnoticed by the flashing alarm system. The hallway past the bedroom was a familiar sight from the many times she'd conjured the image in her mind. She traced the numerous framed photographs as she studied each one with great interest. Each smiling face captured a happy memory she'd never been privy to. Mira had stolen her life.

Nearing the back bedroom, she heard her sister's gentle respiration moving like clouds over her pillow. The yellow moonlight fell across the floor, highlighting Mira's face with a soft glow. She saw age etched in the lines of her sister's skin and the silvery strands of hair blending with the light brown of her youth. She saw herself at the age of fifty-six in her sister's image, a victim without recourse against years of gravity and the loss of youth-sustaining hormones.

A silver glimmer bounced off the moonlight on the nightstand. Emelia recognized it as the locket bearing the inscribed **B** for Brasov that matched her own. In better times, it had represented their bond to one another.

With a youthful slender finger, she almost touched Mira's cheek, then pulled back when she stirred in her sleep. Emelia bent close to whisper like she had as a child late at night, when they'd lay side by side in the huge bed. They'd shared little girl secrets in hushed voices as they waited for sleep to carry them to dreamland. As time went on and their beds became two, the quiet whispers had continued across the small crowded bedroom. Now a lifetime lay stretched between them instead of floorboards, and each one traveling a different path determined by the fate that befell them. The time for secrets was over. The truth was needed to set them free and save Arianne's life.

Emelia rested her hand on Mira's shoulder, and called her from the realm of dreams. "Sister...sister wake up."

Mira startled, grabbing the covers to her chest. Her eyes squinted in the pale illumination. "Who's there?"

"Emelia, sister."

"Emelia? You're lying." She reached for the phone. "Get out. I'm calling the police."

"Will you turn yourself in for kidnapping my children, Mira?"

Slowly she returned the phone to its stand muttering, "My God."

"No, sister, not God. Simply one condemned by Him."

Mira turned on the lamp. "Don't talk to me about God. You made your choice long ago, forcing me to make mine."

Emelia shook her head. "I had no choice in my dark birth; it was a gift from Vladimir. It is a decision I don't regret. I am immortal. But you took everything from me out of blind ignorance, risking my children's lives to play the hero."

"Is that how you see it?"

"Yes."

Mira threw back the covers and slid her bare feet into a pair of scuffs. She wore a determined frown and came face to face with Emelia. "What would have happened to your children had I left them to you? Can you honestly answer that?"

"I asked you to stay. I begged you to help us."

She held a finger to Emelia's lips. "That's not what I asked you."

Emelia turned away, realizing where this was going.

Mira followed close behind. "You would have destroyed their lives, too, by making them vampire and probably me as well. Let's keep it in the family, huh?" She grabbed Emelia's shoulder and spun her around.

Instinct overcame Emelia's judgment and she bared her fangs. Mira's hand dropped to her side, a look of disappointment on her face.

"So you would kill your own sister after all?" She yanked her nightgown's collar hard. It tore into a jagged edge to expose her bare neck. "Go on then, if that's what you came for. You disgust me."

After all the years of pain and torment, Emelia had waited for the moment when she would confront Mira and make her pay. Now, with only inches between them, she knew she could easily take her. Perhaps if Mira had withered before her in fear and begged for her life, it would have been easy. But she'd proven a mighty force, much stronger than she ever gave soft-spoken Mira credit for. A certain relief filled Emelia when she realized this was the woman who'd raised her daughter. She'd no doubt instilled that very same strength within Arianne. For that, she was indebted to her sister, for Arianne would need it in order to survive.

Emelia turned away and laughed bitterly. "I won't harm you, Mira. As easy as it would be, I find no pleasure in it. I suppose you did what you thought you had to do, with my children's safety at heart. For that, I respect you. You risked your very life for them. But I'm angry and jealous over the lost years and memories that you were able to share with them. That will never change."

"And I can't undo the past. I've cried plenty over your fate because unbelievably, I still love you. However, you shouldn't be here. Let it go, Emelia, let your children live with the memory of a mother they loved and lost."

"I cannot do that, Mira. They're in danger."

Mira eyed her warily. "I don't believe you."

"Arianne will die if you don't. While it is true I want her back in Romania where she belongs, there is even more reason for her to become full vampire now. You must help me to earn her trust so I can save her. She'll listen to you."

"Never," Mira spat.

"Then she will die, and you will lose her forever."

"And what about Michael?" Mira stared at her.

"Although his blood is pure, he may be a target of those who seek their revenge against me. I believe he is in danger as well."

"I don't know where he is."

Emelia smiled. "I know you don't. But I can tell you he isn't far. I can feel him nearby when I'm in the city. It is just a matter of time before I find him."

She picked up the necklace and tenderly placed it around Mira's neck. As she secured the clasp, she leaned next to her sister's ear. "Remember, we are Brasov, always Brasov. Together, nothing can stop us, if you chose to help me."

CHAPTER 30

The sun burned bright in the blue sky. Arianne turned into traffic and smiled at the beautiful day. She phoned the lab to explain she'd be a little late, and put Jimmy in charge until she arrived. Guilt reared its ugly face as she left the lab tech with the impression she had important business to attend to. She did—the business of Christmas. Not that her list was as long as Santa's, but finding something special for the aunt who has everything is a difficult task. She thought of David and her hand hovered over the console phone at his pre-set button. He had an imaginative mind; surely, he could help her out with some ideas.

"Admit it. You just want to hear his voice." She turned down Michigan Avenue. Christmas ideas or not, she hadn't heard from him in a while, and hit the button as she continued toward Water Tower Place.

"Homicide. Detective Spears."

"Hello, Detective."

"Well, good morning, Doctor. What can I do for you?"

"Why don't we play hooky together and go Christmas shopping?"

An exasperated sigh escaped him. "I'm really swamped right now. I wish I could...I really do."

"Me, too, but I still haven't gotten anything for Aunt Mira. Which reminds me, have *you* been a good boy this year?"

"Doubtful." He turned away from the phone to answer a muffled question in the background. "Sorry. Things are a little nuts here."

"Listen, I'll let you go. How about I make us both a homemade meal some time this week?"

His brief hesitation gave her the answer before he spoke. "I'd like to, Arianne, but..."

She fought down disappointment. "Hey, that's all right. Really. My schedule is looking a little heavy, too. Some other time."

"Arianne, listen. There's something you should know."

She pulled into the parking garage and landed a prime spot right away. As she cut the engine, she heard the words she'd never expected.

"There was a murder...at least that's what *I'm* calling it, on an international flight. The victim was drained of blood without any signs of a struggle and there were two puncture wounds on his wrist."

"What are you saying?"

"Arianne, I think you should be careful. It could have meaning for you."

Flashes of the night before came to mind. Her inability to sleep and edginess made sense now. After Michael had gone to bed, she'd finished some paperwork and snuffed the fireplace. Lying in bed, she'd only tossed and turned with visions of dark shadows hovering overhead like black hooded figures. Then, in the silence, she'd felt herself drawn to the balcony doors.

When she'd stared out over the vast city of twinkling lights and the bustling sounds of traffic below, she'd felt love, not *for* the city, but rather *from* somewhere close by. The emotion made her ache for the physical closeness of another, to consummate the feeling completely. Touching the glass, she nearly cried out at the sudden heat coming through it. It alarmed her, yet she couldn't pull away and didn't want to. She'd stayed like that for quite a while, listening to her heartbeat, and feeling each respiration, as though they were the links holding the moment in place. Then the feeling was gone.

Another series of background voices crackled over the phone, and then David's apology. "I'm sorry, I have to run. Promise me you'll be careful."

"I will," she said, and disconnected.

Suddenly nauseous, she forced herself to take several deep breaths. Her hands trembled on the steering wheel. Her fingertips were still a dusky blue. Ice water seemed to pour through every bone in her body. Her heart pounded hard in her ears as though it might explode, and she gripped the wheel tight until the sensation subsided. Through it all, she realized the palm she'd pressed to the window the night before still burned with heat. For reasons she didn't understand, she found a strange comfort in this—a comfort she'd longed for all of her life.

After hearing David's warning, she wondered if the incident could have a connection. He didn't have to say it; she knew what he was thinking. Her parents had come to take her home.

* * *

David didn't know what frightened him more—the thought of real vampires loose in Chicago or the disappointment in Arianne's voice earlier on the phone. His frustration had become an almost tangible creature, riding shotgun on his way to the morgue. He sounded off to his invisible partner, and pounded the Camaro's dashboard. "Dammit! What am I missing?"

His childhood love of jigsaw puzzles came to mind, a hobby for which he'd been dubbed "Captain Cardboard." He recalled the hours he'd spent hovered over the dining room table covered with oddly shaped pieces of strangely blended colors, and knew there would come a moment when he'd cry out in despair over the one spot which seemed to have no piece. Pride would fill him when his mother would stop to look over his shoulder. Her *oohs* and *aahhs* inspired the cause, but then she'd point with a painted fingernail over the bare spot asking, "What about *this* piece?"

The incredible feeling of anxiety felt the same now. There was a connection between Brewster's murder and the airline death; he could feel it. What was the missing piece, and what kind of picture would it form once he found it?

When he checked his watch, he saw it was long past quitting time for Dr. Gainor, but the morgue never closed—fortunately for him, not so lucky for others. All he needed was five minutes with the body. He turned up his coat collar against the harsh wind, and pushed his way through the double glass doors looking like James Dean.

The evening crew had already arrived for the graveyard shift and David saw the familiar face of Pete Billings, a young blond of about twenty-two sporting a patchy goatee. His surgical scrubs looked more like pajamas as he scuffed along the gray floor tiles wearing paper shoe coverings. He offered David a high-five.

"Hey, Detective. How's it goin'?"

David followed him toward the refrigerators. "I'm doing all right. How about yourself? They keeping you busy?"

"Shit. I can't believe how much overtime the Grim Reaper's been putting in." He grabbed a clipboard from the wall and began checkmarking a row of names. "So, what can I do for your tonight?"

"I need a look at a body. The guy from the airline."

"Ah. Passenger eighty-nine." He grinned. "That was his number." He crossed the room to the huge freezer-type door and pulled hard on its L-shaped latch. "Be right back."

David tapped his foot to the rock song on the cheap desk radio beside the clipboard. When he checked the roster, he saw passenger eighty-nine's name was Casimir Antonescu.

Eastern European? Romanian? That would explain a lot.

Peter rolled a cart veiled with a white sheet out of the refrigerator. "Here you go. Should I undrape or do you want the honor?"

"I'll get it, Pete. Where are the gloves?"

"That rack over there." He hefted his chin toward the corner.

"Got it. Thanks."

"I have a body comin' in a few minutes. Do you mind if I leave for a bit?"

"Go ahead. I'll just cover him up when I leave, it shouldn't be long."

Pete swung through the gray double doors and was gone, leaving an eerie quiet in the room. Slowly, David drew back the sheet. Every movement seemed magnified in sound. He wished Pete would have left the radio.

The puncture wounds gaped. How could someone suck the blood out of a person without any signs? All of the evidence was the same, yet he couldn't shut down the feeling there was something else. Captain Cardboard to the rescue, he thought.

Icy fingers of alarm brushed the back of his neck. A phone rang somewhere beyond the doors. Illusory shadows fueled the fire of imagination. He was glad it was time to go, and covered the body. He switched off the lights, and let the door swoosh closed in the dark.

He crouched and waited.

Several seconds passed and a tall figure arose beside the cart, stealth in movement as it pulled back the sheet from the body. A narrow stream of light from the doorway cut the blackness. He saw the figure move over the corpse.

David charged the intruder and slammed him to the floor. The man bucked David easily, shifting his weight and grip. A sense of déjà vu struck David as they struggled. The man broke free and scrambled across the room.

There was no time to pull his gun when the body cart suddenly wheeled rapidly toward him. He jumped and rolled, ending in a standing position, ready to fight. He moved cautiously, when he saw the assailant had disappeared. A memory flashed and he knew the attacker was the man from the woods. A Jen-Ku priest.

He reached for his side arm, and felt his head jerk back in a vice chokehold. He quickly reversed the move, and cradled the priest's neck in the bend of his elbow. David rushed the wall of metal drawers, and slammed the man's head hard. Weak and disoriented, the intruder dropped to his knees. David yanked open a vacant body-drawer, shoved the priest inside and slammed it back inside the vault.

The man's muffled yells were barely audible as David leaned casually against the drawer, arms folded across his chest. "So, we meet again, my twisted friend. Now that I have your complete cooperation, why don't we have a little chat?"

Fists and feet pounded from inside. David shook his head. "I can stand here all night, pal. The air on this side is just fine."

Silence.

David's skin prickled at the thought of the man suffocating. He waited a moment longer.

Finally, he heard a calm voice muffled from inside. David switched on the lights and slowly slid the drawer open to find the priest lying peacefully on the slab.

The man swung his legs over the side and jumped down. His deep brown eyes pinned David with a stare of severe judgment, but David wasn't moved. He saw the man was dressed as before, in black loose pants tied close around the ankles and a tunic of the same material over a long sleeved body suit. David was sure the Jen-Ku dagger was securely hidden beneath the tunic, ready for action.

The man stood beside the body. "How did you find me?" It was more of a statement than a question.

"You found *me*. I'm just doing my job."

"And so am I." The man's accent held a hint of Italian.

"So I've heard. The business of vampires."

"Yes. It is a noble service."

"Unlike the homicide detectives who get to clean up your messes."

"I respect your position, but you do not understand mine." He glanced at the victim.

"That's okay. I'm not sure I want to."

The priest lifted the corpse's forearm, and pointed to the wrist. "See these marks? They are vampire. This man was a victim of Satan's strongest force on earth. Even his demons do not have the power to take life like these creatures."

"So, isn't this guy a vampire now?"

"No. He was not given the gift of the dark birth. He is dead."

"Well...uh..." David looked at the man.

"Mandari," the priest confirmed, still studying the puncture wounds.

"Mandari, I have to tell you, noble profession or not, you're under arrest for trespassing."

"You know that will never happen, Detective...?"

"Spears." David rested a hand on his gun. "Why not?"

"I won't be here long enough. Besides, do you really want to waste your time with legalities, when what you came for is answers?"

"All right then, suppose you tell me why *you're* here."

Mandari replaced the sheet, and moved in front of the cart, facing David.

"I heard about the strange death on board the airline and wanted to see for myself. Now, what is it *you* came for?"

"Fair enough," David conceded. "I want to know what or who, really killed this guy."

"Then you believe in vampires. Good. You are much safer in your acceptance. Those who deny their existence are often the easiest targets."

"Which brings me to my final question." David pinned him with a stare. "Why did you try to kill me on the hiking trail?"

"As you say...fair enough. I was trying to save your life, Detective."

"It wasn't in danger."

"I realize that now. After your embrace with her, I assumed she'd lured you out there to kill you. Please understand my war is not with you, but that of the vampire. She is half so, therefore, she is potentially dangerous."

"How do you know she's half vampire?"

He closed his eyes briefly as if speaking to a child. "The Jen-Ku are everywhere, every town, every city, and we're very serious in our pursuit of God's most vicious enemy. We could not be successful without an intricate network."

"You mean spies."

"Something like that. At any rate, you'd be better off staying away from Arianne."

"I can't do that."

Mandari nodded. "I see. Be wise my friend, don't let your feelings cloud your judgment."

"She will not kill. You have my word, Mandari."

"Right now, she is not the prime concern. I'm searching for the monster that did this." He raised an arm toward the corpse. Her name is Emelia Von Tirgov, Arianne's mother. But then, you already suspected as much. That's why you're here."

"And if it's true?"

"If she is here in the city, then it is Arianne who is in danger. Emelia's reasons for risking her own destruction can only be to find her daughter and make her full vampire. Together they would be very strong, capable of ruling any number of covens." After a short pause, he added, "You understand, I can't let that happen."

"When it comes to saving Arianne's life, you'll have to stand in line."

"I admire your courage. You would make a superb Jen-Ku."

David started to go. "Thanks, but I already have a job." He headed for the doors turning briefly to add something, but the room was empty except for the sheeted corpse. It looked like Mandari already knew he'd decided to drop the trespassing charges.

CHAPTER 31

Arianne considered Friday afternoon traffic a true test of patience and skill. The general public was hot on the trail of cashed paychecks, beers to be chugged, and love to be made—in other words, "Let the weekend begin." Arianne felt *her* weekend start as she passed the St. John city limits sign.

She glanced over at her brother, looking handsome in his navy winter jacket and black Levis. He bit his lower lip, the same way she tended to when life proved a little stressful. Admittedly, her own lip was tempting as they drew closer to Mira's. She hadn't told her aunt who the special visitor was, only that they'd arrive in the early evening.

When she'd called Mira the night before, her aunt had sounded nervous, distracted. Arianne knew her better than anyone, her moods, her tone of voice, and the way she paced when she had something on her mind. Although she couldn't see her over the phone, she knew Mira had paced throughout their entire conversation by the static produced by the loose phone cord.

"Aunt Mira? Is everything all right?"

"Uh, yes, dear. Why?"

"You don't sound like yourself. Did I catch you at a bad time?"

"Not at all. I just finished making some dessert cups and now I'm ready to relax and read my new book."

"Uh-huh. Then why are you pacing?"

The static stopped.

"I'm fine, really. When am I going to see you?"

Arianne smiled. "How about tomorrow? I'm bringing someone, so no curlers, okay?"

"Who is it?"

"It's a surprise. But you won't be disappointed. Tomorrow is going to be very special for you."

They'd talked a while longer, then just before hanging up, Mira had said, "I'll see you tomorrow then. Be careful, Arianne, promise me?"

She'd assured her aunt she would, and had hung up wondering why she was concerned for her safety. At first, she'd thought it had to do with driving, but with the milder temperatures, the roads were clean and dry. Forties in December were equal to a spring day.

What could her warning mean?

Now, only minutes from her destination, Arianne's stomach was a theme park ride of loops and twists as they drove past a pasture of cows enjoying the unusual warmth of the season. Second thoughts reared up to confuse her as she tried to picture the reunion. Clouds of doubt, as ominous as thunder, hovered over her bright hope of family closure.

As if reading her mind, Michael asked, "Are we doing the right thing?"

"Absolutely." She forced a smile.

"You know, I've always dreamed of meeting my family, and of course, you were a wonderful surprise."

"Of course," she teased.

"But now that it's happening, I'm having second thoughts."

"Let me put your mind at ease, big brother. Aunt Mira is the most gracious, loving woman on earth. Look what she went through to save us. I know she gave you up, but that was out of love, not because she didn't want you."

He nodded. "I have no ill feelings toward her. She did what she thought best. I just don't want to disappoint her."

"You won't, I promise you." She turned on the radio and grinned. "Do you mind a little rock, or should I find a Gregorian chant?"

"I could use a bit of solid ground right now. Rock will be fine."

* * *

Arianne held tight to Michael's arm as they stood on Mira's front porch. Her heart galloped, and she wondered if her brother could hear it. As the door slowly pulled open, they glanced at one another. This is it, she thought.

At first, Mira only stood staring, as though she didn't see them at all. Her pallor and the dark circles under her eyes alarmed Arianne. Something was very wrong. Then her aunt's expression broke into sunshine as she opened the screen door wide.

"Come in, come in," she said.

In the small foyer, Mira hung their coats on decorative wooden wall-pegs, then turned to greet the newcomer.

Arianne clasped Michael's hand. "Aunt Mira, this is a day for miracles, and if anyone deserves one in their life, it's you. Michael has come home."

"Michael?" She stepped forward, never taking her eyes from him. "*My* Michael?" Her voice cracked.

Mira faltered a bit in her step. Michael wrapped a supporting arm around her waist and led her to the couch.

Arianne followed, still trembling. She brushed away the tears trickling down her cheeks, and grabbed a tissue box from the table on her way to join them. This was better than any tearjerker movie she'd ever paid eight dollars to see.

Mira hadn't let go of him and clutched his hand as they sat side by side. "After all these years, how did you find us?"

"It was Arianne who found *me*. It was the best surprise of my life."

Mira tenderly palmed his cheek. "Michael, can you ever forgive me?"

"There's nothing to forgive. Arianne explained the situation and the difficult position you were in. I want to thank you for saving us."

Mira was silent as she fought for composure, burying her nose in a tissue. When she looked up, she said, "I thought I'd never see you again. That day at the orphanage...it was so hard...I wanted to die."

Arianne watched them find closure and peace after years of questions and doubt.

Mira she sat back still dabbing at her eyes. "Were you treated well?"

"Very well," Michael said.

"My, you turned out to be handsome. Any special lady in your life?"

Arianne grinned at her brother's crimson cheeks. "Michael's a priest, Aunt Mira."

It was Mira's turn to blush. "I'm so sorry. Arianne, for goodness sakes, you should have told me."

"It's all right, Mira," Michael assured her. "My looks are deceiving. I'm currently on a sabbatical and don't wear my priest's clothing."

"When will you return to the church?"

"I'm not sure. That's a decision forthcoming. Right now I'm here to help Arianne."

Suddenly Mira's expression darkened and she became quiet. Once again, Arianne felt there was something her aunt wasn't telling, something very wrong. Before she could ask, Mira stood.

"How about some homemade dessert and fresh coffee?"

* * *

In the kitchen, they caught up with each other's lives, laughing at stories of young Michael in seminary, and enjoying Mira's fresh fruit tarts with whipped cream. When the conversation lulled, Arianne began clearing the small table. As she placed the delicate china cups and plates in the sink, she was surprised to hear her aunt's serious tone.

"Leave those, Arianne. I need to talk to both of you and I need your complete attention."

They moved to the living room, and each took up a comfortable position as Mira took center stage before the fireplace. Arianne's nerves knotted when she saw her begin to pace.

"You certainly gave me the gift of a lifetime today. I suppose it's timely, considering recent events in my life. Now that we're all together again, I'm sure you're aware *we* are not all that is left of this family. Although it all seems like a lifetime ago, it's never far away."

"What are you saying, Aunt Mira?" Arianne glanced nervously at Michael.

"We all need to be careful, especially now that we're together again." She turned to Arianne. "You gave me a wonderful surprise, my dear. Unfortunately, I have unexpected news for you, that isn't so wonderful."

"What is it, Mira? What's wrong?"

"Your mother came to see me the other night. She's here to find you."

* * *

The rusty mailbox resembled a squeezed loaf of bread, with deep indentations on both sides. Batting practice from a car window is the second great American pastime. MONROE danced in crooked black peel-and-stick letters on its side.

David turned down the gravel drive crunching toward the faded blue cracker-box that Gunther Monroe called home. Tan roof shingles curled like potato chips under the winter sun, trimmed with worn Christmas lights clinging to sagging gutters. A retired cop should have all the time in the world to keep up his home, unless that time is spent peering into the bottom of an upturned whiskey bottle, David thought.

At the doorstep, a dim yellow light glowed behind frayed front room curtains the color of dirty sand, while the television blared through the closed door loud enough to hear the game show host's voice, "…and the answer is…"

David felt the doorbell grit in the socket from disuse. After several seconds, the television applause lowered and the door opened enough for David to see his old friend and mentor wearing a dingy tank-style undershirt, gray trousers, and a warm smile.

"Spears! You sonofabitch, get in here!"

The forty-year veteran carried a few more pounds and a lot less hair since his retirement several years ago, but his box-like chin and Boston terrier nose were permanent fixtures.

David stepped inside to the pleasant aroma of something Italian filling his nostrils. Somehow, the image of Gunther in an apron didn't fit. If brass cannolis were any indication of longevity, Gunther Monroe would still be standing long after Armageddon. He was the only homicide detective David knew to hold his ground, right or wrong, with the Chief, earning him the nickname of "Bulldog." The fine line between brave and stupid had been crossed many times by the brazen detective, but he always knew when to fold his hand and walk off with his dignity. David knew Chief Mags never openly admitted it, but he liked Gunther and was sorry to see him go. At the retirement dinner, they'd shaken hands, called each other a sonofabitch and parted with watery eyes.

David had partnered with Bulldog during his first two years in homicide, enough to learn the ins and outs, and right and wrong of the job. Many times, it seemed they were on the slippery edge of ethics in order to get the job done. And they had. Together, they'd solved more murders in one year than the other teams combined. David learned the real nemesis isn't always the bad guy with a .45; it's the invisible enemy that lives within.

Bulldog had a heart attack after the second year, forcing him to finish out his time on the force behind a desk. There were worse ways to lose a partner, David realized, but watching Gunther day after day, shrivel under mountains of paperwork, made him wonder if going out guns a blazin' wouldn't have been preferred by the hard-edged veteran.

That's when the drinking started and David knew it was over for Bulldog.

"Come on sit down." Gunther motioned to an easy chair as he padded barefoot to the couch, his hefty gut hanging over his pants. "Can I get you a beer or somethin'?"

"No thanks, Gunther. I'm fine." When he sat down, the easy chair cushion nearly swallowed him to the waist.

"So, what's going on Spears? I haven't seen you for a while."

The man's faded watery eyes seemed to ask why he was alone in his twilight years after giving so much. *"Why doesn't anyone come 'round anymore,"* they asked.

"Things have been crazy down at the station," David said. "You know the drill, it seems like it comes in waves. And right now we could all use some life preservers."

"I don't doubt it." Bulldog muted the TV completely, returning the screen to the silent movie era as the seven o'clock showcase started with *Casablanca*. "Sure you don't want something?"

"I'm sure." David squirmed in his seat. "Listen, Bulldog, I need your advice."

His gray eyes sparkled, and he hefted his posture straight. "Of course, you do. What's up?"

David explained the details of the case expecting an exploding belly laugh from his ex-partner. But instead, Bulldog held a serious expression, taking it all in until David stopped.

"Whew. And I thought I'd heard it all." He glanced at Bogey's sneering smile on the television. "I love this movie. You ever see it?"

"Not all of it."

"Yeah, well you oughta rent it. It's got a lot of heart. It's more than just a sappy love story, ya know."

David stared at the shell of a man whose granite tone and icy stare had melted confessions out of the toughest criminals imaginable—he'd even brought a few to tears.

Bulldog reached for a Pepsi. "So, anyway, you were saying about forensics and the paper fragment."

"Right. They confirmed it's part of a surgical shoe covering. Could be from the lab, or maybe not."

"And nothing turned up in the first victim's apartment?"

"Nothing unusual."

"What about co-workers?"

"They all check out. It's a dead-end case, only I can't let that happen."

"It wouldn't be the first, Spears. Sometimes it can't be helped. Why, I *still* have nightmares over some of the unsolved cases I worked. Not often, but once in a while."

"There's too much at stake."

Gunther thought a minute, staring at David. "You're in love with her."

"Who?"

"The girl with the bad blood."

"Arianne?"

"That's it. Listen, I might have screwed up two marriages because I was married to my job, but it doesn't mean I don't know about love. And that bozo's got it wrong, I can tell you. A kiss *ain't* just a kiss, it's heart and soul meeting, *that's* what it is." That said, he pressed his back to the couch and propped his feet on the coffee table.

David looked around at the shaving of carpet worn thin by time; a lame barrier between thirty-year old furniture and faded floorboards. Bulldog's bare feet jiggled in nervous habit, apparently right at home on top of the table with no one around to lovingly shoo them off. Is this what he had to look forward to?

Bulldog rested the back of his head in his hands. "My advice to you, Spears, is to step back."

"Step back?"

"Right. You know that old saying about blind trees in the forest?"

David smiled. Bulldog had a way with words.

"Well, the same applies here. Sometimes we just get so caught up with the details, or lack of them, that we lose sight of the big picture. You have to look at more than the evidence. Consider all possibilities, even if they don't fit and even if they seem outside the ring of the investigation. I remember one case about twenty years ago that had me by the short hairs. I hadn't slept in days. Then one afternoon I stopped at one of those Stop-N-Shops for a slush drink. I wasn't thinking about anything in particular, not even the case, when I spotted a rack of those fancy gold and silver lighters. Suddenly it clicked for me and I knew my next move. Arrested the killer two days later and as far as I know, that asshole is still providing service for the nice fellas down at the house of corrections."

They talked of old times, old friends, new policies, and everyone's favorite, Chief Mags. They talked until Bogey sent Bacall on her merry way amidst the tears and airplane's rumble.

Bulldog slapped David hard on the back as they shook hands at the door. "I miss the old times, David. I really do."

"We could use your eagle-eye down at the station, Gunther."

"Yeah, well this old bird wears bifocals now. But I have my memories, don't I?"

As David fired up the Camaro, he saw the lights in the house go out, leaving a black silhouette in the night.

Friends are still friends, he thought. As time goes by.

CHAPTER 32

Heading for home, the Camaro held its traction on the road as the outside temperature dropped. David drove slower than usual, turning the conversation with Bulldog over in his head. Step back, his long-time friend had advised. Easier said than done. Time was running out and he had everything to lose.

He recalled the rundown condition of the house and the man. It pained him to think of it. Still, maybe things weren't as grim as he thought. Although Bulldog had offered him a beer, he himself had been drinking a Pepsi. Had he finally wrestled the demon into a cage? If so, how secure was the latch?

Bulldog might be right; chasing your tail gets old and frustrating. Maybe he would take Arianne up on her dinner offer. He couldn't remember the last time he'd eaten a dinner that hadn't come out of the freezer or a fast-food joint. A homemade meal sounded real good. Memories of their last date came to mind as they'd curled together on the couch—her ebony hair so soft against his cheek, and the sweet taste of her full lips lingering long after the kiss.

A jolt of reality brought him to attention at something Bulldog had said. *"You're in love with her."* He decided that it felt all right. But was it true? After all, Bulldog was a romantic, maybe seeing things he *wanted* to see in this cruel, treacherous world.

"You have to look at more than the evidence."

Suddenly, he needed to hear her voice and found he'd already begun dialing. Her phone rang a seemingly endless drone of disappointment. He pictured her at his apartment taking in his photos, with her simple method of character judging. Then it clicked, like Bulldog's gold and silver lighter.

David turned the car donut-style on the deserted street and headed the other way. The home photo theory was about to have its first test.

* * *

David stifled a grin. Paul Bently's landlady, Mrs. Gish, was in curlers again. Her fuzzy pink robe and matching scuffs brought images of the crime scene back all too clear. She drew her robe tighter over her chest to cover a high-collar nightgown. Tired green eyes examined his badge closely as he held it up for her to see. Finally, a nod of approval gained him entrance, and he followed the sixty-something woman upstairs.

"I wish his family would come clean out the place," she huffed up the sagging steps. "I got renters waiting."

"The crime scene wasn't released that long ago. I'm sure they'll be along any day now."

"Yeah, well, if the stuff isn't gone by the end of the month, I'm junkin' it."

"You're all heart," David mumbled.

"What's that?"

"I said that's a good start."

The key slipped the lock easily with a sound click. Mrs. Gish pushed open the door. "There you go, Detective. Lock up when you leave. I'll be downstairs if you need me." With that, she trudged toward the stairs stopping briefly at the top. "I'm not really that heartless, Detective. It's just that I have bills to pay like everyone else and I count on my leases to finance this place. I feel real bad about Paul's death. He was a nice young man, and all his friends were that way, too."

He watched her clutch the wobbly railing, and make her way downstairs slowly. Apparently, he wasn't nice enough. *Someone* murdered him.

Inside the apartment, all signs of the tragedy had been erased, including the crime scene tape and rancid cigar stench. It looked as though Paul Bently might come walking through the door any minute, wearing his white lab smock and green scrub pants. The paper shoe coverings would be absent, unlike the killer who'd worn his to eliminate prints.

The furniture was early yuppie, although a lab tech's salary probably couldn't quite compare with that lifestyle, it seemed Paul had found a way. Maybe some of his nice friends had pitched in and bought it for him. Black and white sketches of Chicago's buildings were placed in the living room on tables and walls. Perhaps Paul's friends had hired a Feng Shui consultant as well.

Books by Patterson, Clancy, and King lined the small waist-high cabinet against the far wall with several lab reference books. No surprise there. Paul's video collection held such classics as *A Bridge Too Far, The Guns of Navarone,* and *The Ten Commandments,* mingled in with a multitude of adventure/karate flicks. He wandered into the master bedroom and found that it, too, had been cleansed of the demons, save for a six-inch snake of yellow crime scene tape left by the crime lab. The four-poster bed remained untouched since the morning Paul had made it for the last time.

On his way to investigate the bathroom, David stopped short, catching sight of Paul's cluttered dresser. An array of diverse frames from 5x7's to 8x10's lined the top in lieu of the average guy stuff like cologne, concert ticket stubs, dirty socks, and extra rubber packets. None of the good stuff. Just photographs.

Several family pictures started the set, with Paul standing arm and arm with a woman who could have passed for his clone with the exception of age and gender. She looked to be about sixty, her smile the same pose in each shot. There were quite a few with Paul in fisherman's gear, right down to the hip-boots, for the times when the fisherman feels compelled to get right in the water and wrestle the fish into the net. David knew the feeling well.

Toward the end of the line, David's pulse quickened. There it was. The missing piece. A 5x7 photo framed in black with silver etching showed Paul wearing a bowling league shirt and standing beside another man in a matching shirt. The two were all smiles, arms draped over each other's shoulders as they held a trophy between them. Paul Bently and Roger Thomas were apparently bowling buddies as well as co-workers. So why had Roger denied knowing Paul very well, giving the impression he only knew him from the Research Center?

Maybe he didn't want to get involved in murder. Maybe he didn't even like Paul and figured it was a moot point. Or maybe he'd veered out of his strike zone after one too many exploding pins. Game over for Paul.

*   *   *

Half empty cartons of fried rice and beef chop suey sat on Arianne's coffee table. The fireplace crackled into the quiet room providing pleasant white noise. Arianne stared into the yellow blaze feeling relaxed to the point of hypnosis after the filling meal. Michael lounged beside her on the couch. After returning from Mira's, they'd decided on Chinese take-out and a cozy evening at home. There was a lot to think about.

Mira's warning that Emelia had arrived to find them brought a sense of alarm and, strangely, a twisted sense of relief. Arianne had known there would come a time when she'd be forced to face her parents, and for the first time in her life, she felt ready. The time for hiding was over.

"What are you thinking?" Michael asked softly.

"The same thing you probably are," she said.

"What's that?"

"About our visit with Mira and her warning."

"We only have the nights to fear. As long as one of us remains awake we should be all right." He got up and checked the door once more. Arianne wanted to comfort him and make him believe what he'd just said, but she didn't believe it either. Not really. Emelia would come for them; it was just a matter of time.

Arianne felt drained and achy, and she rested her head back, with her eyes closed. Every day she grew weaker. She'd lost enough weight to make her look drawn, and the dark circles under her eyes could no longer be covered up with makeup. She saw the concern in her brother's eyes when he looked at her and was helpless to ensure him it would turn out okay.

She forced herself up before she fell asleep. She pulled the patio drapes closed, jerking her hand back in sudden pain. The silvery cord had caught her finger, drawing blood. Her eyes widened as she looked at the thick, dark spot forming on her finger. It was black. The tarry substance trickled slowly down her finger like a snaking oil spill.

"Is the patio locked?" Michael asked.

Quickly she wrapped her finger in the tissue from her sweater pocket. "Yes, everything seems secure. You wouldn't mind if I went to bed, would you?"

"Of course not." He stroked a lock of hair from her face. "You look exhausted. I'll stay up and keep watch."

Inside the bathroom, she ran her finger under the faucet and watched the water flow black at first then fade to gray as the wound stopped bleeding. After applying antibiotic ointment and a bandage, she dressed for bed.

A vibrating tingle consumed her whole body as if in warning. Her nerves were suddenly sharp and she listened carefully. Her pulse quickened at a sound outside the window. Before she could react, it blew open. Wind howled inside the room. The curtains leapt toward the ceiling, and billowed violently. Arianne rushed to close it, but stopped short when a figure flew inside, landing without a sound.

The woman was dressed in black velvet with long hair flowing over her shoulders. Arianne saw the high cheekbones and full lips and knew it was Emelia. She stared into the woman's crystal blue eyes and found she couldn't move.

As the woman moved closer, she spoke in a rapid whisper that echoed in Arianne's mind. "Arianne, I am your mother."

She shook herself from the trance-like state and stepped back.

Her mother pleaded. "Please don't fear me. I love you. You were taken from me before I could be a mother to you. It was beyond my control."

Something stirred within Arianne. Was it longing for her mother's touch? Could this be her true fate? She felt the warmth of forgiveness spreading through her and wanted to try. But Mira's warning remained in her mind and the harsh reality shattered the warmth.

"I will never kill or return with you to Romania. You're wasting your time here." She saw darkness surface in her mother's expression.

"Mira has poisoned you."

"Mira loved me enough to save me from your curse. You should be thankful."

"I am. I'm grateful she raised such a strong daughter. For you will need your courage before much longer."

"Is that a threat?"

The woman's gaze traveled to the bandage on Arianne's finger. A black spot seeped through.

"It has already started." Her voice faltered with emotion. "Arianne, you must listen to me. You are dying. There is no way to save you, except by taking the blood. If you don't become full vampire soon, you will not survive."

"Then I will die!"

"Your soul will never rest, don't you see? It is the only way. I lost you once and have found you. I will not lose you again."

"Is that your wish for me? To be a creature of the night, selfishly draining the life from innocent victims in order to survive?"

"It is necessary. You will have immortality and eternal youth. We can be together ruling the night as it was meant to be."

Arianne stepped back. "No. You're wrong and there's nothing you can say to change my mind."

"Then you have sealed your fate. But I won't forsake you. I'll stay with you until the end. No matter what happens, Arianne, you are still my daughter and I love you."

Her mother stood close now and raised a slender hand to her cheek. "You *do* believe me?"

Arianne fought the emotions welling up inside, wanting to turn away from Emelia the vampire, to shun her evil forever. An inner voice cried out from her heart, alone and frightened.

"Why, Mother? Why did it have to be this way?"

"Fate had the last word. But I don't regret my life, only what I've lost."

Arianne's eyes brimmed as her mother folded her into an embrace. She nestled in her arms and took in the scent of lilac talc. She wept for all the time they'd missed together, for what should have been between them. Her fears consumed her at the very real possibility of what could lie ahead if the procedure didn't work. They sat together on the bed's edge, holding each other for a long time. She allowed herself to be rocked like a child, safe against the world. Arianne no longer feared the woman she'd come to dread, and realized her mother had come home to her heart.

"Oh, Arianne, I can't stand to lose you."

Arianne pulled back and wiped her tears. "There is a way, Mother. It's my only hope."

She explained the procedure to Emelia, and told her it would be done soon.

Emelia's eyes were wide. "And you say you must be vampire in order for it to work?"

"Yes. It's like any disease process. The patient can't *potentially* have cancer in order for the clean DNA to work. They must already have it."

"I see. Then how will you become vampire?"

Arianne closed her eyes to the explicit detail. "I'll have to drink blood."

"No, Arianne, that won't work."

"What do you mean?"

Emelia stood before her. "In my quest to find you and your brother, I was taken in by a coven-master named Daegon. He was very old, very wise, but in the end, very foolish. He trained me, taught me the most ancient secrets of the ways of the vampire with the understanding that I'd govern the coven with him. He predicted what is happening to you now and warned that in order to become full vampire, your fangs must pierce the skin. There is no other way."

"But surely—"

"No, Arianne. It must be done in order to consummate your dark spirit and your soul. Once they join, nothing that can change it. I hope your procedure is the key you need."

Before Arianne could answer, Michael pounded on the door. "Arianne? Are you all right? Unlock the door!"

Emelia shifted her gazed to the lock. It turned neatly with a soft click. She wore an unreadable expression, as the doorknob turned. The reunion was about to become complete.

CHAPTER 33

The batch of genetically altered cells was invisible in the petri dish. Usually the lab techs culled out the cells that didn't accept the clean DNA, but this time Arianne took it upon herself. As her fingers held the pipette, it shook unsteadily now and then causing her to wait until she steadied herself. As she peered through the lens, she felt as though she were viewing her future in microscopic form, like a god mapping someone's life. She sat back on the stool and sighed. The cells with the clean DNA were properly aligned and ready to go. Roger sauntered by on his way to the break room as Arianne finished.

"Roger, will you refrigerate those dishes in stall three?"

He shrugged and detoured from his route, moving like a slug on muscle relaxers. "You want me to take these, too?" He nodded toward the dishes at her station.

"I'll take care of it, Roger. Thanks."

"No problem, Dr. B."

When she stripped off her latex gloves, she saw her bandage had gone with them. The wound had scabbed over, but remained a dark reminder of her mother's ill-fated words, *"You're dying, Arianne."* It hadn't been a new revelation, as a physician she knew the signs of a body hell-bent on self-destruction, and hers seemed to harbor a death wish.

The soulful expression of fear was a strange emotion to see on Emelia's face. She'd always pictured her mother as a strong, willful monster, who feared nothing. But last night had proven her wrong.

When she saw her mother's tears and heard the torture in her voice, she knew she'd misjudged her. Perhaps she really was a mother who loved her children, who fell victim to a set of circumstances out of her control.

She recalled the expression on Emelia's face when Michael had entered the bedroom, a look of excited disbelief stretching her lips into a hopeful smile.

"Michael? Is it really you?"

His eyes were wide, first looking at Emelia, then settling on Arianne to ask, "Are you all right?"

"I'm fine. Everything is under control, Michael. She isn't here to harm us."

He moved in front of Arianne, never taking his eyes from Emelia.

"Mother. I pray for your condemned soul. But you aren't welcome here. Please return to Romania and let us live in peace."

"Michael?" Emelia moved toward him. "Please don't fear me. I love you, you're my son."

"How can you claim to know love, when you're filled with such evil. The two can't live together. A house divided will fall."

"Don't quote scripture to me. Doesn't the good book also say to honor your father and mother?"

"I honor your memory; the place you would have held in my life. But there is no future between us because you are an affront to everything I stand for."

Arianne took his arm. "Don't you see, Michael? She's a victim as much as we are. Can't you forgive? Isn't it time to stop throwing stones and start healing?"

"It isn't that simple—"

"Forgiveness never is, but who are we to judge?"

He'd stared at her, and fingered the cross dangling over his chest. She heard him mumble something she didn't understand, *"Sins of the father,"* then his expression softened as if he suddenly understood a great secret. He took Emelia's hands and pulled her close.

The memory lingered as Arianne cleaned the lab station. Before she could re-bandage her finger, the doors pushed open and David came through wearing a determined frown that said, official police business. She met him halfway across the room.

"David, what is it?"

He cupped her elbow. "Can we use your office?"

"Of course." She led the way.

Inside, she waited until he closed the door. "You're scaring me."

"Sorry." His eyes softened. "Is Roger here today?"

"Yes. Why?"

"I need to bring him in for questioning, Arianne."

"But, why?"

"He might be Paul Bently's killer, and if that's true, he most likely murdered Fred, too. But right now, I just need to talk to him."

"I'll call him," she said on her way to the door.

David gently turned her to face him. "Hey, are you all right?" He stroked her cheek and leaned close. "I'm worried about you. You're working too hard."

She closed her eyes at his touch and wanted to tell him everything. But this wasn't the time.

Instead, she forced a smile. "I've been pushing to get the cells ready for the procedure. The sooner the better. Then I can get some much needed rest."

His eyes held her. "Promise?"

She nodded. "I'll get Roger."

As she reached the door, he said, "Is your homemade dinner offer still open?"

"Absolutely."

"How about tomorrow night?"

"Great. Do you like Italian?"

"Love it. I'll bring the wine."

"Seven o'clock, and don't be late."

A short time later, Arianne watched Roger leave quietly with David, wide-eyed and red-cheeked. His reaction to David's request to question him at the station had been one of shock under hooded eyes.

"I already told you what I know," he'd said lethargically. "There's nothing more to say."

"Maybe a few pictures will jog your memory," David quipped as they headed out.

Chills crawled up her arms at the thought of working side by side with a killer. How many times had she worked late, alone with him in the deserted building? It could easily have been her.

If Roger turned out to be the killer, Fred's call of the young man would have to be amended. He may not be the sharpest scalpel, only the most dangerous.

* * *

Coffee slopped over the cup's side and settled in a neat brown ring on the table. Roger looked from the spill to David and back again. A lock of hair covered one eye and part of his curled lip. He sat in a lazy slouch with his feet propped under the table on the opposite chair.

David yanked the chair back, forcing Roger to sit up straight. He turned it around and straddled it. His eyes were stone. "I said make yourself comfortable, not take a nap."

Roger winced and clasped his hands on the table. "I'm awake. What do you want from me?"

"The truth."

"I already told you all I know about Paul."

"Like I said, the truth."

David waited for an answer. It was an old trick, probably invented by King Solomon in all his cunning and wisdom, and just as effective today. The waiting game could break the most stubborn criminals into talking. No one likes the awkward silence that follows a question—even if the answer tends to incriminate. Eventually, they feel they have to say *something* and that something, David had found, usually ends up moving the case forward. He could wait all day if necessary. He doubted Roger felt the same way.

The heavy silence melted into more than a minute before the lab tech shook his head in defeat.

"I knew Paul from work and eventually we ended up bowling together. That's all."

Another silence followed as if Roger were waiting for applause. David cocked his head, keeping their gazes locked.

An exasperated sigh cut the quiet as Roger squirmed. "Man! What do you want from me?"

"Why did you say you didn't know him outside of work? Afraid we'd take the trophy back?"

"No, no. Nothin' like that."

"Then what?"

"I just…I just got scared. That's all. I figured it would be easier to say I didn't know him that well so you'd leave me alone."

"You'd think if he was only a bowling buddy, you'd want to help all you could."

"But I don't know anything, so how can I help?"

"What were you doing while Paul was performing a dive in the toilet, Roger? Where were *you*?"

Roger's apathy fled as the smoking dragon of anger surfaced. "I was standing in his bathtub holding up a big card with a 10 on it!" He slammed his palms on the table for emphasis.

David stared at him, unmoved.

Still trembling after his outburst, Roger ran a hand through his hair exposing full facial features.

"I was at home watching football," his voice shook. "No one was more surprised to hear about Paul than I was. He was a nice guy—too nice. He trusted people and they took advantage of him. We weren't close, but I liked him."

David nodded. "Okay. Can anyone vouch for your whereabouts?"

"My mom. We watched the game together."

"And on the night of Dr. Brewster's death you were...?" David held his hands palms up.

"At home, mostly."

"What's *mostly*, Roger? Do we have to have this dance again?" David heard the strain in his voice. He was losing patience, fast.

"I drove by the Research Center."

"What time?"

"Around eight, I guess."

"Why were you there?"

"I didn't stop, just drove by. I'd left my Walkman in my locker and thought I'd pick it up. But I saw Dr. Brewster's car from the road and kept on goin'."

"Why's that?"

"He was always riding me about something, and I'd already been late twice that week, so I just kept going."

"Is the lab usually open that late?"

"Only if Dr. Brewster or Dr. Brasov are working. Now if it had been Dr. Brasov, I would've stopped. She's always decent to me."

"So you had a problem with Dr. Brewster?"

"Yeah...I mean, no! He was okay. He just rode me once in a while."

"Uh-huh. Did you see anything else that night? Anyone else on the premises, anything unusual?"

"There was another car in the lot, parked further out. But I don't know whose."

"What did it look like?"

"I think it was dark blue or black. It's hard to tell under the sodium lights. They have that weird orange glow. It was some kind of small job."

"Make? Model?"

He shrugged. "I don't know. A two-door, I guess. I didn't pay much attention. Like I said, when I saw Brewster's car, I just left."

"Why didn't you say anything the first time you were interviewed?"

He shrugged. "Guess I didn't think it was such a big deal."

The rest of the interview didn't provide much more information and David released the tech with a renewed dislike for CD headsets. Too much loud music *can* fry your brain. Roger was living proof.

David sat at his desk, and reviewed his notes from the Brewster investigation, noting all time cards had been checked for that day. No one had stayed any later than five o'clock. Whoever had been in the lab that night had been there with one purpose in mind—too kill Fred Brewster. So, whose car had been in the lot that night?

According to Arianne, the Research Center did not have cameras mounted in their parking lot. They were lucky to have enough funding to supply test tubes and microscopes; videos of the parking lot were beyond necessity. David frowned. This time he had the puzzle piece and nowhere to put it.

CHAPTER 34

The winter night wrapped itself around the city like a heavy blanket. Temperatures plummeted, winds howled, and Chicagoans were fearlessly enjoying the Holiday Season. Ice skaters covered the ice of a man-made rink near Michigan Avenue, some gliding, some sliding, and most laughing at the elements from under muffling scarves. Others, of a more timid nature, preferred the sport of shopping on Michigan Avenue.

Arianne checked off a mental list of market items for her dinner date—Ricotta cheese, peppers, tomatoes, fresh garlic, and, of course, breath mints. She pictured the scene in her mind of the dining room table dressed in her favorite ivory linen tablecloth with matching tapers in ornate brass holders. A pale candle glow softly illuminated David's handsome features, turning his eyes into emerald lasers, as he held her gaze. Her mind's eye traveled over the scene, and caught like a glitch on videotape onto her faded purple blouse—the one with the missing pearl button. She'd already decided on comfortably casual, something suitable for cuddling on the couch, but realized as she drove home, that her wardrobe needed a serious make over. Too much time spent in a lab coat can destroy a woman's sense of style. It was time for a fashion treat, she decided, and headed for Marshall Fields.

Red, gold, and green glitter caught the lights, and splintered bright shards of color over the intricate decorations and elaborate displays. The department store was alive with Christmas spirit, enticing customers with everything from the latest seasonal music to the sensual aroma of chocolate. Arianne forced herself past the Frango mints, moving toward women's fashions.

Silk and velvet in every color and style bombarded her, and confirmed her sinking feeling that this could take some time. Usually quick in making most decisions, her brain seemed to slam to a crawl when picking out her wardrobe. She recalled the food items in the trunk of her car and reasoned the cooler temperatures would keep them cold enough for a while. She had time for one outfit, she decided, and hurried to make her choice.

A spacious dressing room provided ample room, and the soft lighting offered a romantic look to any outfit being considered. Arianne's arms ached as she pulled a ribbed turtleneck sweater over her head. A burning sensation curled upward inside her throat as she detected a fresh, sweet aroma. The enticing warmth seemed to emanate through the dressing room walls. She was distracted from her mirrored image and wondered where the scent was coming from.

Her reflection blurred as the overwhelming sensation of intense hunger consumed her. Her keen hearing picked up the sound of soft breathing to the left and she realized with sickening dread that there was someone in the next stall. There was something else, too, although her clouded mind could not focus on it clearly; it was a feeling, a tingle of warning. She tried to shake herself from the daze.

She fought to see herself clearly in the mirror as the distorted image slowly returned to normal. Or had it? Suddenly, a stranger stared back at her with eyes of ebony. Her raven hair was a tangled mess tousled over skin the color of white jade. The hardened lines of her jaw were well defined as she felt the thrust of her canine teeth grow more intense. Gripped by an insatiable appetite for blood, she closed her eyes and prayed for it to pass. She had to get out of here before she lost control.

A timid knock at the door drew her attention as a voice asked, "Excuse me? I hate to bother you, but could I ask you to zip me?"

Arianne's body trembled with desire, when she smelled the sweet, human scent so close now.

"Just a minute," she called.

She stepped to the mirror and opened her mouth wide, confirming her worst fear. Her fangs had fully protruded; their deadly tips glistened sharply. "I'll be right there," she said calmly.

When she opened the door, there was a young blonde standing outside, in a red satin dress held up in front by a slender, manicured hand. Her blush matched the crimson garment.

"I'm so sorry to intrude, but I can't reach the zipper. Would you mind?" She turned, and pulled her long hair to the side, exposing her bare neck.

Arianne reached out with shaking hands to accommodate. The throbbing pulse in the woman's throat beckoned to her. "This looks lovely on you. Just your color."

"Thanks. I wasn't sure if it was too…you know…red."

"Well, it *is* Christmas. Why not?"

"That's what I say." The woman seemed to relax.

Arianne felt the hunger burning within. Her jaws ached with desire to close around the creamy skin and drink. She zipped the dress and adjusted the silk trimmed collar. Her fingers brushed the spot where the pulse was strongest.

She fought the urge, but the longing was too great. She leaned close with her mouth open wide in anticipation of the first incredible rush of warmth.

Someone came into the hall, and Arianne quickly pulled back. A clerk carrying several blouses on hangers made her way toward Arianne.

"Here you go. I hope these are to your liking. I think the cranberry knit will compliment your coloring."

Puzzled at first by the sudden assistance, she saw it was Emelia.

The young girl thanked Arianne again and hurried to find a mirror.

Emelia's voice was a harsh whisper. "We have to get you out of here."

The feeling had passed, and Arianne changed her clothes quickly. Guilt filled her at the thought of what she'd almost done. Nausea rose in great writhing tides inside. She felt numb as Emelia led her to a chair in the footwear department and sat beside her.

"Just hold on for a minute. You'll feel better soon." Emelia stroked the hair from her cheek.

Arianne's hands were trembling ice as she searched her purse for car keys. Her eyes brimmed with tears and blurred her vision, finally causing her to give up. Her mother's hand rested on her own.

"It's okay to be frightened. But remember, you didn't hurt anyone."

"This time," Arianne choked out.

"You must do the procedure as soon as possible, or next time I might not be able to restrain you. Daylight has no power over you yet, and won't until you become vampire. If you should weaken during the daytime, there will be no stopping you."

Arianne nodded. "Everything is ready for the procedure, but I need to complete the cycle. I need to be vampire in order for it to work. But I can't make myself take a victim. I won't kill."

"You won't be able to stop it, Arianne. You see now how overpowering the desire can be. But you do not have to kill. There is another way."

"How? You said my teeth must pierce the skin."

"Yes, but if you only partake, the victim doesn't die."

"What does that mean?"

"You only take a small amount and the victim recovers without any real memory of the incident. However, they will slowly grow weak and disoriented, eventually going insane."

She watched in amazed horror as her mother described the act as if it were no more than the facts of life. In this case, they were the facts of death, and not an option.

Emelia's expression was grim. "I know your thoughts. To you I'm no more than an animal. But it is survival, nothing else. While it's true I've come to accept my life, and enjoy the immortality, I am not a killer at heart. When I came here, it was with the intention of finding my children and returning with them to Romania. I see that is not possible. You've built a life for yourself, as has Michael. For me to take that away would be equal to me losing my life with you so long ago. I love you both too much for that. Life is about choices, Arianne. Now, you must make yours."

Arianne looked at her mother for a long time. She saw the timeless beauty and knew it was hers for the taking. Yet her determined heart made it impossible to accept the gift. She believed in miracles and had faith in herself and her own convictions. There would be no sell-out.

"I won't do it," she said.

"Then you will die."

"Then so be it."

Her mother's voice was pleading. "I spoke with Michael and he's volunteered to let you take him."

"No. Leave him out of this he's done enough. Besides, the victim must be someone else or the cells with his DNA will be rejected. Don't you see, mother? It's hopeless."

In that moment, Arianne knew her fate as she had always known. There was nothing to save her dark soul.

* * *

Across town, Emelia's hotel room held the obscure silhouettes of furniture against the dim green light of the digital clock. A tall shadow moved easily in the darkness, a stealth creature of the night.

The intruder searched the drawers and nightstand and found what he'd come for. A thin smile grazed his lips as he read the name on the passport. It seemed *Olga* had entered the United States without the proper welcome. Something must be done about that. Justice must be served.

He pocketed the penlight and allowed his hand to brush the weapon at his side. It's cool steel was shocking against his skin. As he gently stroked it, he assured himself it wouldn't be long until the fires in his heart crying for atonement would be quenched. Very soon there would be one less vampire in the world.

* * *

By the time Arianne arrived home, her pain was so intense her mother had to carry her from the elevator. Michael met them at the door.

"What happened?"

"She's dying, Michael. There's not much time left." Emelia helped put her to bed, dressing her in a comfortable nightgown.

Arianne moaned at the shooting pains that burned her every movement. Her body felt leaden and she couldn't raise her head. A dim shadow moved above, gently caressing her face with a damp cloth.

"Mother?" She struggled to catch her breath.

"Yes, darling? It's me. What can I do for you?"

"Don't let me die alone."

Emelia held her hand at the bedside. "I won't let you die."

"It's too late. Just don't leave me."

The door pushed open then, and Destiny came in, howling softly at the commotion. The wolf licked Arianne's hand until she responded with an ear scratching.

"It's all right, baby. Mommy isn't feeling well, that's all."

Destiny whined as if to ask why, then lay down beside the bed.

"My four-legged child." Arianne tried to smile.

"Some day you'll have a baby of your own."

Arianne tried to object, but Emelia quieted her with a finger to her lips, as she continued, "Then you'll know how much I love you and why I can't let you go."

The room grew dim and Arianne felt as if she were moving down a slow-moving slide, feeling the darkness enfold her.

CHAPTER 35

Sounds of the Big Bopper *bopped* across the small fifties-style diner. The rancid smell of grease explained the severe wear and tear on the cook's pimply face. A waitress wearing a pink dress with a white apron slapped the bill face down on David's table mumbling, "Have a nice night," never breaking stride on her way to the next table.

He sat back in the red high-top booth trying to find a little breathing room after the big meal. Another greasy spoon, he thought with a frown. His dinner at Arianne's tomorrow sounded more enticing than ever. Concern crept through the veil of pleasant anticipation of their date. Arianne had looked so tired this morning in the lab. Her color was almost gray under the bright lights. The dark circles under her eyes haunted him, and when he'd touched her cheek, it had been ice cold.

A different kind of fear settled in his gut, not the usual on-the-job anxiety, but a deep overwhelming terror that comes from helplessness. It hit him harder that a sucker punch, and with just as much pain—what if Arianne died?

His cell phone rang twice before he fished it out of his coat pocket. "Spears."

The silence on the other end lasted only a few seconds before he heard Michael's voice. He sounded old and tired.

"David? I hate to bother you, but—"

"What is it? Where's Arianne?"

"She's bad. I don't know what to do except pray."

"I'm on my way." He pocketed the phone and started to scoot out of the booth when his pager went off. The department's number flashed across the small device's window. By the time he reached his car, the beeper went off again.

"Not this time," he said turning it off.

*   *   *

Arianne awoke and saw Michael at her bedside. He'd fallen asleep in the chair with a book propped open over his chest. Dear, sweet Michael, she thought. He'd proven a dedicated, loving brother. A small weight rested on her chest and she saw his beloved crucifix had been draped over her head.

When she reached for his arm, she saw how suddenly far way he seemed. The farther she stretched her fingers, the more distance spread between them. He seemed to be moving away from her.

"Michael?" Her voice was scratchy.

Suddenly she began to sink into the mattress.

"Michael!" Terror filled her when she wondered if she'd really screamed. Was she awake? Why didn't he hear her?

She clawed the edge of the mattress above her. It was sucking her in. Her hands slipped from their hold and it was too late to stop. The bedding closed over her face, stifling her scream.

This is death, she thought. The fear of life's last moments escaped her as she found the experience strangely comforting and somehow even peaceful. She wondered if she was about to be reborn into another life as the warm blackness cradled her.

The veil cut open above her and she slid through the shadows onto solid ground. Her bare feet pressed into spongy grass, soggy with dew and cool against her soles. The gripping pain was gone, along with the aching bones and nausea. The sky wore several pale shades of lavender and pink, although there didn't seem to be an actual sunset or for that matter, a sun.

In the distance, she saw what looked like a tall woman, bending low at the waist, with hair falling in great long tendrils to the ground. Arianne made her way across the wet sod, and found it wasn't a woman at all it was a weeping willow. The tree folded over the ground surrounding it with its soft green spirals bowing in submission.

As Arianne walked through the soft curtain branches, they seemed to caress her face. Her cheeks were damp with their dew and she tasted the droplets still clinging to her lips. Salty, like tears she decided, and brushed the wetness away. Near the huge trunk, she heard a low moaning, the wailing sound of a woman. There was no one near, only the tree, with its great groping fingers. The pitiful sound grew into sobs and she realized the tree was crying.

The branches became entangled around her neck and arms. When she tried to break free they tightened their grip. Leafy ropes held her fast as they wrapped about her ankles. She fought to break the vines, but it was no use. The arm-like branches shoved her back violently toward the trunk and she fell to the ground.

In the willow's torso was a tall mirror that reflected her image, yet it was different. The Arianne in the mirror moved independently like an animal trapped in a cage. She watched her move behind the glass in search of a way out. Her eyes were wild in terror as she pounded and screamed against the mirror.

Arianne pressed both palms to the glass and called to the woman. "Over here! I'm over here! Can you hear me?"

The woman kept hitting the barrier, now thrusting her full weight against it in an effort to break through. Arianne heard her muffled pitiful cries.

"I'm innocent," she screamed. "Help me!"

Arianne rapped fiercely. "I'm trying. I want to help you!"

"Please," her mirrored reflection begged. "Don't punish me. I'm not guilty!"

The word struck a cord, and she realized the one thing that could keep her from the cleansing her soul needed was guilt.

All at once the woman behind the glass stopped. Her face shifted into a stern expression with eyes glowing yellow. Her voice echoed fiercely as she spoke.

"You see the truth of what you are. It is denied no longer."

"No." Arianne backed away, trembling.

She watched the woman's skin turn a pasty shade. Her eyes sunk deep into pitted sockets. At last, she opened her mouth as if to scream, but instead she bared razor-sharp fangs.

A slicing pain shot through Arianne's foot as she looked down to see Michael's crucifix on the ground beside her foot. She grasped it by its top and saw it looked like a dagger in her hands.

The image behind the mirror hissed a raspy taunt, "You are me! There is no release. Be damned!"

Arianne's mind was a blur as the ill-fated words repeated in her head. She tried to see her as the pleading victim like before and recalled her declaration of not guilty. Then everything fell into place and she realized what she had to do. In order to break free of her life-long guilt, she must face the dark side and defeat it. No more running. She had to stand and fight.

Arianne rushed the mirror with the cross raised high. She brought it down hard against the glass and shattered the mirror into exploding shards.

* * *

Michael jerked awake to find his book on the floor beside Destiny. The wolf's sad eyes asked for an answer, an answer he didn't have. Arianne lay sleeping, but her skin was a dangerous shade of gray. Her face was covered in sweat, yet felt icy to the touch. He knelt on the floor beside her, clasped her stiffened fingers and began to pray. "My gracious heavenly Father, I pray for your mercy—"

The bed shook.

He stopped and looked around, but found no one. He closed his eyes and continued. "I come before Your throne with a humble spirit, seeking Your wise council—"

This time the floorboards buckled and he was tossed like a small boat at sea. He landed palms down against the floor, nearly hitting his face. A great moan blared throughout the room in deafening volume.

Michael forced himself back to Arianne's side to lay over her in protection. He raised his voice in the Lord's Prayer and shouted above the din.

"Sins of the father!" the groaning voice drowned his prayer.

Blood trickled down the walls as they writhed in and out. A sweet-sour stench filled Michael's nostrils causing him to gag. His knees slipped on the dark fluid flowing across the floor.

"...Thy will be done..." He continued to pray.

"Sins of the father!" The voice roared.

"...Lead us not into temptation..."

"Penance!"

"...but deliver us from evil..."

The walls heaved as though they would explode and wailed a mixture of anger and pain. Michael held tight to Arianne as Destiny howled a mournful cry of despair.

* * *

Arianne awoke in the quiet shadows of her room. Her brother's motionless silhouette remained in the chair close by. Destiny's warmth emanated beside her with his chin propped on her thigh. His eyes glistened against the white moonlight spreading through the room. She caressed the wolf's face and felt the comfort of unfaltering love and companionship. She knew she was home now, far from the willow's grip and the tormented apparition in the mirror. Her brother's crucifix remained in her hand, and it occurred to her, it had been more than a nightmare. The dream's frightening aura lingered even now, and she realized she'd crossed a threshold with no turning back. If she were to defeat the curse, she must face her dark side by becoming vampire.

Her hunger was dormant for now, but how long would she be able to control it? How long before she would give in to her vampire's lust and take her first victim? Hot tears rolled down her temples toward her pillow.

"There has to be another way," she cried softly.

Michael stirred in his sleep at the distant sound of the doorbell. Arianne already knew who it was. Her mind's eye saw David as he entered the living room and greeted Emelia. Their conversation seemed guarded with frequent glances toward the bedroom. David's expression showed concern as he listened to her mother.

Arianne left the bed and moved past Michael. Her strength had returned. She glimpsed her reflection in the dresser mirror and saw herself as the woman in the dream, the same pale skin and haunted eyes. She craved the taste of warm blood now, as the sensation coiled up from her center and move to her throat. A slow snarl curled the edges of her lip when her fangs caught the bright moonlight. She stepped back from the mirror and waited in the shadows. The sweet human scent just outside the door would soon sate her ravenous craving.

* * *

A single lamp, creating a dim glow, lighted Arianne's living room. Emelia continued her explanation to David as she paced before the patio windows.

"If Arianne doesn't become full vampire tonight, she will die. No one will be able to save her."

David glanced toward the closed bedroom door, unable to shake the sensation he was being watched. When he turned back to Emelia, he saw the pain etched on her face, and heard the torment in her voice.

"I know you are a man of the law, and I don't expect you to condone what must be done. But there is no other way, David, Arianne must take a victim."

He tossed his jacket onto the couch and headed toward the bedroom.

"Where are you going?"

"Making good on my promise to serve and protect."

* * *

Yellow light cut across the room as the door slowly opened. Arianne sniffed the air like a wolf when the silhouette entered. She knew it was David.

"Who's there?" Michael's voice came abruptly.

"It's David. I need to see you in the hallway."

Arianne heard the muffled voices rise and fall just beyond the door, with Michael's becoming more high-pitched as the conversation went on. A brief lull alerted her they were finished, and she crouched on the bed in defense. She'd never felt paranoia like this before, but realized it could be a necessary ally for a vampire.

David entered the room and closed the door behind him. "Arianne?"

She watched his shadow move closer.

"Arianne, it's David. Are you awake?"

Her senses perceived calm, yet she heard his heart pound hard. She sensed he feared her and that meant he was probably unarmed.

She turned on the bedside lamp. His gaze fell over her, taking in the changes with a subtlety reserved for seasoned cops. No breathy gasp or cringing shoulders, only a brief, almost undetected widening of the eyes. Then it was gone and he moved toward her. The first two buttons of his shirt were undone and the collar pushed aside. Something stirred within as she watched the throbbing pulse in his neck. She forced her eyes closed and tried to avoid the temptation. *This is David, the man I love.*

She held up her hands. Her voice was raspy and harsh. "David, stop. Get out before it's too late."

"It's already too late, Arianne. You're dying."

"Please leave me. Please."

"I can't do that. I'm in love with you."

His arms enfolded her, drawing her close.

She fought the urge, but it was too powerful. "David, go. I can't stop this."

"I know, and I'm not afraid."

He pressed his lips to hers tenderly, with the lightest touch, then trailed seductively down her neck. She melted into his embrace, and felt his gentle, yet firm hold. It felt as though he'd never let her go and she knew she didn't want him to.

As she kissed him back, she felt the searing hunger return and consume her. The sweet taste of his skin rolled over her tongue as her fangs grazed his neck. She allowed him to pull her on top as they lay back onto the bed. Their eyes met as she bent to kiss him once more, and whispered against his ear, "Please forgive me."

She found the throbbing place on his throat and sunk her fangs deep. His skin yielded like warm butter, the liquid heat pouring swiftly into her mouth. She closed her eyes, and drank deep, savoring the taste.

His grip loosened as she drank, and finally let go altogether. The throbbing continued against her lips. She felt it grow weak. David was dying, but she couldn't tear herself away.

A sudden vice grip on her shoulders yanked her from David's throat. Blood streamed from his neck and onto the bedspread. Arianne fought her mother's restraint, but Emelia was much stronger.

"Get him out of here," Emelia ordered Michael.

Arianne leaned back against her mother. Her vision spun out of focus and nausea curdled her stomach. "I'm dying." Her voice was barely audible. "Hold me, I…can't…do this."

Emelia stroked her forehead. "You aren't dying. You're being born."

CHAPTER 36

Arianne was aware of being held for what seemed like a very long time. Each tick of the nightstand clock echoed into a long pause before the next one. Her respiration was as distinct as a balloon being blown up then slowly released. Gradually, she felt her heightened senses and strength return to normal. She turned to Emelia, whose eyes were a blaze of azure ice. Did she see fear or pride in them? Arianne couldn't tell.

Emelia's tone bespoke confidence. "You will soon be full vampire. I can see the changes in you already. Don't fight it, simply let them come."

Before Emelia finished speaking, Arianne pulled out of her mother's arms and fell to her knees. She was racked by the burning sensation of acid pouring through her. With each gasp for breath she saw scenes of her life from cradle to the present flashing by as one tremendous film reel. Strange voices beckoned from beyond the grave and wailed her name in unison as she watched visions of decayed corpses claw their way out of their cemetery plots. The fetid stench of rotted skin and embalming fluid flooded the air. The walls of her bedroom cried blood and then tears, eventually fading away. Her ivory nightgown was tinged pink at the hem.

Emelia seemed to be frozen in place and offered no readable expression. Finally, the strange effects ended and her bedroom returned to normal. Arianne experienced a powerful surge of strength and clarity she'd never imagined. She saw the crumpled bed linens where she'd taken David and she was consumed with remorse.

"Where's David? Where did Michael take him?"

"He's resting. He'll need time to regain his strength, but he'll be all right."

Arianne hung her head. "He'll go mad."

Emelia didn't answer.

"How long does he have?"

Her mother looked away. "Weeks, months maybe. Plenty of time to cleanse him with the procedure."

"I wish he'd never come. He didn't deserve this."

"No one forced him, Arianne. He wanted to do it for you because he loves you. But for now, you must sleep. The sun will rise soon."

Arianne peered out into the black winter night. "Where will I stay now?"

"Michael will tape the windows with black plastic. The shades and curtains will cover the rest. I'll be leaving now, and won't return until tonight."

Arianne stared at the bloodstained sheets. "The procedure will be at the lab this evening. The cultures can only survive one more day."

As Emelia turned to go, Arianne said, "I don't want to feed again, Mother. Promise me you won't allow it."

"I promise you." Then she was gone.

* * *

A major-league headache, stiff neck, and complete disorientation led David to believe he was in the middle of a very bad hangover. Bright sunlight flooded the room through patio windows and somewhere in the misty twilight of waking, he thought he heard a door close.

He winced as he sat up, and rubbed his neck. He felt two small scabs. What had he gotten into last night? It must have been one helluva fight, he decided, seeing his sidearm on the coffee table. A good ol' fashioned fist-a-cuffs.

The strong aroma of coffee lifted his awareness and he realized he was in Arianne's living room and that he needed a shower and clean clothes. First things first, and clear the old head with a cup of java. He jumped at Michael's voice.

"David, you're awake. Would you like some coffee?"

"Please," he heard himself say past the ringing in his ears. He tried to recall the previous evening and buried his face in his palms. He remembered eating at the diner and getting a call. After that, it was pretty much a blank hard-drive.

Michael came back with two mugs. He wore the expression of a parishioner about to make confession. His silence spoke volumes.

David fought for his bearings and allowed the first steaming sip to take effect. Finally, he asked, "What happened?"

Michael leaned his elbows on his knees and met David's stare with tired eyes. Apparently it had been a rough night for him, too.

"How much do you remember?"

David shook his head. "Not much. Where's Arianne?"

"Resting." He nodded toward the closed bedroom door. "You were bitten last night, David."

He ran a hand through his tousled hair, and tried to bring up the memory. "And?"

"She's full vampire now."

"Thanks to me." David felt his liquid breakfast churning in his stomach. "Is she all right?"

"Fine, as far as I can tell."

"So what happens now?"

Michael sighed. "You should start feeling better soon. The blood loss you experienced was little more than giving blood."

"So where's my o.j. and cookies?"

Michael chuckled, but it didn't sound sincere. His expression grew serious. "The procedure must be done tonight or the cultures won't be any good. Once Arianne is back on her feet, you'll need to undergo the same process."

"Or what?"

"Or you'll eventually lose your mind."

"Pardon me, Father, but I'm a homicide detective. That can't be a very far stretch."

"Seriously, David. You'll go mad."

"How much time do I have?"

"Emelia said it would be weeks or months. Time enough."

"Right," David said, draining the mug. "That gives me time to settle the matter of murder." He stood. "Can I bother you for a hot shower and change of clothes?"

"Certainly. And, David?"

"Yeah?"

"Thank you."

He stared at Michael for a moment, wondering what he was

thanking him for, then simply nodded and headed for the shower.

His bare feet sunk into the thick peach carpet of Michael's bedroom as he viewed the clothes on the bed. Not bad taste, for a priest, he concluded and dropped the towel from around his waist. The hot water had cleared his head and he felt his energy returning. He still had no memory of the night before. When he checked the mirror, he saw the undeniable proof he'd been bitten and pulled the shirt collar up higher.

David raised his eyebrows at the new look. No doubt, heads were going to turn when he entered the department this morning. The chief would be especially impressed with the gray turtleneck and black jeans, but then, he'd probably put him on desk-duty anyway, for ignoring the pages last night.

At the window, he tested the sunlight on his face for ill effects. What were the dangers after being bitten? Perhaps he'd pick up a pamphlet at the free clinic later just to be sure. Somehow, he realized it wasn't funny and he suddenly felt very alone, the way Arianne probably felt every day. His hand grazed his face. No smoldering skin or pus infested boils, instead the warmth felt good. He'd never appreciated the sun like today.

As David passed Arianne's cluttered desk on his way out, he noticed a stack of papers on top. He recognized them as the documents Dr. Brewster had translated. They were the valid proof she was daughter of Emelia and Vladimir and had a brother as well. These papers had started the proverbial ball rolling full speed into the catastrophic events that followed. Perhaps, in more ways than originally thought, he realized as he picked up the receipt on top. The crumpled yellow carbon showed the translation service fee. At the bottom, there was a neatly scrawled signature, not likely made by a doctor. Jimmy Stolo had signed it. Apparently, Brewster had his lab tech pick up the documents for him. Had Jimmy peeked inside and found the truth before turning them over? Even if he had, it didn't prove anything. Or did it?

* * *

The sickening smell of room deodorizer couldn't cover the lingering human scent in Emelia's hotel room. Tonight the scent was fresh. She shook the feeling, convinced she was imagining things. Still, there was that smell.

As she dressed for bed, she thought of Arianne now sleeping in the blackened tomb of her bedroom. Would she miss the sun's glow or its final dance toward slumber in the evening? It hadn't been easy to give up that beauty in her own life; she'd always loved the sunshine on her face. In time, she'd learned to enjoy the moon's white light falling over her and the shadowy fields each night as she rode Borak. The familiar evening light offered an almost romantic illumination for the night-dwellers, both human and otherwise. If Arianne's procedure failed, she would be one for eternity.

She settled herself under her protective coverlet, and felt the trance-like state fall over her, taking her to the place where only vampires go in their twilight sleep; the place where they are most vulnerable.

Suddenly, Emelia awoke. She sensed the human scent close by. Her eyes saw the intruder clearly beside the bed, with his curved dagger poised above her heart. She fought to regain her cat-like reflexes, but was not fast enough. The blade descended.

Before she could react, she saw fingers grip the man's throat and lift him from the floor. Emelia watched as the attacker sailed like a rag doll across the bed and slammed into the wall. He recovered quickly and was back on his feet with the dagger's blade ready to strike.

Fully awake now, Emelia focused on her savior and realized it was Vladimir. His eyes were black ice as he met the intruder with a powerful thrust kick, and sent him backwards against the door. The attacker scrambled to his feet and groped for the doorknob. Before Vladimir reached him, he pulled it open and was gone. Calmly, Vladimir closed the door and latched it.

Emelia touched the spot where the blade had sliced her skin and watched it close up without a trace. She rushed to Vladimir, who held her tight.

"How did you know?" she asked against his cheek. "What are you doing here?"

"My dark conscience led me to believe you and Arianne are in great danger. I had to come."

"Shylock?"

He nodded.

"Where is he now?"

"He's at peace. I gave him his freedom. He served me well."

"I don't believe he did."

"You underestimated him. Shylock convinced me of the true dangers you face. He risked his eternity to make me see the error of my ways. For that I had to repay him. When I realized he spoke the truth, I had no choice but to see to your safety. I was a fool to let you come alone."

"But how did you get past the Jen-Ku?"

"I know you don't want to believe it, but Shylock helped a great deal. The important thing is that we're together. Have you seen Arianne?"

"Yes...she's become full vampire but..."

"But what?"

Emelia explained the procedure as best she could, not fully understanding the science behind it, only that it had the potential to release her daughter from the curse.

Vladimir listened intently, his expression serious. When she'd finished, he remained silent, as if deep in thought. Finally, he said, "This procedure, how do we know it will work?"

"We don't. It has only proven successful on one person. And, of course, the woman was not a vampire. But it's Arianne's only hope."

"If it fails?"

"She will remain vampire."

He frowned. "A fate we would share without enthusiasm, I'm afraid. Nevertheless, she is vampire and must return to Romania. It isn't safe for her here."

"Arianne has made it clear she will not feed again. If she doesn't, she'll die, Vladimir. She is your daughter, so much like you in finding no joy in her immortality."

"And you have accepted her decision?"

"Yes. I respect her wishes. It's the only way I can prove my love for her."

"And what about Michael?"

She hesitated. "He's a priest."

"There was a time when that would have made me very happy. Now there is no hope to gain his love."

"You're wrong, Vladimir. He loves us still. We have found our children after all the suffering and loss. We finally have them back. But we can't have them the way we wanted. They will not join us. I guess I've come to accept that after seeing how happy Arianne is in her life. She is content without immorality. We have to let her go, let them both go."

Vladimir nodded. "Then let it be. But we must be extremely cautious now that the Jen-Ku have found *us*."

Emelia spied the attacker's weapon near the door and picked it up. She ran a finger along the blade and eyed it carefully. "Perhaps not."

"What do you mean?"

She turned it slowly back and forth. "This dagger is not Jen-Ku."

CHAPTER 37

Sunday at the precinct was no less hectic, but seemed relatively quiet today. David hit enter once more on his computer and swore under his breath.

"I heard that," George Johnson called from his desk nearby. He frowned at David and came up beside him with coffee sloshing over the rim of a dingy cup. "Hey, what's with the duds, Spears? Not your usual style."

"At least I have some," David countered.

"Looks like somebody's not gettin' enough, and with those clothes it's no wonder."

David let the banter drop. He didn't have time.

George leaned over and scanned the roster of names from the Research Center, sipping his coffee.

He pointed an ink stained finger at the page. "Stolo, huh? Sounds like it's short for something."

"What do you mean?"

"You know. Like it's been chopped off or something. A lot of people do that when their name's too long—they just shorten it. Makes life easier for everyone."

David double-checked his notes and nodded. "You're right. Jimmy Stolo is actually James Stolojan. No priors, no unusual background at all."

"Why the name change? Stolojan isn't that bad. By the way, what is that, German?"

"Good question." David reached for the background information he'd collected. He thumbed through the papers and wrapped the last one hard. "Look at this. James Stolojan, age twenty-five, born in the U.S. to *Romanian* immigrant parents!"

"So?" George looked confused.

"So...no one else had access to the Romanian documents Brewster was holding or has the ethnic background that might allow him to read them. If Jimmy's prints are on those papers, I can get a warrant to search his place."

"He doesn't have any priors. How can you match the prints?"

David reached for the phone. "Every Research Center employee has been printed for security purposes."

* * *

When David's suspicions turned out to be correct, he found himself knocking on his old partner's door once again.

"Jesus, Spears. Twice in one week?" Bulldog stepped aside to let him in.

This time the living room was filled with the sounds of the big band era, with Glenn Miller leading. As he followed his former partner into the kitchen, he noted a hot, tangy aroma, like Cajun. His white T-shirt resembled the aftermath of a horror scene and he wondered how many tomatoes had given their lives in the name of a good sauce.

"Have a seat, Spears." Bulldog motioned toward one of the bar stools beside the counter. "Would you like a drink? Pepsi, or something?"

"I'll get it." David helped himself in the refrigerator.

"So what's up? You've got that hungry look in your eye."

David popped the top and sat on the stool. "I need a quick search warrant."

"How quick?" He stirred the bubbling contents of a large pot on the stove.

"An hour ago."

"And you think I've got one ready?" Bulldog chuckled and wiped his hands on a nearby towel. "I'm not *that* good."

"C'mon, Gunther. I know you still have connections. Somebody out there must owe you a favor. This could break the case, or I could lose it altogether. Time is crucial."

"Gumbo?" The man held up a large dripping ladle. "It'll put lead in your pencil."

"No, thanks."

"Suit yourself." He heaped a hearty portion into a bowl.

"Gunther, what about the warrant?"

Bulldog sat next to him and began eating. David watched his eyes water as the first taste kicked in.

The man wiped his chin and mumbled, "Don't sweat it. I think I can help you. However," he raised a pudgy index finger, "it's going to cost you."

"Doesn't it always?" David grinned.

"No, *really* cost you."

"What's the catch?"

"I want in."

"In?"

"On the action. The chase. These four walls and this happy homemaker shit just aren't getting it for me."

"You're coming out of retirement?"

"Not officially. But I *have* been toying with the idea of my own private investigation service. This would be as good a jump-start as any. So, what do you say?"

"The hot sauce has cooked your common sense. What about your heart?"

"Vegetating on the couch is far worse for circulation than chasing sickos. You said yourself you could use my eagle-eye."

"You won't do this any other way?"

"Course I will. I'm just asking you as my friend."

David mentally weighed the request, and considered the health risks as well as working with a partner again. He'd been a lone wolf since Bulldog retired and preferred it that way. For one brief, shattering moment, he pictured himself in Bulldog's situation and felt the pain. The loneliness.

David handed him the phone. "Looks like we need a warrant, partner. Do your magic."

*   *   *

Voices...familiar voices coming closer from down a long tunnel...

Arianne awoke to blackness. Slowly, her eyes adjusted, and she saw her bedroom clearly through a sheer gray veil. Nothing seemed to escape her attention, her senses were magnified beyond measure, even her skin tingled as she arose. Very aware of tremendous energy and strength within, she was also aware of something else—hunger. The gnawing sensation for blood grew stronger at the sound of voices outside, and she went to the door to listen. She recognized her mother and Michael, and struggled to place a third, deep, unfamiliar voice. The conversation lulled and she sensed they knew she was awake, both Emelia and the other man. She seemed to connect with their minds and heard them beckon to her. Then she realized the man was her father.

Michael was speaking when she opened the door. "Father. We finally meet."

"Not for the first time, my son. There was a time when you called to me with great love."

"So much has happened." Michael's voice broke.

"I'm still you're father. I do love you. I can't help what I am."

"My divine Father teaches us not to judge. You were a victim in my eyes. We'll have to learn to put the rest behind us."

Arianne felt the warmth between them and knew they'd bonded after so many years. She joined them, uncertain of what to expect. The familiar surroundings of her living room took on a surreal quality, almost as if they belonged to someone else in a different place and time. While she felt strangely removed, she also felt in full control, and alert to every sight, smell, and sound.

"Arianne." Her mother saw her first.

She looked past her, and realized her father was just as she'd pictured him. His salt and pepper hair gave him a distinguished air; his facial structure and nose reminded her of hers. His black eyes drew her to him.

"Father?"

"Yes, Arianne. I'm here."

She folded into his embrace, and rested her head against his chest.

He pressed his cheek to the top of her head. "I'm so sorry you have to go through this. If I could have saved your mother any other way—"

"You did it out of tremendous love, Father. I understand that now."

"Yes, but the pain and torment it's caused. I'm responsible for it all."

"You're responsible for nothing. You were a victim, too. But now there's hope we can defeat this curse and be free. If it works, you can have your old life back, we all can." She turned toward her mother.

Emelia's expression remained unreadable. "We should be going to the lab now, before your hunger becomes too great."

Arianne held her mother's gaze to remind her of her earlier promise not to let her feed. She prayed she would be true to her word.

"Perhaps I should go in first in case of the Jen-Ku," Michael said.

Vladimir nodded. "Yes, we're extremely vulnerable tonight with three of us. The Jen-Ku would have quite a victory at our destruction. Your mother and I will stand guard during the procedure, but I'm afraid you must do it as quickly as possible. The longer we're there, the more likely they'll attack."

Arianne looked at Michael. "It won't take long once we get started, I'll have help from my lab tech. "

"All right then, let's get going." Vladimir led the way.

Michael moved close taking Arianne's arm. "Are you ready?"

She nodded. "I want to get this over with before the hunger gets too strong."

"Remember, I'm here for you, and I won't leave you. Sometimes we must face the darkness to see the light. But you won't be alone."

"I know, Michael, and I love you for it." She squeezed his hand. "It's time."

Michael's words filled her mind as they headed for the lab. He was right—she wasn't confronting this alone. Many lives depended on it.

* * *

David tucked the warrant inside his jacket pocket as he got into the Camaro. The low-bodied vehicle sunk considerably as Bulldog nearly fell into the passenger seat.

"Jesus, Spears, you need an elevator to reach the bottom of this thing." He grunted as he stretch the seatbelt over his paunch.

"Suits me fine. It moves when I need it to. Now are you going to whine like a little girl or should we get going?"

"Hit it," he said.

David saw the squad secured in front of the apartment building and headed inside with a couple of officers and crime lab technician. Bulldog nodded to his old coworkers as David motioned for the small group to follow him.

He pounded on the door and announced their business. When no one answered, the men forcefully entered the apartment with guns drawn. It wasn't long before they realized the dwelling was empty.

Jimmy's apartment was quiet, save for the soothing sound of a bubbling fish tank.

They moved along the darkened hallway that led to a rather spacious living room and kitchen. Jimmy's decorating tastes were young bachelor, with a vinyl sectional couch, glass tables, and framed posters of the original Soldier Field for artistic flair.

The two officers who'd gone ahead of David came back into the living room. "There's no one here," the taller one said.

"What a dump," Bulldog concluded. "No recliner."

"Why don't you take this area while I check the bedrooms?"

David headed past the cramped bathroom to search the master bedroom first. Experience had taught him it was usually the best place to start. People liked to keep their prized possessions and deepest secrets close, but out of easy reach to others. Their bedrooms provided for both.

The queen-size bed was unmade with a black and maroon comforter entangled with cream-colored sheets. The room was fairly kept, except for the bed. Perhaps Jimmy had over-slept and left in a hurry.

He rifled through the double closet and dresser drawers, and found nothing unusual, nothing linking Jimmy to anything except the not-so-good housekeeping award.

Suddenly, Bulldog's voice barreled from down the hall. "What the hell?"

David found him standing outside the spare bedroom.

"What did you find?"

"The reason cops like us get up every mornin'. The taste of victory."

CHAPTER 38

Arianne and Michael entered the lab with Emelia and Vladimir standing guard in the hallway. Michael had checked the lab first and found it clear.

Arianne fought the building urge for blood and hurried to get started.

"Is there anything I can do to help?" Michael asked.

"Not now, but keep an eye open for anything strange. Don't get too close. Your scent is starting to affect me."

Looking hurt, he backed up a few steps.

"Don't take it personally, big brother. Everyone has a scent. I didn't say you stink." She offered a teasing grin that she didn't really feel. Right now, it was all she could do to keep her nerve, but she didn't want Michael to fear her when she needed him the most.

Jimmy came out of the back room with the vial containing the culture cells, and placed it carefully on the tray beside the mock surgical table, which was nothing more than a long wheeled cart and a sheet. Masks, gowns, and gloves were ready on a nearby table to ensure a clean environment. It wasn't a surgical suite, but under the circumstances, it would have to do.

Arianne nodded a silent greeting to her assistant as she double-checked the syringes and vials. Satisfied everything was in order, she glanced over at Michael. He'd gone pale, seated on a lab stool next to a counter, nervously tapping his foot. Her gaze moved to the door where she knew her parents stood waiting. So much depended on this procedure, there was no backing out. The longing to feed was more than uncomfortable now, painfully tearing at her throat. It was time to end this.

When they'd all donned their masks, she boosted herself up onto the cart, and rolled up her sleeve. "Do you remember everything, Jimmy? If not, now is the time to say so and I'll review it."

"I've got it all in here," he smiled, tapping a temple.

"Once I'm sedated, I won't be much help to you. At that point you'll be pretty much on your own. Just monitor my blood pressure and keep the IV running at the lowest possible rate. Okay?"

"No problem."

She drew up the correct amount of cultured DNA cells into one syringe and the sedative in the other. "Everything's ready, Jimmy. Go ahead and start the IV."

He put on a gown and sterile gloves with a nervous glance first toward Michael and then at the door. A thin line of perspiration had formed over his brows as he tightened the tourniquet into place. "Here we go, Dr. Brasov. This won't hurt a bit."

* * *

David's jaw dropped as his eyebrows rose. It was rare for him to be out-and-out surprised. He'd seen many strange scenes over the years, but this one definitely caught him off guard.

The room held no signs of residence. No bed. No dresser. Instead, a large, makeshift altar sat against the far wall in front of the windows. On the wall to his right, several items hung from nails, crudely pounded into the drywall—a black sleeveless tunic with black pants, a pastoral collar of royal purple, both exactly like Mandari's. Beside them was a curved dagger, probably ordered from some weapon magazine and definitely *not* like Mandari's. While it was cheaply made, it would certainly do the intended job. Was this the murder weapon used on Brewster?

"Jeez, would you look at this?" Bulldog said viewing the altar.

It was covered with melted wax from over fifty pure white candles across the back. In front of them appeared to be a shrine of some sort with a framed picture of Jimmy. David bent for a closer look and saw it wasn't Jimmy at all. The man in the photo was several years older, but with the same facial features, he could have easily passed for his brother.

Bulldog covered the closet doorknob with a hanky and opened it.

"Empty."

On the floor in the opposite corner, David noticed a manila envelope with papers sticking out. He put on a pair of rubber gloves, compliments of the coroner's office, and picked it up. He didn't read very far before he recognized the documents as copies of the ones Brewster had held for Arianne. As he leafed through them he found the birth certificate with Emelia's name listed as mother, circled in red ink. He headed for the master bedroom with Bulldog close on his heels.

David dropped to his knees in front of the closet and began taking out a dozen pairs of shoes. He reached deep into the corner and grabbed the last pair. The tattered old sneakers had seen better days with frayed shoes strings and missing eye holders. Flipping them over, David saw what he'd dreaded but suspected.

Bulldog bent closer, hands on knees. "Would you look at that? The damned soles are partially melted!"

"Yeah, could be from a chemical spill."

"What kind of chemical melts rubber?"

"Acid. Like Dr. Brewster was splashed with."

On the tip of the right shoe, stuck into the sole, was a small blue paper fragment. David recognized it at once as part of a surgical bootie like the fragment found in Paul Bently's place. He motioned for the evidence tech to bag it, while he headed for the front door.

"Come on, let's move," David called out to Bulldog.

"Hey, where you going?" Bulldog huffed along behind.

"To get to Arianne before it's too late."

* * *

Bulldog had barely closed his door when the Camaro took off. The shiny black bullet sped toward the lab as David punched Arianne's number on his cell phone.

"Damn! No answer. They must have left already."

"What about back-up?"

"Can't do that. If they go busting in there during the procedure, Arianne's chances are gone. Besides, we don't know what the situation inside the lab is. If things are relatively calm, I'd like to keep them that way. We'll be there in five minutes."

He tried calling the lab, but got no answer. He pressed the accelerator. "We'll go in through the back. You can cover me from behind."

Bulldog huffed indignantly, his eyes not quite meeting David's.

"Cover you with what?"

"That cannon you've got stuck in your holster. What's it, a .45?"

Looking sheepish, Bulldog tugged at his jacket for better concealment. "Yeah. When I turned in my rank and pride, I decided to keep just *one* memento of the job. This was it. Ol' Betty and I have seen some tough spots, but she's never let me down. Kind of like you and me. I just hope I don't let you down tonight."

"You'll do fine."

"It was kind of ballsy of me to insist on coming along after being out so long. I know what this case means to you."

"We're almost there. Don't get cold feet on me, now."

David slowed for a traffic jam and then went around toward the intersection. Just as he reached it, he slammed on the brakes as a small import collided with a minivan. Glass shattered and fragments of twisted metal went airborne.

A horn blared continuously as the unconscious driver in the import lay slumped against the steering wheel. People ran to aide, as David jumped out and yelled for Bulldog to radio for help. He flashed his badge as he tried to maintain calm and prevent further injuries.

By the time he reached the import, the driver was stumbling out with the help of two men. His bleary eyes and disoriented expression told David he was either in shock or very drunk. He hoped it was the former.

Suddenly, a bystander screamed as the front of the minivan caught fire, filling the inside with dark gray smoke. David saw a small set of palms pressed up against one of the side windows, and the silhouette of a little girl. When he reached the van, he watched in horror as the child beat the glass with her tiny fists behind her muffled cries. The smoke was too thick to see anyone else inside.

David yanked at the door handles, but they were all locked. He realized he had little time.

"David! Try this." Bulldog came running with a tire iron.

David called to the child in hopes she would hear him. "Get back from the window! I'm going to break it. Cover your head!"

There was no response. The tiny palms had disappeared from the window.

With a forceful swing, he shattered the window. Putrid smoke poured out as David reached inside and unlocked the door. He crawled inside to find the child huddled on the floor behind the driver's seat.

"Mommy! Mommy!"

David picked her up gently and rushed her to the first paramedic unit on the scene.

A burst of flames shot up from the engine as David raced back to the van.

"Wait!" A medic yelled, "The fire trucks are arriving now!"

"There's no time," he called back.

David could see the slumped figure of a woman behind the wheel. Much of the smoke had cleared, allowing him to see there was no one else in the van. He squeezed between the two front seats, unlatched her seatbelt, and pulled her out through the passenger side. He'd only taken a few steps away, when the van exploded into flames

Bulldog grabbed him securely, and led him toward the ambulance. "C'mon, David. We gotta get you checked out."

David couldn't stop coughing. He took several cleansing breaths and pushed ahead. "I'm fine. I need to get to the lab. Can you stay here and help out for me?"

Bulldog's expression was solid. David saw the old Gunther Monroe return. He nodded. "You bet."

David watched him force his way through the crowd to take charge. With precious moments lost, he hurried from the scene. He hoped it wasn't too late.

CHAPTER 39

Jimmy's voice sounded far away. Arianne wondered briefly where she was and why she couldn't move her arms. She focused her eyes with great effort and felt like she wanted to give up and just sleep. Something told her that would mean certain death. She squinted under the bright lights at the blurred image overhead. Then the voice came again, this time clearer.

"How are you doing, Dr. Brasov?" Jimmy asked.

"So...sleepy," she said with a cottony feeling in her mouth.

"I'm getting ready to start," he leaned close, "but before I do, you should know I've been looking forward to this moment for a very long time."

"You...have?" She forced her eyes open again.

"Yes. Although, I feel bad that I have to kill you, it is necessary."

Her memory started to clear and she recalled what was happening. She saw Michael across the lab on the stool with his head bent in prayer. He had no idea what was going on.

She tried to call for him, but only managed a light croaking sound. He couldn't hear her.

Jimmy's face loomed closer yet. "Today is the day of atonement. You are about to pay the price for your mother's evil."

Michael called to Jimmy, "How's it coming over there?"

"Everything is going as planned. She's resting comfortably and I'll be starting in just a moment."

Arianne strained to lift her head and try to catch her brother's attention, but Jimmy moved into her line of vision.

"I've always heard that doctors aren't good patients. Now, try and cooperate, Dr. Brasov."

"Why are you doing...this?" she managed to ask.

His laugh was incredulous. "You really don't know, do you? But then, how could you when you just recently became full vampire? Yes, Dr. Brasov, I know all about you and your work with Dr. Brewster. I know why you are here tonight. It has nothing to do with a blood disease like you told me. But Dr. Brewster can't help you now."

"*You* killed him."

"No. Your mother did."

The world was growing fuzzy again and Arianne struggled to hold on. She felt a breathy whisper against her ear and shuddered as he spoke.

"Your mother is responsible for Brewster and Bently's deaths because she murdered my brother. It is because of her evil they had to die."

"But why?"

"Dr. Brewster was helping you. Hell, he found the cure! I couldn't let that happen. Poor Paul just happened to find out the truth about what I was doing and had to be dealt with. You see I want Emelia to suffer the loss of someone she loves, like I did. My mother died of a broken heart after my brother was killed. Now it's time to serve justice."

She watched in sickening dread as he held the syringe containing the cultured DNA cells and wasted it onto the floor.

"Very soon, your mother will die of a broken heart, too, when I hand her yours."

Arianne fought to stay awake as he held a scalpel overhead. The instrument gleamed against the bright lights as it lowered to her chest.

* * *

Emelia glanced at the wall clock in the hallway. The procedure seemed to be taking longer than planned. She watched her husband's grim expression grow more tense as time went on.

She tried to reassure him. "It shouldn't be too much longer."

"Perhaps we should check."

"I don't want to disrupt anything. Besides, Michael..."

She stopped as an inaudible cry reached her mind. "Arianne?" Emelia whispered in response.

Vladimir suddenly lifted his chin, at a scent he'd not detected a moment ago. "Jen-Ku," he said, turning back.

Emelia rushed into the lab, with Vladimir following, and stopped short at the sight before her.

Jimmy stood beside Arianne holding a scalpel, dripping with blood. His eyes were wide, and fixed on a man dressed in black with a curved dagger. A Jen-Ku priest.

"Don't come any closer, or I'll cut out her heart," Jimmy warned.

Michael tried to push past the priest, but the man grabbed his arm and stopped him.

The man's tone was firm, as spoke to the lab tech. "I am Mandari, a Jen-Ku like your brother. Don't do this, Jimmy. Step back and leave her."

"If you were truly Jen-Ku, you wouldn't ask that. She's a vampire!"

"It is not your place." Mandari took an easy step forward.

Jimmy's eyes were full of hate as he looked at Emelia. "You killed my brother by turning him into a vampire! I had to be his replacement. That's why I tried to be like the Jen-Ku. Because of your evil, I lost everything. Now you will know what it is to lose someone precious to you."

Mandari moved closer. "Your brother died doing what he was born to do. It was an honorable death. Do not disgrace his memory by this act of vengeance." Mandari was now close enough to reach the tech, but remained still. His dagger hung at his side, readily available.

Jimmy glanced at it and licked his lips nervously. He put down the scalpel. "You're right. This isn't the way to do this at all." He yanked the dagger from Mandari's belt, slicing him across the stomach. The priest doubled over and fell to the floor, blood pouring through his fingers as he held his abdomen.

Emelia rushed forward, but stopped when Jimmy poised the dagger over Arianne's chest.

Suddenly, the back door of the lab opened and Roger came in looking confused. "Hey, what's goin' on?"

Jimmy smiled a twisted grin of pain. "You're just in time to see justice served, Roger." He plunged the dagger in deep as gunshots pierced the room.

Jimmy's white smock splattered bright red. His eyes widened as he bucked backwards and fell. He was dead before his head hit the floor, crunching like an eggshell.

David holstered his gun and ran to Arianne.

Emelia pulled the dagger from her daughter's chest and watched as the gaping wound slowly sealed itself.

Michael crossed himself. "What now? The cultured cells are destroyed."

Roger had gone pale and leaned against the counter. "There's...another...vial."

"What do mean?" Michael asked.

"Dr. B had me hold on to one, although at the time I didn't know why."

"Then we can still do the procedure?" David asked.

Roger shrugged, looking more like the himself. "Sure. She explained it to me. Said she wanted to be sure I understood what to do in case something happened. Guess I was her insurance."

Arianne stirred and slowly opened her eyes.

"It's all right," David assured her. "It's all over, you're safe."

Emelia took her other hand. "Don't be afraid. Your new life is just about to begin. Your true destiny."

CHAPTER 40

Days later, Arianne awoke to the sweet high sounds of waltz music from another era, with a harpsichord and violins riding the romantic, graceful melody. Her bedroom was warm with sunlight and the rich scent of roses as she got out of bed. The thick peach carpet hugged her bare feet as she made her way toward the living room and followed the music. She heard a deep voice murmuring and thought of David, but she realized it wasn't him. Then the blushing tone of a woman's voice followed, and Arianne hurried to see what was going on.

The living room furniture had been pushed back to make room for dancing, and the balcony drapes were open with the sun's light shining like a wide spotlight. A man and woman held close in a lover's embrace, swirled effortlessly about the room, laughing and smiling, their gazes locked upon each other.

As the couple rounded the room once more, Arianne caught a glimpse of the familiar long chin and flashing dark eyes. It was Shylock. She watched in shock as the woman's bustled, teal gown swayed gracefully as they danced. Her crystal blue eyes never left him as ruby lips formed a loving smile. Black, silken tendrils cascaded along the back of her head with a single white tea rose tucked in along the left side above her ear.

Arianne closed her eyes. This couldn't be happening. She was dreaming. Suddenly she froze. If Shylock was back, it must mean the DNA procedure had failed. This was her world now, with ghosts and entities of all possible realms, of vampire covens and ravenous death.

She saw Shylock's cape strewn casually over the back of the couch, as though it belonged there—as though *he* belonged here, and she cut across the room to grab it.

Suddenly the music stopped and the couple turned to stare at her in apparent surprise.

Arianne pitched the cape at him. He caught it and offered a sly grin. "Welcome home," he said.

"Get out." Arianne heard the hurt in her own voice. Her hopes were gone, her chance for release destroyed. She knew what lay ahead and did not need her dark conscience to remind her.

"I said, get out!"

Annoyed by her feelings of guilt, Arianne reminded herself they were ghosts, and she held no power over them. This time, she tried for the sound of reason. "Please, Shylock. I need time alone. I know the truth—you were right all along. It is my fate."

Shylock stepped away from the woman and cupped Arianne's chin. His fingers had lost their icy jolt. "Arianne, you have misunderstood. You are free."

"What do you mean?"

"We're both free. We've been cleansed and released."

It was true. She could see him clearly now, his skin had lost its transparent whiteness and had taken on a warm hue that gave his eyes a brilliant sable color.

"Then why are you here?"

"To say good-bye, my dear. Angelique and I will be leaving soon."

She stared, still afraid to trust him.

He led her by the hand to the bright light pouring through the balcony windows. The sun's rays fell over her bare feet in a blanket of golden yellow. He stopped when her entire body stood flooded by the light, her face turned upward to fully greet the sun.

"There, you see? You are no longer vampire."

She felt him let go and opened her eyes. He seemed less clear to her now in the bright wash of light, but his voice remained strong.

"You see, Arianne, God always stands ready to forgive. But it is when we forgive ourselves, that we truly find our final redemption." With that, he held out a long-stemmed rose—a white rose this time, and offered a gentleman's bow. Angelique came to his side, and took his arm. Arianne watched them fade together slowly, until all she saw was the skyline of the city beyond her balcony windows.

* * *

The lab was quiet except for the hum of the autoclave machine in the far corner. No one would be in for a while and Arianne wanted to be alone when she checked her blood for the first time since the procedure. She placed a drop of blue dye on the slide and prepared it for viewing. When the timer dinged beside her, it signaled that the slide was ready.

Her hands shook as she secured it on the microscope. She straightened to get a clear view and saw the miracle she'd prayed for. The blood cells were textbook perfection in shape, color and quantity. She was cured. The slide blurred from her vision as tears spilled down her cheeks.

"Oh, Fred, I wish you were here to see this."

"I'm sure he is, in some way or other." David stood in the doorway.

She ran to him, and buried her head against his chest. "Oh, David, I'm free. *We're* free."

He kissed her deeply and drew her close. She tasted his sweetness, and felt the tender passion quenching part of her desire and creating another. She was finally free to love without dread or penalty.

Her lips brushed his cheek. "I have good news for you, too."

He kept a firm grip around her waist. "What's that?"

"Your results are normal. You won't have any residual effects from the bite. The DNA took."

"You had doubts?"

"There was a slight risk. After all, I've never dealt with vampire DNA before. But my theory proved right. When you were bitten, I became your vampire mother, so to speak. Our DNA commingled, changing yours forever. Fortunately, it made us compatible. Simple."

"If you say so. That means no more poking me with needles?" He grinned.

"Yes, you big baby. You're in the clear."

"Speaking of that, Mandari's been cleared. He had nothing to do with Fred's death. He was there that night, but after it was too late. He saw first-hand what Jimmy's sick revenge did to an innocent person."

"What was he doing in the lab that night?"

"Looking for you, in hopes of finding your mother."

She shook her head sadly. "I hope this is over now, too many have died."

"He'll be in the hospital a while. It'll sure give him a lot of time to think."

He checked his watch. "Well, it's midnight. Depending on how you look at it, what do you say to a late dinner or early breakfast?"

"Sounds great," she said grabbing her coat.

Outside, the temperatures were single digits in the kind of tempest wind found only in Chicago. They huddled close as they made their way across the parking lot, when a dark shadow stepped out from behind David's car. Arianne felt his arm tense through his bomber jacket as he went for his gun.

The lot's lights cast an orange glow about the figure, as it moved toward them. Emelia brushed back her hood.

"Mother," Arianne said startled. "What are you doing here?"

Her smile was warm as she watched David holster his weapon. "I've come to say good-bye. Your father has regained his strength since the procedure and we'll leave soon."

Arianne felt disappointment. She'd hoped they would choose to stay. "Where will you go, now that he's mortal again?"

"We're returning home, Arianne. He wishes to live out the remainder of his life there. I will care for him until the end."

There was a deep sadness in her tone Arianne had never heard before, and she wondered if Emelia regretted her decision not to become mortal.

"Mother, it's still not too late...we could cure you."

Her eyes reflected the light like sparkling gems. Was it pride she saw in her mother's expression? Was it the look of acceptance of who she is right or wrong? Whatever her reasons, Arianne knew she would not change her mind.

"What about the Jen-Ku?" Arianne asked.

"Mandari and his forces will always hunt me. I know that. His wounds will heal and he will be fit for the fight again. That's why we will be leaving soon."

For all that her mother was, for all she'd chosen to be, Arianne still loved her. She bit back tears, as she held her for the last time. "I love you, Mother."

"I love you, too, my darling. Nothing is stronger than that."

"Will I see you again?"

"Only if you come to Romania. It is still your home."

A sudden wind caught the darkness and screamed a high-pitched wail. When Arianne looked back, Emelia was gone.

They stood together against the bitter gusts, wrapped together like Eskimos, and the night fell over them as they awaited a new day and the hope it would bring.

EPILOGUE

.

A gentle breeze fanned Arianne's hot skin as the sailboat pulled out of Monroe Harbor. Blue skies, a picnic basket full of fresh sandwiches, and a bottle of sparkling grape juice promised a beautiful day. Destiny padded along in an effort to gain his sea legs before circling once and lying down.

Arianne adjusted her sunglasses to see David carefully working the boat out onto the vastness of Lake Michigan. His bare arms covered in tiny beads of sweat, glistened under the sun, causing a sensual shiver to grip her. Had anyone ever made love on a sailboat, she wondered? She shook away the thought and concentrated on opening the bottle of juice.

"Are you getting hungry?" she called.

He turned back, with a sly grin and wriggled his eyebrows.

"For lunch," she confirmed.

"Oh. Not yet. I'm just enjoying the view."

"I wish Michael could have come with, but he had to perform a wedding this afternoon."

David let the wind take the sails for a bit as he moved to sit beside her. "Speaking of weddings, today is a special day for us."

"You remembered." She grinned.

"You doubted me?"

"Uh-huh."

"Gee, thanks, and a happy six-month anniversary to you, too."

She handed him a glass and proposed a toast. "Here's to our new life, just beginning."

David raised his glass before she finished, but quickly lowered it as she continued.

"Beginning with a new life."

The plastic champagne glasses *clunked* as David formed a puzzled expression. "A new life? You mean?"

Arianne nodded. "We're having a baby."

David pulled her close, tenderly kissing her. He stroked her cheek and looked into her eyes. "Thank you for coming into my life and making it whole."

"Don't thank *me*, it just happened. And I'm so glad it did."

"I believe it was more than that. It was our destiny."

With that, Destiny raised his head and howled softly as if he agreed.

SCARLETT DEAN

Horror fiction author, Scarlett Dean, has been a true horror fan since childhood, and has always enjoyed creating her own dark worlds and characters. "I remember racing home every day after school to catch the last fifteen minutes of my favorite daytime soap, *Dark Shadows*. It was also a Friday ritual to curl up with a big bowl of popcorn and watch scary movies late into the night. The horror world intrigued me so much that I started writing my own stories."

She is an avid reader who is always looking for a really good scare. As a full-time author, she has published her own quarterly magazine of other author's works in fiction, non-fiction and poetry. She enjoys motivational speaking at area schools to promote the gift of writing and encourage reading.

In addition to her love of books, Ms. Dean finds music, especially Rock, to be her second greatest passion. "Since I can't dance, sing or play any instrument well, I'll stick to writing."

She has three children, and a Siberian Husky who is more like a fourth child than a pet. Her husband is the computer genius who bales her out of her e-messes with the patience of God, and supports and encourages her in all of her writing endeavors. Of course, her characters are practically family when she's writing a book, often keeping her awake at night. "Being a writer allows you to get away with hearing voices, without being committed!"

You can visit her website at: www.scarlettdean.com

Amber Quill Press, LLC
The Gold Standard in Publishing

Quality Books
In Both Print and Electronic Formats

Action/Adventure	Suspense/Thriller
Science Fiction	Paranormal
Mainstream	Mystery
Fantasy	Erotica
Romance	Horror
Historical	Western
Young Adult	Non-Fiction

Amber Quill Press, LLC
http://www.amberquill.com